# Only With the Heart

### Linda Steinberg

Only With The Heart

ISBN 978-0-9897546-3-7


Copyright © 2013 by Linda Steinberg


Printed by Create Space

# Acknowledgments

Thanks to Rae Monet for working with me to create the perfect cover.

Special thanks to my technical advisor James McNeely for his input on the tech lingo and his engineering advice on how a Suite Smart and talking robot might really work, and for his calm, easy-going nature and general support in sharing my life.

And, as always, thanks to my critique partners, Pamela Stone and Juliet Burns, who began years ago as writing buddies and evolved into best friends.

# ONLY WITH THE HEART

*It is only with the heart that one can see rightly. What is essential is invisible to the eye.*

Antoine de Saint-Exupery, *The Little Prince*

## Chapter One

Someone was in the laboratory.

Setting aside his blueprints and sandwich, Brian flattened his palms against the metal desk and listened. Thirty seconds after the security beep, he heard the grinding of a gear.

He took in a shallow breath. He didn't expect Connor back from lunch for at least two more hours. And no one else had a key to the lab.

Possibly some street kids had broken into the converted warehouse, thinking it was unoccupied. Brian mopped his brow with the tail of his flannel shirt and silently exhaled. Slipping his feet out of his sandals so they wouldn't flop against the concrete floor, he threaded his way through the graveyard of electrical circuits and wires. As he passed the unassembled fileserver rack, he grabbed a four-foot metal rod and shouldered it like a baseball bat.

A rash of static crackled through the stale air. A raspy, inhuman voice grated. "Helllooooooo."

The intruders had activated Victor.

Clenching his weapon tighter, Brian stepped over a stack of computer science magazines, raised the pole and prepared to swing it at--

A woman? He lowered the pole to the floor.

The female hunched over the platform supporting the VICTR 001 prototype was blond, shapely, and definitely hot, though from her provocative position, he couldn't see her face. The feature that first drew his attention was her compact, heart-shaped backside.

An eyeful of tanned legs lured his gaze from the short, classy tennis dress to the spotless white sneakers with cheerleader sock pompoms kissing her ankles. Upper crust Valley girl. Connor's type.

She didn't turn or look up. Brian's military stealth training served him well. Though females rarely noticed him even when they were looking straight at him.

The woman reached a hand under the hem of her flared mini-skirt. Skimming pink pearl fingernails over a bare buttock, she yanked a wedged cotton panty over the mouth-watering expanse of skin.

*Whoa.* He cleared his throat to alert her to his presence.

The woman straightened and whirled around. "I'm so sorry; I didn't know anyone was here." She pointed to Victor. "I was just so intrigued by..." She fidgeted with her skirt, tugging it down as far as it would go. "I'm with Connor McKay."

*Had that figured.*

The woman twisted her honey gold ponytail out of its holder and shook out thick, luxurious hair. Her cheeks--the ones on her face--flushed. "How long have you been standing there?"

"Long enough." The face was as pleasing as her other assets, and looked vaguely familiar. But then, most of these debutantes were digital copies of one another. This one had the fresh, peaches-and-cream complexion of a soap commercial model. Her wide eyes were so blue they looked artificial.

The office door slammed. "I see you've met Dr. Frankenstein." Connor strode into the lab wearing a preppy blue shirt and a sneer. He draped a proprietary arm around the woman's shoulder.

So subtly the action looked unconscious, the blonde shrugged free, extended her hand to Brian, and smiled. "I'm Paige Anderson." The brilliant flash of her perfect teeth brightened the room like southern California sunshine.

"Brian McKay." His palm melted against soft warm flesh.

"Nice to meet you, Mr.--McKay?" She glanced at Connor. "Relative of yours?"

"Half brother," he responded. Connor never failed to include the 'half.' "I ran into Paige at the country club," he explained. "I brought her over to see the business."

The woman's gaze returned to Brian, her aquamarine eyes scrutinizing him as if he were a lab experiment. "You're the older brother from Reno," she said, finally placing him. "When I was a kid, we lived next door to Connor's family. I don't remember meeting you, though."

"Brian spent summers with us," Connor said.

"Two weeks," Brian corrected. The first two weeks in July from the year he turned eight until he was old enough to refuse to go. It might have eased his father's conscience, but Brian had hated every damned minute in that house.

He nudged his glasses farther up on his nose. Of course Paige didn't remember him. But now he remembered her. Before shipping out on his first tour of duty, he'd stopped by Gil McKay's Beverly Hills home with the stupid hope of making his father proud. A vain hope.

Connor's friend Paige had been at the house with a couple of other thirteen-year-old girls. The snotty brats had acted as if Brian's Airman Basic uniform made him a non-person. Except for Paige. She'd been friendly, interested. A beanpole of a girl, wide-eyed and curious. Her figure had matured, in all the right places, but her face held the same open, innocent expression.

Her lashes flitted. "So you're working for Connor now?"

Brian ground down on his teeth. "We're partners."

"Oh." Paige cocked her head. "Connor didn't mention that." She giggled. "You must be a *silent* partner."

Connor stepped forward. "Brian's my one dollar partner." A million dollar smile barely masked his contempt.

Paige didn't seem to notice. With her eyes still focused on Brian's, she raised a hand slowly, intently to his face.

The glitter of diamonds bounced off her tennis bracelet and reflected on his glasses. Low intensity tremors rumbled inside his chest as she extended a finger and gently wiped the corner of his mouth.

Brian's feet rooted to the floor. His glasses fogged.

"Mayonnaise," she said, holding up a greasy finger.

He refilled his stalled lungs with the mist of a fruity, expensive perfume, then slipped off his glasses and rubbed the steamed lenses with his shirt.

Connor touched Paige's shoulder. "Well, it's been great catching up on old times," he drawled, "but I promised Paige I'd give her a tour of the Suite Smart demo."

Brian bowed aside. "Go ahead."

"Milady." Connor's hand slid down Paige's arm to her hip, his fingers inches from her derriere.

When the couple was out of earshot, Brian turned to the robot. "What are you staring at? She's not your type either."

Victor made no response.

"'Bro'!" Connor turned around and yelled. "Come with us. Paige might have some techie questions for the geek side of the partnership."

Brian squelched a snicker. Not much chance a society debutante like Paige Anderson would ask any penetrating questions.

But they wouldn't have to be very deep for Connor to be in over his head.

*   *   *

Paige searched the laboratory for a paper towel to wipe her hand, but found only dirty rags. Wordlessly, Brian McKay pulled a starched white handkerchief from the pocket of his faded jeans. The cloth was immaculate, gift box-creased as if it had never been used. And monogrammed: BGM.

She patted her hands delicately, refolded the hankie and tried to return it.

"Keep it."

Did he have a strict daily word limit? Every reply was a two word sentence. He really was the silent partner.

Tucking the handkerchief into her waistband, she followed the two men through a jungle of wood and metal. The high narrow windows let in slivers of mid-afternoon sun. Tangled wires snaked across the concrete floor and disappeared into shadows.

How could anyone work here? Connor's ash wood desk in the sunlit, air-conditioned office area was neat and polished. But Brian's in the middle of the lab looked like an outpost in an electrical war zone, under attack by a futuristic army.

"You'll have to excuse Brian's playground," Connor said. "He never got past the sandbox stage."

"Creative genius expressing itself," she retorted, winning an appreciative look from Brian. The place was beyond messy, but innovation apparently thrived in the chaos. Not many great ideas were conceived at a neat desk.

A pair of worn leather sandals sat beside the scarred metal desk. Paige looked at Brian's feet. White socks. He wore his plaid flannel shirt unbuttoned over a snug black T-shirt. In the middle of June! With the white socks and sandals, all he needed to complete the "nerd" outfit was a pocket protector and white tape holding the nosepiece of his wire rimmed glasses together.

Brian adjusted the bridge of his glasses, and shoved his feet into his sandals, shuffling ahead of her. It was hard to believe the brothers came from the same gene pool. Connor had inherited not only his father's blond good looks and muscular build but also the easygoing 'bedside manner' of the man who'd played the handsome Dr. Mike Devlin on *Medical City, USA* for twenty seasons.

Brian must favor his mother's family. The taciturn brother was an inch or two taller than Connor, lean and spare, all meat and no fat. Her gaze wandered to his faded jeans. Softened from a thousand washings, they hugged his tight butt as if they lived there. Which they probably did.

She pulled the handkerchief from her waistband and dabbed the perspiration on her upper lip. It must be eighty degrees in here. She glanced up at a single ceiling fan hanging from the high rafters, its blades moving as slowly as a speedboat propeller after engine shutdown.

The men stopped in front of a plasterboard wall encompassing a room the size of a three-car garage. Connor faced her and waited for her attention like a tour guide. "The Suite uses voice-activated technology to create a luxury, self-service environment for guests in five star hotels." He touched a paneled area in the center of the wall, looked at Brian, and then called out, "Doors open!"

The paneling, which she now realized was a set of double doors, swung eerily open like the entrance to Ali Baba's cave. Refreshingly replete with a cave's cool temperature.

"Front light on!" Connor said.

Paige gasped. The model of a luxurious hotel suite lit up to reveal a king-sized bed, cherry wood and marble night stands with lamps. A sleek granite bar gleamed with all the expected amenities from coffee pot to toaster oven. A leather sofa and club chairs made up a small sitting area. The suite even had fake windows built into the plasterboard walls. "This is so cute!"

Her description earned a wince from Brian but Connor beamed as if she'd complimented his first born. She eyed his immaculate Brooks Brothers Oxford shirt and khaki Dockers, wondering how much he'd actually worked on this project.

"Lamps on!" he ordered and the two bedside lamps cast a warm, cozy glow.

Paige moved into the room. The designer silk comforter and cluster of pillow shams looked inviting. She smoothed a hand over the spread, and then sank down to try out the bed. But instead of a soft mattress, her bottom jarred against wood and wires.

"Ouch!" Flailing, she struggled to sit up before she punctured her backside.

Though Connor was standing beside her, it was Brian who grabbed her hands and lifted her up. "No mattress," he said.

His grip was stronger than she expected. As Paige's feet hit the floor, her body kept going. Pulled off balance, she slammed into Brian's chest.

His body was as hard and unyielding as his personality. Strong fingers pressed against her back as he steadied her. A rough chin grazed her cheek. Paige inhaled the scent of coffee and mayonnaise and soldered metal.

Recovering her breath, she pushed out of his arms. "With all the care you put into the appearance of this room, couldn't you have outfitted it with an actual mattress?"

"Took it out to work on the wiring," Brian explained.

Paige silently counted his words. Eight?

"You'll be able to change the bed height, head and foot level and angle just by voice command," Connor added.

"Oh, like a hospital bed."

"Or a massage table," Brian said.

Was he being suggestive? A glance at Brian found an innocent, oblivious face. The inference must have been hers, responding to the awareness of his arms against her back. Her gaze turned to Connor, who was leaning against the granite bar, looking amused. He glanced at the empty coffee pot. "Make coffee," he said loudly.

Within seconds the aroma of fresh brewed coffee filled the suite.

Brian spoke from across the room. "A cup of coffee, please."

A Styrofoam cup dropped from inside the apparatus and the decanter above dripped coffee to fill it. Nice, but nothing so special here. She'd seen a million vending machines do the same thing. But who had pressed the button?

Tentatively she took a sip. The coffee tasted as good as any Starbucks latte. She winked at Brian. "It's nice to have a man serve coffee, even if you didn't have to lift a finger."

"Brian's good at serving," Connor said with a superior smile. "Been doing it all his life."

It sounded like good-natured banter, but Brian didn't return the jibe. His lips set in a thin line.

"Now boys, play nice and I'll fix you both a cup." She faced the coffee machine, trying to remember the voice commands Brian had used. "One cup of coffee," she ordered.

Nothing happened.

Connor glanced at his brother with a worried frown.

"You didn't say please," Brian said.

The machine was fussy about manners? "A cup of coffee,

12

please," she amended.

Still nothing. "You're playing with me, right? When Brian diverted my attention, Connor was pushing the buttons in the back of the machine."

Connor grinned. "Nope. No buttons." He showed her the back of the apparatus.

"You try it, then."

"Okay." Merely by speaking, Connor produced a cup of coffee for himself as easily as Brian had.

"So what's the deal? It doesn't like women?"

She thought she heard a chuckle from Brian McKay's throat. "It doesn't recognize your voice."

He motioned her toward a narrow wire rack with two computers sitting on it. After inserting a flat disk into a slot on one of the towers, he handed her a script of several nonsensical sentences and had her read them into a microphone.

Brian typed some gobbledygook, ejected the chip and inserted it into a wired box. "Okay, you're set up. Go for it."

She served a cup to Brian with no problems. "This is cool. Do you have a patent?"

"We will. Soon," Connor said with a pointed look at Brian. "Then we sell this baby to every five-star hotel in the country and make millions."

"Wow. What'll you do with the money?"

"Connor's going to spend all his the first night, drinking and doping." For the first time she heard an edge of steel to Brian's voice.

Connor grinned. "Nah, it'll take me at least a week." His cell phone rang. Excusing himself, he disappeared through the paneled doors.

Staring into his cup, Brian sipped his black coffee. "So," he said after an awkward silence, "You want the rest of the tour?"

"Sure."

He showed her how the windows opened with just a word, silently shutting to a different command, and explained the workings of the voice-activated thermostat. When he talked about his work designing and programming the product, quiet Brian McKay seemed to find his voice.

She studied the intense eyes behind the thick glasses. "Do you have orders for this already?"

"Connor's meeting with a prospective buyer on Tuesday."

"Just Connor? Not you?"

Brian shrugged. "Connor's the salesman. I'm the guy behind the scenes."

A fitting division of labor. Connor's connections and outgoing personality were definite assets for a startup business. Brian lacked his half-brother's poise and charm, but he was clearly the brains of the outfit. "What is that robot thing I saw when I came in?"

"Victor." Brian switched off the coffee pot and all the lights with a single 'Shutdown' command, then ushered her out of the Suite Smart lab, ordering the doors to close behind them.

"Victor? That's its name?"

"It stands for Voice Initiated Custom Talking Robot. He can be programmed to perform simple tasks, or answer questions." Brian led her to the apparatus. "Shake hands, Victor."

The robot lifted a wiry appendage. Paige gingerly touched the sharp-ended coils.

"How are you today?" Brian focused on the machinery as if he were talking to a person.

"I'm. Fine. Thank. You," a raspy voice responded. "How. Are.

You."

"That's amazing." Paige applauded. "Can I ask him stuff or do I need a chip for that too?"

"He's not coded. Knock yourself out."

She asked, "What is your name?" to which the robot responded, "Victor." "How old are you?" brought forth the disconnected response, "I. Am. One. Point. Four. Years. Old. How. Old. Are. You?"

"Victor," Brian admonished, "You should never ask a lady her age." With a crease in his cheeks that on someone else might have been a smile, Brian moved to the robot. "Apologize."

"I'm. Sorry." The robot's 'voice' actually sounded contrite. "Please. Forgive. Me."

"Of course I forgive you." Good grief, she was talking to a piece of metal as if it had feelings. "I'm twenty-five. Years. Old," she added whimsically. She ran her fingers over the skeletal 'chest.' "Victor, how do you like working in this laboratory?"

The robot made a belching sound, and then fell silent.

"Ah, so I stumped him." She looked to Brian but he was busy typing on a keyboard next to the machine.

"I like it," the robot screeched suddenly. "The pay stinks but they give me all the metal filings I can eat."

Paige blinked. "How did you do that? And why was his voice smoother that time?"

"I keyed it live." Brian looked up from his keyboard. "The other responses were pre-programmed, one word at a time."

"Pretty neat." *Good grief, Paige, that sounded lame.* 'Neat' didn't begin to cover it. It was positively brilliant. "So what's the market for something like this?"

Brian looked embarrassed. "There isn't one. Victor's just... a toy."

"I bet there'd be a huge demand for a toy like this." She thought of Elena. And Jose and Jesse and Katie. An idea tickled her brain. "He could be an educational tool for the blind."

"The blind?" He adjusted his thick-lensed glasses. "How?"

She sat on the swivel stool beside the robot, crossing her legs carefully to gain maximum coverage from the short tennis skirt. "I work at a day camp for disabled children. The kids in my group are visually impaired. Some are difficult to draw out."

Particularly Elena Ramirez, a quiet seven-year-old she'd so far been unable to reach. Paige suspected abuse, but couldn't get close enough to the girl to discover the truth. She drummed her fingers against her knees, envisioning the excitement in the children's faces if Brian's robot visited camp. And maybe, just maybe, it could help Elena to open up.

Brian leaned against a wall. Under the overhead light, the red paint stains on his black tee shirt looked like dried blood. "How can Victor help your campers?"

It was so adorable that he called the robot Victor. As if it was a pet. Or a friend. "Are you familiar with the practice of using dolls in psychotherapy? Sometimes children can share their feelings easier with a doll or puppet than with real people."

"So, use a doll or puppet."

"I've tried puppets. The kids enjoy it, but they know it's a game. They know my voice. And they can feel my hand. Victor has his own voice. And you can control him remotely." She smiled hopefully. "I'm thinking the kids might respond better to a friendly robot than an authoritative adult."

"Friendly, huh?"

Well, maybe she'd have to help him with that part. Brian seemed as socially insecure as some of her kids. But there was a way to connect with him, surely, just as there was a way to reach her shy and troubled campers. She just had to find the right buttons to push.

Victor's buttons.

"Paige, we need to go." Connor burst out of the office, pointing to his Rolex.

"Darn, I almost forgot." Paige scooped up her canvas satchel. She'd promised to meet Shelly at three to select the music for her engagement party. Paige's car was still at the club, and with Saturday afternoon beach traffic, she'd barely make it to the studio on time.

She turned to Brian. "Do you have a card? I'd like to talk more about this."

Connor sprinted to his desk and handed her a white business card with 'Suite Smart' printed in big block letters, and under it, in letters almost as large, 'Connor McKay, President.'

"Where's your name?" she asked Brian.

"It's the same phone number," Connor answered for him.

Silent partner. Invisible partner. Why didn't Brian demand more of the spotlight? Suite Smart and Victor were his creations, start to finish. Was he just shy? Insecure? Or a misanthropic loner who related better to machines than people?

Brian grasped her extended hand with a firm shake. Electricity tingled in her palm as if she were a wire in one of his inventions.

"Why don't you come visit the camp sometime?" She dug in her satchel for the brochure and scribbled her cell phone number on it. "Then you can see the kids yourself."

This time she'd be proactive. This time she wouldn't wait for hard evidence when her gut told her something was terribly wrong. Brian McKay's robot might be the key to opening up timid Elena Ramirez. Before it was too late.

He folded the paper and shoved it in his jeans pocket, but shook his head. "I'm sorry but--"

She covered his lips with her forefinger. He flinched under her touch and she lowered her hand. "Don't say no. Say you'll think about it."

His dark eyes met hers, probing, suspicious. "I'll think about it."

Hardly the enthusiastic response she'd hoped for. Thawing this cold, hard man might prove just as difficult as reaching Elena. But behind the frown that seemed permanently etched into Brian McKay's face, she sensed a smile lurking, daring someone to lure it out.

A challenge Paige couldn't resist.

\* \* \*

Brian unlocked his desk drawer and placed the Suite Smart blueprints inside. Unfolding the Camp Sunshine brochure, he sniffed the still pungent aroma of damp towels and sunscreen.

"Valley girl," he muttered but there was nobody to hear him except a lifeless robot. She was probably just working at that camp as community service for a D.U.I. charge she'd gotten out of with her rich Daddy's help.

He crammed the brochure beneath the pile and locked the drawer. He didn't have time for charity. There would always be somebody in need. And if he didn't deliver the Suite program within the next two months, he might be one of them.

*Too damned cocky for your own good.* When Connor's slick, high-priced lawyer slipped that two-year deadline clause into the partnership agreement, Brian had almost laughed. He'd been playing with voice activation technology since the Air Force. How long could it take to build the prototype and test it? He'd figured a year, eighteen months at the outside. He *hadn't* figured on all the paperwork required to apply for the patent. Nor the endless modifications that kept the project in a perennial state of almost-but-not-quite perfected.

*The strong defeat the weak, but the smart triumph over the strong.*

Brian stiffened his spine. He could still meet the deadline and win back his birthright. With his fifty percent share of the profits, he'd never have to kiss up to another self-absorbed, over-privileged, golf-playing asshole again. Suite Smart was his ticket to financial independence and nothing was going to interfere with his timeline. Certainly not a perky debutante with sea blue eyes and a smile that could melt a polar ice cap.

As he headed out to grab dinner, Connor came strolling back in. "Forget something?"

"Business cards. I gave away all I had at the country club today." Connor refilled his sterling silver card case and dropped it in his shirt pocket. "I'm going to the Manhattan Club tonight and it wouldn't hurt to have some on hand." He jingled his keys. "What's wrong with the mattress wiring?"

"Nothing. Minor adjustment."

Connor narrowed his eyes. "You promised I'd recoup my investment in two years. If this project's not ready--"

"It's ready," Brian said, matching his brother's glare. It would be. "I've done my job. Do yours." He trained his eyes on Connor's to avoid looking at the framed poster on the wall above him. A head shot of the kind and compassionate Dr. Mike Devlin advertising the hit soap opera that had made Gil McKay a household name.

*Phony bastard.*

He grabbed his helmet and slung it over his arm. "Going out with Paige tonight?"

"Hell, no." Connor grinned. "I never have lunch and dinner with the same woman. It gives them serious ideas."

"She turned you down?"

Connor kept his smile but Brian caught the hint of a snarl. "She had a prior engagement."

Paige had turned Connor down. Perverse satisfaction danced in Brian's gut but he kept his expression neutral.

"No great loss. I know Paige Anderson from way back. With her it would be three or four dates of kisses and hand-holding before I could even think about getting in her pants."

Brian winced.

Unfortunately, Connor saw it. "You're hot for her," he taunted, just like the summer Brian was fifteen and ten-year-old Connor had caught him mooning over airbrushed models in the Sports Illustrated swimsuit issue.

He flipped him off. "She's attractive, so what? One more shallow blonde whose deepest thoughts are about doing lunch and playing tennis."

"She's a damned Do-Gooder." Connor said it like an epithet. "Paige taught Special Ed in a D.C. public school last year. Retards and kids like that."

Okay, so she wasn't doing community service for drunk driving. She was a certifiable halo-wearer. Maybe she could wave her angel wand and create her own damned robot. "Why'd she come back from D.C.?"

"Her mom died." Connor set the warehouse alarm and followed Brian out. "You gonna visit that camp?"

"Nah."

Connor hurtled behind him down the outside stairs. "You want my advice, Bro?'"

"No." Brian started his Harley and revved the engine to drown him out.

"You need to get laid," Connor shouted over the roar. He wrapped his fingers around the handlebar. "I've got a sure thing going tonight. Todd has a new wild woman and she promised to bring a couple of friends for me and Boozer." He winked. "She could probably scare up one more."

"Thanks, but no. I can get my own dates."

Brian accelerated out of the parking lot before he was tempted to take Connor up on the offer. He didn't care for the nightclub scene, even less for his brother's company, but he sure as hell needed a woman.

A real woman, not some kiss-and-run Beverly Hills tease who'd use him for his brains and then move on to a handsome, rich stiff. He knew the game. And he wasn't playing. He couldn't wait to sell Suite Smart and get the hell out of this southern California paradise.

He shot down Santa Monica Boulevard and turned into Ocean Avenue. Bikini-clad blondes wearing see-through sarongs strolled along the sidewalk, slowing traffic to a crawl. Soliciting honks and catcalls with their fake boobs and vacant smiles.

God, he hated this town.

Miles beyond the city, on the Pacific Coast Highway, he sucked refreshing sea air into his lungs. His heart lightened as he raced across the sand, slid the bike sideways in a cloud of flying sand and came to a stop.

Ditching his helmet, he let the ocean breeze ruffle his hair. *Freedom.* He took off his splotched glasses and tilted his face to catch the sun, licking the salt spray from his lips. The chatter of gulls silenced the traffic noise. The gentle crash of surf on sand washed away the images of brash businessmen, movie moguls, and swimsuit sirens.

But he couldn't erase the mental picture of a society sophisticate with a girl-next-door smile. Nor ignore the memory of her pearl pink nail skimming white cotton panties and a smooth, bare bottom.

His body stirred against his will. The woman had no respect for personal boundaries. She'd invaded his space. Touched him.

He fingered his upper lip, releasing a whiff of mayonnaise and the lingering fragrance of expensive perfume. Damn, the girl had literally gotten under his skin.

# Chapter Two

"Circle." Paige threaded her fingers through five-year-old Jesse Ortega's and guided them over the felt template. "It's round."

"A ball is round," the little boy said.

"Yes. Good." A leaf fluttered across the picnic table. Paige brushed it away and placed a tennis ball in Jesse's hand. "Dig in the toy box and see how many more round things you can find."

The afternoon sun glinting through the trees settled on Jesse's blond hair like a halo as he eagerly searched through the cardboard box. Paige strolled around the table, praising the other children's art projects.

The distant roar of an approaching motorcycle wove percussive chords through the strings and woodwinds of Beethoven's Fifth Symphony. Paige had brought her CD player and asked her campers to draw or paint what the music made them feel. A few of the children had created beautiful paintings. Such a shame they could never see and admire their own talent.

Elena sat in her usual position, legs crossed beneath her, on a woven mat under a California black oak. Despite Paige's efforts, Elena wouldn't join the others. What awful secret was that terrorized little girl hiding? How could Paige help her if she couldn't even reach her?

The sounds of chirping birds mingled with the gnashing of car tires on the gravel road beside the campsite. Parents arriving to pick up their children.

"Okay, campers, time to wash the brushes and get ready to go home." Under Paige's supervision, they stowed the pine cones and other treasures they'd collected on the day's nature walk in their backpacks. "Now join hands and follow Mrs. Carroll."

It was Jenna Carroll's turn to serve as bus monitor on the ride back to the city. Her colleague announced a loud "Let's go, campers," as she approached so the children could identify and follow her voice.

"I have to go to the potty," Katie Royce announced.

"I'll take her." Pulling Katie out of the line, Paige took her hand and guided her to a wooden structure housing the toilets, sinks and showers.

As she'd been taught, Katie felt her way in along a heavy corded rope. Trying not to smother her charge's independent efforts, Paige waited outside. She massaged the back of her neck and rolled her head. The children had been unusually wound up for a Monday. It might take the rest of the week to calm them down.

Footsteps crunched pine needles behind her. She jumped and spun around.

Brian McKay moved out of the shadows. "You have enormous patience with those kids."

Paige clasped her hand to her chest and caught her breath. "How long have you been there?"

"Long enough."

Paige blinked. Was she having déjà vu? She studied his faded jeans, gray t-shirt, and moss-colored Dr. Martens boots. "Are you planning to sneak up on me every time we meet?"

He shrugged. "You invited me."

"Yes, but I assumed you'd call first."

"You didn't say anything about calling."

Why did he think she'd written her number on the camp brochure? The man had absolutely no social skills.

"And I wasn't sneaking, I was observing."

A matter of semantics. "Never mind. I'm glad you came." Paige listened for cries of help from inside the bathroom facility, but heard only a child's singing.

"You were kind of hard on them," Brian said. "Making them clean their own brushes and put their art supplies away just so."

"Their disabilities shouldn't excuse them from the tasks they *are* able to perform. It builds their confidence." She smoothed her hands against her shorts. "Each container is a different shape or size to make it easy for them." She bit her lip, regretting her defensive outburst. "What else did you observe?"

Brian stroked the shadowy growth on his chin. His face couldn't seem to decide whether or not it wanted a beard, and he'd apparently given up trying to convince it one way or another. "Happy campers?"

Was that an attempt at humor or a snide remark? With Brian, it was hard to tell. Frustrating. She could usually read people better. "Did you notice the girl sitting apart from the others?"

"The little pixie under the tree in green shorts with sad brown eyes who swiveled her head every three point five seconds to follow the sound of your voice? No."

"Well, she--" Paige stifled a chuckle. He'd caught her off guard again. "Her name's Elena. She sits like that every day. Doesn't talk. I know she can, I saw the verbal test scores from her pre-school."

"Is her hearing okay?"

"Slightly impaired. But she wears an aid and I just put in a new battery."

"Maybe she's just shy."

Hopefully that was all it was. "I've tried everything to get her

24

to talk to me. Why can't I reach her?" *Why am I asking advice from a man who speaks in two-word sentences?*

"Give her time. She exists in a dark, lonely world. But it's comfortable for her. She may be afraid of rejection if she ventures out."

How could he get this from a five-minute observation? Unless he wasn't talking about Elena. Paige checked the area to be sure no one was too close. "I'm concerned because...well, I'm afraid she may be abused."

His brown eyes narrowed behind his glasses. "You've seen evidence?"

"No, it's just a gut feeling." She brushed a loose hair away from her eye. "But my instincts are usually good."

She told him about Michael Marsh, her shy second grader who'd refused to play sports. "I had a bad feeling, but I was afraid to speak up. At the health screening, the school nurse found cigarette burns on his back."

Brian winced.

"I hope I'm wrong about Elena. But... maybe your robot could help her come out of her shell."

"Ms. Paige, who is that?" Katie shuffled out of the bathroom, struggling with the band of her designer shorts.

Paige tugged the girl's pants together and fastened the snap. "This is Mr. McKay. He's a friend."

"Is he my friend?"

"Yes, I am," Brian said without hesitation.

The little girl beamed. Walking her fingers up his pants leg until she found Brian's hand, she wrapped her fingers around his palm. Paige started to suggest he bend over to let the child touch his face, but before she could speak, Brian crouched down and placed the little girl's hands on his cheeks.

25

"You wear glasses," Katie said, feeling his face. "I used to wear glasses."

"I'll bet they were pink with sparkly stars in them," he said.

"Blue. With a pirate patch over one eye."

Katie knew colors? She wasn't blind from birth? Paige had worked with the child two weeks and hadn't known that. "We'd better get to the parking lot. Your mom is probably waiting."

Brian got to his feet. With her small fingers entwined in the man's large ones, Katie skipped confidently, without a trip or a fall, toward the parking area.

Paige hiked her satchel over her shoulder and followed redundantly behind. She amended her initial impression: Brian McKay just lacked *adult* social skills. He'd won over Katie with barely an effort. Kids seemed to know instinctively whom they could trust.

She wasn't surprised though, that the child had latched on to Brian. Katie could be sweet, but she was a spoiled little rich girl who demanded more than her share of attention. Paige felt challenged to find the time for the underprivileged children who most needed her help.

Like Elena. But Victor the robot would help her, Paige was relying on it. *If* she could persuade Brian to program his robot creation for her kids. Watching him with Katie, his lips curved in an almost-smile, she guessed her task was half done.

Jenna was already loading the campers into the bus when they arrived at the parking area, but she was having a difficult time keeping them in line. Half a dozen or more, some in wheel chairs, gathered around gawking at a monster motorcycle. Several of the blind children ran their hands over the sleek machine. Paige glanced around the clearing. Her silver Infiniti was the only other vehicle in the lot.

She turned to Brian. "Yours?"

Nodding, he handed off Katie to her and sprinted to rescue the gaping, excited campers. "Careful! The motor's still hot."

"Can I get a ride, man?" A mentally challenged boy of about twelve pushed his way past the others.

"No, me."

"Me."

"Me!"

Paige fought her way inside the circle. She shook her head firmly at Brian. "Liability laws," she whispered. To the campers, she said loudly, "Sorry, guys. Mr. McKay's not allowed to give rides to anyone under twenty-one years old."

"Awwwww." Disappointment chorused. Paige shepherded the children back to the bus with a relieved sigh.

"How old are you, Ms. Paige?" a young voice asked.

It was one voice. Paige decided to ignore it.

"Ms. Paige can ride," another boy cried out. Several more took up the chant. "Ride. Ride."

They wanted to ride so much, even vicariously. The mentally impaired, physically handicapped, the blind, imagining themselves on that bike with the wind in their hair and the sun on their cheeks, hearing the engine rev, soaring off into a place where they were whole and normal.

"Come on, Ms. Paige."

She looked to Brian for help but he stood with his helmet hanging from his arm, his brown eyes twinkling behind his thick glasses. "I think your fans have spoken." He handed her the helmet and whispered. "We'll just make a few laps around the clearing."

*It's for the kids,* she told herself, handing Jenna her satchel to hold.

A cheer went up as she put on the helmet and tightened the strap. For the sake of the blind children, she described her motions

27

and reactions in the detailed commentary of a radio sports announcer. "My head feels like it's in a tunnel. I hear you all but you sound so far away."

She climbed onto the bike behind Brian and clasped her hands around his waist. Nice abs. She'd been right about his being all meat. And muscle.

She chose not to describe that sensation to the kids.

They took off with a jerk. The helmet's shield slammed against Brian's back as he did a one-eighty and careened across the clearing. Paige dug her knees against his thighs and held on.

They made only three or four rounds around the lot, but to Paige, it was a mini Indy 500. She squeezed her eyes shut and clutched Brian's tight stomach, exhilaration charging through her body. When they slowed and finally stopped, after probably a two minute ride, she panted as if she'd run a marathon.

And the kids cheered as if she'd won.

Slowly she untangled her legs from Brian's and let go of his waist. He steadied the bike while she dismounted, his long legs straddling the heavy metal machine like a cowboy on a tamed bronco. When she handed back the helmet, his dark brown eyes locked on hers. Heat simmered in his gaze. Fighting to catch her breath, Paige melted in the afternoon sun.

"Okay, everybody on the bus now." She waved the last campers through the door.

Jenna glanced at Brian, wiggled her brows and winked at Paige.

*Don't start,* she warned Jenna with her eyes as she took back her satchel.

Brian turned off the motorcycle's engine. "Sorry if I scared you," he said when the busload of campers and their chaperone had driven off. "I was just trying to put on a show for the kids." He swung his leg over the bike and dismounted.

"They loved it." She undid her pony tail and shook out her hair, combing the tangles with her fingers. "And I wasn't scared."

Shaken was more like it, but more from the man than the machine. Paige had piggybacked on a motorcycle before, but didn't remember ever feeling that rush of adrenaline, the sensual thrill of body crushed against body.

Suddenly she became aware that they were alone in the clearing. And that she was much too aware of *him*. Brian's intense gaze scorched a line from her eyes down the row of pearl buttons on her cotton blouse. The tips of her breasts tingled as if he'd stripped her naked. Not an altogether unpleasant sensation.

Reminding herself that her interest in Brian McKay was his brain, she fumbled with the strap of her day pack and switched it to the other shoulder. "Katie really took to you."

"Yeah, I'm a big hit with females under seven and over seventy."

She giggled. His dry sense of humor kept her off guard with its infrequent, unexpected appearances. And drew her in. "You understood Katie. She responded to you. But not all kids are that easy. That's why I think Victor would help."

Paige envisioned the awe in the children's faces if they could hear Brian's robot speak, and feel him move. "The kids can ask him questions and he responds. Maybe you could program him to ask questions for the kids to answer." Her pulse raced with anticipation. "Or they could type into the keyboard, or touch him to activate him, or--"

"Whoa. Slow down, lady. Victor's just a prototype. He can speak a few sentences, answer standard questions. Programming him for your little dog and pony show would take a lot of work. And time."

Time he needed to spend on the Suite Smart project. His business. "I'm not asking you to do this for free. I'd pay you." She raised her chin and offered a promising smile.

\* \* \*

*That smile could be your downfall, McKay.* Brian couldn't tear his eyes from Paige's face. He'd never met anyone who glowed with such joy and hopefulness. As if there were no problem she couldn't fix with determination and a positive attitude.

He hadn't intended to come out here today. He'd left the lab to grab a burger, but the bike had found its way toward this camp as if some invisible force were driving it. The perky debutante/do-gooder had somehow reeled him in. And though he fought to maintain his usual detachment, Brian sensed she was about to drag him into her optimistic fervor.

"I know you could make this happen." Paige's bright shining eyes cajoled and caressed. "Can I commission this project? What would you charge?"

"How much do you make?"

She frowned. "At the camp? Nothing. It's volunteer work."

Great, she was not only volunteering her time but willing to spend her own money and he was supposed to charge her for it? "Forget it."

She jutted out a stubborn chin. "I'll pay whatever you feel your services are worth. What's your price, Mr. McKay?"

"Brian."

"Paige." Her blue eyes flashed like a laser, melting all they surveyed.

*Oh, hell.* He pushed up the bridge of his glasses. "Twice your salary."

Her eyes widened, then relaxed into a twinkle. "You drive a hard bargain." She reached for his hand, sending a blip of low level current through his veins. "You'll have time for this? What about Suite Smart?"

"Almost done." *Almost* being the operative word. Every time he thought the programming was finished, some little glitch popped out to send him back to the circuit board. He hoped he wasn't making a promise to Paige he couldn't keep.

The cocky little demon inside him egged him on, assuring him he could do both. After all, there were plenty of wasteful hours spent eating and sleeping he could put to productive use. He'd catch up on his sleep when they sold the Suite.

Paige rubbed the pad of her thumb along his palm. "Can I at least help?"

He swallowed his breath. "That's part of the deal."

"So when do I start?" This time her smile combined little-girl excitement with a flirtatious grin.

"Whenever you want. I'm at the lab every day." It wasn't like he had to check his appointment book.

But damned if Paige didn't pull a pocket calendar out of her satchel and thumb through the well-used pages. "Tomorrow? Wednesday?"

He shrugged. "Drop by whenever. You don't have to call first."

Her light laugh was warm and ingenuous, not the over-the-top cackle typical of empty-headed Valley girls. "Well, I guess I'd better get home and clean up."

Paige's creamy face glowed. The slender threads of her sun-bleached hair groomed themselves as if they wouldn't dream of falling out of place. Though she'd been out in the woods all day in the sweltering summer heat, the society princess looked as fresh as a morning shower.

Brian tried to picture Paige dirty--or at least less perfect, her hair mussed and tussled, her blouse wrinkled, her lipstick smeared from his penetrating kiss. A hard ache pulsed between his legs. He attempted a seductive smile. "What's your hurry?"

"I'm meeting Connor at six-thirty."

*Connor.* Brian's chest tightened.

"We're attending a preview of the David Hockney exhibit at LACMA. "Would you like to come? It'll be fun."

"No, thanks." Tinkering with robots and motors was fun. An art exhibit sounded like a colossal bore. Rooms full of uptight socialites making small talk, wasting time, money and life. The kind of scene where Connor shone.

The kind of scene Paige apparently enjoyed. What the hell had he been thinking, fantasizing about a girl like that? Paige Anderson lived in a world he wanted no part of, and where he'd never be accepted. She might not be your typical shallow, self-absorbed Valley girl, but she was still Rodeo Drive and he was everything's-cheaper-in Reno.

He watched her drive off in the late model Infiniti, then kicked the Harley's tire. He'd program Victor for her campers as he'd promised, but that was as far as it would go. She was Connor's type, in heart and mind. As incompatible with Brian as a Mac to a PC.

*Right.* He might be able to program his mental software not to want what he couldn't have, but he was finding it damned difficult to fight his body's hardwired response.

\* \* \*

Paige linked her elbow through Connor's and maneuvered him into the spacious rooms of the Los Angeles County Museum of Art. "Isn't this a magnificent exhibit?"

"Yeah." Connor snagged a flute of champagne from a passing waiter and drained the glass with one gulp.

"Mrs. Foster-Ricardo is delighted you've joined the Art League. You must have really impressed her."

"What impressed her is, I'm Gil McKay's son," he said dryly. "The frumpy old battle axe probably figures I have Hollywood connections."

Cynicism was apparently the only quality the McKay brothers

had in common. Paige stopped in front of a watercolor self-portrait featuring grand, opulent brushstrokes. "Don't you love Hockney's unconventional use of color?"

"Whatever."

"Not your taste? You prefer more traditional art?"

Connor set his empty champagne flute on a linen-covered table. "Between you and me--" He plucked a petit-four from a silver tray and winked. "--I don't know much about art, and I care less."

"Then why did you sign up for the committee?"

"Contacts." He popped the small square cake into his mouth.

She propelled him away from the dessert table. "I don't think anyone on the Junior Art Committee is in the hotel business."

Connor shrugged. "It never hurts to get your name out there to the ultimate consumers."

"You mean your product name."

"That too." Connor grinned. "When Suite Smart is a household word, customers will demand to stay in hotels that provide it. And Connor McKay will be known as a pioneer in voice activation technology."

Instead of Gil McKay's son. Paige squeezed his arm. "You may not be an art aficionado, but you do know your marketing. With your business acumen and Brian's technical skills, you could incorporate Suite Smart and make a splash on Wall Street." She scanned the smartly dressed men and women promenading the museum halls as if strolling the Champs Elysees. "Is he here tonight?"

"Who?"

"Brian." She countered his blank stare. "Your brother?"

"What am I, my brother's keeper?" Connor scooped up two glasses of champagne and handed her one. "Brian wouldn't be

33

caught dead in a place like this."

"He doesn't like art either?"

"I wouldn't know. He doesn't like crowds. Especially crowds of rich people. Brian thinks we all belong in the seventh circle of hell."

Paige touched the rim of the glass to her lips, surveying the men in four thousand dollar suits and women wearing fur coats in the middle of June, young couples dripping with old money. *Sometimes I agree with him.*

"Paige. There you are."

She turned to see her sister standing in the museum, her hand glued to her fiancé's. Shelly looked beautifully exotic in a slinky magenta gown slit to the thigh. In her simple black sheath, Paige suddenly felt like a Sunday school teacher.

A formidable-looking older woman joined them. Cocking an inquisitive brow at Connor, Shelly purred, "Paige. You know Nick and his mother."

Nicholas Foster-Ricardo sported a sparse goatee and an earring dangling from his eyebrow. His mother, a member of several charitable boards and the hostess of this evening's exhibit, wore a Sixties bouffant that started at the nape of her neck and rose into the ozone layer.

"Mrs. Foster-Ricardo." Connor rushed up to the dowager and grasped both her hands. "What a magnificent exhibit. I was just telling Paige how much I admired David Hockney's unconventional use of color."

Swallowing hard, Paige introduced Connor to Shelly and Nick.

"Connor is Gil McKay's boy," Mrs. Foster Ricardo added. "Astounding resemblance."

Connor's smile stayed in place but an angry spark flashed across his blue eyes.

Mrs. Foster-Ricardo took Connor's arm. "I'm so glad you're enjoying the exhibit. May I show you our newest acquisitions?" With a nod to Paige, she ushered Connor into the next room of paintings.

"Nick, be a dear and scavenge me some champagne." Shelly smiled at her fiancé. "Paige and I need to powder our noses."

"Sure." Looking grateful for the opportunity to escape, Nick bolted off in the opposite direction from his mother.

Shelly tugged Paige's arm and steered her to the Ladies lounge. "God, my face feels like it's frozen in a permanent smile. And my feet are killing me." She slipped off her Ferragamo sandals and sank into a stuffed armchair. "So that's Dr. Mike Devlin's son? From *A Wonderful World*? God, he's sexy!"

Paige took the seat beside her. "*Medical City, USA*. And the actor's name was Gil McKay. Connor's father died a couple of years ago."

"Dr. Mike died?" Shelly's eyes widened. "I wondered why he didn't have much of a part anymore."

Paige swept her sister into her arms and hugged her. "Muffin, I love you to pieces, but sometimes I think you're missing a few brain cells."

Shelly giggled. "That's what Nick says. He loves that I'm wild and crazy. And I love that I'm marrying a rebel."

Paige chuckled. To Shelly, multiple body piercings qualified her fiancé as an ultra radical. Never mind that Nick's mother was a well-respected patron of the arts and his father sat on the board of directors of an oil company "So why are you drooling over Connor?"

"I can still look, can't I? We're not officially engaged for two more weeks." Shelly stood and faced the mirror, primping her hair. "You are bringing Dr. Mike, Jr. to the party?"

Paige crossed her legs at the ankle. "I don't think so."

"Why on earth not?"

"We're just friends, Shelly."

Her sister rolled her eyes. "You say that about every guy you go out with. What kind of man does it take to get your passion meter going?"

"For openers, somebody I haven't known since kindergarten." She sprang out of the armchair and freshened her lip-gloss.

Shelly slipped on her shoes and followed Paige out of the lounge. As they entered a room of portraits of David Hockney's family and friends, she jerked Paige's arm. "Uh-oh."

Paige looked where she pointed. Like a king holding court, Connor stood laughing and talking inside a circle of four young women. Each lady hung on his arm or fluttered her lashes in a bid for his attention.

No surprise. At the club the other day, Connor had charmed the tennis socks off every woman within ten feet, and was probably equally skilled at enticing off more intimate articles of clothing.

Paige was more impressed by a man who could charm children.

"You'd better go stake your claim if you want to sleep next to that gorgeous face and ultra-hunk body tonight," Shelly whispered. "I'm off to catch up with Nick."

Paige studied Connor's perfect physique. Too perfect. Was something wrong with her? The thought of sex with Connor McKay held as much appeal as sleeping with a life-sized Ken doll.

She backed out of the room. *What* does *charge up your passion meter?* She'd dated a lot of Connors: handsome, well-toned, charming, and totally predictable. None of them set off her bells. No one had ever inspired the fervent, fiery urges she'd felt this afternoon.

*It was the motorcycle.* The rush of adrenaline, her body pressed against his. She'd been caught off guard, her expectations shaken. And she still trembled from the experience.

She needed air.

Crossing through the exhibit rooms greeting friends and acquaintances who popped up in her path, she finally pushed open the glass doors to the outdoor plaza.

The evening breeze was crisp and refreshing. Paige settled at a café table and listened to the unwinding of rush hour traffic on Wilshire Boulevard. It was good to be home. She belonged here. She'd enjoyed her year of independence, and missed her students in D.C., but her family needed her now.

"Paige Anderson?"

A gray-haired fortyish man and a striking redhead in her late twenties crossed the plaza toward the museum exit. Paige recognized Katie Royce's mother and stepfather. The Royces were generous sponsors of the summer camp, providing scholarships so kids from east L.A. like Elena could attend.

Dr. Royce clasped Paige's hand. "How's your Dad? He owes me a golf rematch since he beat me so badly last time."

"He's been busy. Performing surgery almost every day."

"'Laser surgeon to the stars,' huh? Perfect vision is the mania these days." A trace of bitterness tinged his voice. Katie had been Daddy's patient since Dr. Royce married Katie's mother three years ago.

"Katie loves camp," Mrs. Royce offered. "She comes home every day talking about Miss Paige and the fun activities. She was especially excited today, for some reason."

Brian. Katie had basked in his special attention. Paige wished she could give personal time to each of her campers, but with eight special needs kids under the age of ten, there was never enough to go around.

"We're heading home," Dr. Royce said before she could explain about today's visitor. "We left Kyle babysitting Katie. Usually he's pretty good with her, but you know teenage boys. If we're away too long, he might invite friends over and forget Katie."

Paige nodded in understanding. Special needs children required constant attention. As did emotionally needy adults.

After the Royces left, she propped her leg onto a wrought iron chair and stared up into the darkening southern California sky. She should never have left home. Maybe if she'd stayed, or if she'd apologized...

*If.* Such a useless word. Hindsight wouldn't save Mom. Paige tried not to let guilt overwhelm her, but the least she could do to make amends for her selfishness was caring for her family. Mom would have wanted that.

Daddy claimed he was okay, but since Mom's death he hadn't taken proper care of himself. Paige's older sister Helene, seven months pregnant and overcommitted at her law office, was delighted to have Auntie Paige home to help take care of her rambunctious five year old. And Shelly had begged her to plan the wedding details. As the middle sibling, Paige was the one to whom both sisters turned. She felt needed here, and being needed filled a gnawing hole she barely admitted was there.

Footsteps sounded behind her. Hands clasped her shoulders and slid slowly down her dress. "I've been looking all over for you."

Maneuvering out of his touch, she stood and faced Connor. "I didn't think you'd miss me, surrounded by all those beautiful women."

"But you're the most beautiful woman here." He bent his head and kissed her. His tongue forced her lips open and slithered inside her mouth as his hand slid down her bare shoulder and inched toward her breast.

She pushed him away. "We're in public, Connor."

"That can be easily remedied."

Was he born with that ego or had cockiness just grown on him? She led him back inside. "We should mingle."

Connor bounced back easily from the rebuff, smiling and greeting old friends as they took in the remaining rooms of the exhibit. Downing glass after glass of champagne.

"Haven't you had enough to drink?" She frowned. "You said you had an early plane tomorrow."

"So? I'm not the pilot." Connor danced his fingers down her neck. "Why don't you come with me to Chicago?"

"I have to work." She shook off his hand. "Why don't you take your business partner?"

"Brian? He'd be worse than useless. The suits I'm meeting with don't care about the techie details, they're interested in the bottom line." Connor sipped at yet another drink. "This trip requires somebody who can schmooze 'em and booze 'em up so they'll report favorably to the guys who sign the checks. Geeks need not apply."

She sighed. "He's your brother. Your only living relative, besides your mother. You two should look out for each other."

Connor shot her a disbelieving smirk. "I look out for Number One." He steered her to a cozy loveseat and set down his glass. "I know you think we should all be a loving, happy family, but I didn't even know Brian existed until he showed up on our doorstep one summer." He leaned close to her ear. "The fact is, he should never have existed at all."

"What a horrible thing to say."

Connor took a slow drag of his champagne. "Brian was a mistake. My father only married Brian's mother because she got pregnant."

Paige winced. "Does he know that?"

"Of course."

She squeezed her eyes tight and clasped her stomach. No wonder Brian had a chip on his shoulder the size of Nevada.

Connor high-fived one of his buddies as he passed, then turned back to her. "Brian's not like you and me, Paige. His mother works nights at some Reno hotel. Brian worked there too, when he was just a kid."

"So what's wrong with that?" Paige had worked Saturday mornings at Daddy's office since she was old enough to clean eyeglasses.

"Face it." Connor pulled her close and slid his finger under the shoulder strap of her dress. "Brian doesn't fit in our class and never will."

Paige gritted her teeth at the outright snobbery. She'd grown up with it, she knew it thrived among her friends and neighbors, but she'd never liked it.

*Yet you accepted it.* Paige redirected her indignation inward. After her one naive effort that ended in disaster, she'd never again attempted to stand up against class elitism.

But now, suddenly, it was personal. "*Your* class, Connor." She stood, unsnapped her evening bag, and shook out her car key. "Excuse me if I don't prefer to hang around in the seventh circle of hell."

## Chapter Three

With trembling hands, Brian unclasped the nine-by-twelve envelope and eased out the document. He scanned the patent's legalese until he read the words *Brian G. McKay, Inventor.*

*Sweet.* A smile edged its way to his lips. Connor could print all the damn business cards he liked with his name in gold letters four inches high, but he could never screw him out of his legal rights. The patent proved the Suite Smart program was Brian's alone. That and his labor entitled him to fifty percent ownership in the partnership.

Brian G. McKay, Business Owner. Satisfaction simmered in his gut. He was through making rich people's beds, serving their food, and kissing their gold-plated asses.

Barely audible footsteps approached. A sweet scent filled his nostrils. Pine and cedar mingled with a fruity perfume.

Paige.

He laid the document atop a stack of file folders on the left side of his desk, pretending not to notice the quiet footsteps stealing up behind him. When she placed her hands over his glasses, he even considered wasting a guess or two to feel her soft curves against his back and her warm breath in his hair a moment longer. "Hello, Paige."

She dropped her hands and came around to face him. "Darn it, how'd you know? I thought I was going to sneak up on you for a change."

"Never gonna happen."

She wore her honey blonde hair down today, tucked behind her ears. The top button of her crisp white blouse was open, revealing the end of a tan line and the beginning of soft white flesh. Nothing actually showed, but the hint was enough to quicken Brian's breath.

Bracing her hands behind her, Paige hiked herself up onto the right side of his desk. Her khaki shorts embraced her thighs as snugly as a pair of caressing hands. "Katie asked about you today," she said, running a casual finger over the metal desk's scarred ridges. "She wanted to know when her friend was coming back."

"She's a cute kid."

Paige swung her legs casually as she scanned the large open room. "When's Connor due back from his trip?"

She'd been with Connor last night. Like he needed the reminder. "Tomorrow." He ground out the words through clenched teeth. "How was your date?"

"With Connor? It wasn't a date. Just a charity function for the art museum."

*Right.* She had that look about her, face flushed and eyes shining, that a woman wears after sex or in the presence of her lover.

"Connor seemed pretty confident about making this sale." Paige leaned forward. "Are you excited?"

"Yeah."

She scrutinized his eyes, getting close enough to define the expression 'in your face.' "If you were any less excited, you'd be comatose."

And if she were any more bubbly, he could pour her into a fluted champagne glass. He picked up the patent and started to slip it back into its envelope.

She caught his arm. "What's that?"

"Nothing. Just a document."

"It's your patent!" She jumped down off the desk, almost falling into his lap. "Can I see it?"

"It's a lot of legal mumbo jumbo," he protested, but she was already reading over his shoulder. Her eyes rolled down the page through 'party of the first part' and Latin e pluribus hocus pocus and stopped where his had.

"That's your name!" She looked as thrilled as if it were her own.

"Yep."

"What does the 'G' stand for?"

*Someone I'd rather forget.* "Geek," he said, conjuring a teasing smile.

"Cute." She studied his face. "I've never seen my name on anything like that. Well, once. In fifth grade I wrote a poem that was published in the school newspaper. Not a very big circulation, but I was so excited to see my name in print. Does this feel anything like that?"

"Yeah." The understatement barely concealed the pride he was too embarrassed to share. Brian slipped the document into the envelope and locked it in his drawer. "Did you come here to chat or to work?"

Paige feigned a serious expression and offered a mock salute. "Private Anderson reporting for duty, sir."

She probably thought she looked cute. Okay, so she did. She was so damned adorable he could--

*Connor's girl*, he reminded his libido, pushing his glasses farther up on his nose.

He moved two stools next to the VICTR 001 prototype. A stuffed trash bag that hadn't been there before sat on the floor beside Victor's platform. Brian looked questioningly at Paige.

"Have a look."

He untied the string and peered inside the bag. It was packed with foam squares and cotton rags.

"To make Victor soft," she said. "You *were* planning to stuff him and cover him with fabric, weren't you?"

"Why would I? What does it matter what he looks like? The kids in your group can't see."

"They feel. Everything." She scooped a piece of foam out of the bag and brushed his face. "Would you want to touch a bunch of plugs and wires or feel something soft and cuddly?"

Was that an invitation? He glanced at her eyes. Completely innocent.

"Let's measure him for clothes," she said brightly. "I think he'd be really cute in some denim overalls and a soft flannel shirt."

"You've got to be kidding. How the hell am I going to make clothes for a robot?"

"*I'm* going to do it. I'll make him a shirt and pants from a children's clothing pattern."

"You sew?" He barely hid his surprise. Brian's mother still made her own clothing from an antique Singer sewing machine, but she was the only person he'd ever known who did.

"I'm not totally useless. I can do lots of handy things."

Erotic images flashed through his mind. Heat seared him at the thought of her hands touching his body, caressing, teasing... Dammit. She was doing it again. And she didn't even realize it. He wiped his brow with his sleeve.

"Do you have a tape measure?"

*For the robot.* Struggling to keep his own measurements from increasing, he dug out a tape from his cluttered desk drawer and placed it in her hand. His fingers sparked against hers like an electric charge.

Paige measured the robot's 'arms' and 'legs' and estimated the diameter his 'waist' would be when stuffed and recorded the numbers in a small notebook she pulled from her ever-present satchel. "I'll bring patterns and material next time," she said.

Swiveling her round derriere onto the stool, Paige propped the notebook on her knees like an eager student. "Can I see what you have?"

*The programming.* Determined not to let his hormones get the best of him, Brian clicked open his file and angled his laptop so Paige could read the screen. "Let's build on Victor's basic vocabulary." He scrolled down to the program notes. "For starters, let's say he introduces himself and asks the child's name."

Paige agreed.

"The child responds. Victor repeats the name in his next program." He typed *Space for Child's Name.*

"So what is his next program?"

He shrugged. "'How are you?'" he suggested.

She shook her head. "The kids'll just answer 'Fine.' If we want them to open up, it should be an open-ended question. 'What did you do today?' Or 'What's your favorite part of camp?'"

"Or, 'What do you want to be when you grow up?'"

"Good one." Paige slid off the stool and sat cross-legged on the floor, leaning over the spiral notebook. As she jotted notes, her blouse rode up and untucked from her shorts, revealing drawn lines of colored ink just above her tailbone.

A *tattoo?* Debutante Paige Anderson had a tattoo on her behind?

He squinted to make out the subject, but most of the design was hidden inside her shorts. A flower? A butterfly? A bird? He rubbed the American eagle imprinted on his shoulder, courtesy of his first R&R in the Air Force, then hunkered down on the floor beside Paige. He never would have figured little Miss Perfect to have a wild streak.

For the next half hour they worked on Victor's language and actions, Brian diagramming the program, Paige making suggestions. As always, a rush of excitement coursed through him as the ideas took form, but today he found himself unusually distracted. By the aroma of strawberries in Paige's shampoo. The way she rubbed her thigh with her thumb when she got an inspiration. Just being close to her. Alone.

*Connor's girl.* He shoved up the bridge of his glasses. "I could use a soft drink." And a cold shower. Wiping the sweat from his upper lip, he tramped to the small refrigerator in the back room and returned with two sodas.

"Thanks." Paige popped the tab on her Coke and took a sip. "It is warm in here."

*And getting warmer by the minute.*

She crossed her legs and propped her soda can on her thigh. "So if Connor makes the sale, then what? You sell to other hotel chains, until all five star hotels feature the Suite Smart product?"

So now she was a business analyst? What had prompted this question? *She's interested, McKay. Making conversation. Don't get all defensive.*

He sat on the floor beside her and took a swig of his soda. "There's only going to be one sale. If Allied offers enough money, we let them buy us out and dissolve the partnership."

She eyed him skeptically. "After working on Suite Smart for years you'd just give it up?"

"That's the whole idea." Make the product, sell it, and get the hell out.

"And then what will you do?"

"Whatever I want."

She drew her knees up to her chest. "That's a pretty generic answer."

"To a pretty open-ended question." His hands fisted at his sides. "You trying to get inside my head like you do your campers?"

"Sorry." She smiled sheepishly. "Your head is harder than theirs." She stretched out her legs. "I guess I was just curious about what drives you, what you want from life."

*That would make you the first to care.* "What about you? What does Paige Anderson want out of life?"

She blinked as if she'd never thought about it. "Nothing monumental," she said after a pause. "I just want to leave the world a little better than I found it." She looked into his eyes and winced. "Sounds sappy, huh?"

He grinned. "Sounds like a Miss America speech."

"Well, I'm the middle child. I've always been the peacemaker." She shoved a blond hair behind her ear. "I guess it's just my nature to want to help people."

She looked at him expectantly. Brian stared into her wide blue eyes, as intelligent as they were innocent. If anybody could teach the world to sing, he'd bet Paige could.

She was still watching him. Waiting, he realized, for him to speak.

He adjusted his glasses. "My goals aren't quite so lofty."

"Doesn't matter."

She reached for his hand and covered the back with hers, her warm fingers twining between his cold ones. The gesture stirred him in private places deeper than his erogenous zones.

"I want financial independence." He blurted out his thoughts without censoring them. "To be able to buy my mother a house--any house she wants. I want to look these rich, arrogant bastards in the eye and tell them what to do with their attitude. Then I can leave Tinseltown and never look back."

Paige scrunched up her eyes. "What about Connor?"

"What about him?"

"You sure he wants to sell out?"

He slipped his hand out from under hers. "Why wouldn't he? He gets to make a sh--a boatload of money without having done any work. He can take a world cruise with his coke-sniffing friends and live off the sale proceeds until his trust fund matures."

She looked doubtful. "How well do you know your brother?"

Was that a trick question? How hard was it to know a pompous, self-aggrandizing slouch? "Say what you mean, Paige."

She spoke carefully. "I think Suite Smart means more to Connor than just the money. It gives him an identity, a title, something of his own. It's got to be hard living your life as Gil McKay's son."

"I wouldn't know."

She winced. "I'm sorry. That came out wrong. I'm sure it was tough growing up without a father, but you were strong enough to make it on your own. Connor's not. He needs Suite Smart. And frankly, I can't believe you'd actually sell your patent."

"Why not? It's just a piece of paper."

"It's your blood, sweat and tears. Your baby. I know it's no comparison, but I still have that school newspaper with my poem in it up on my bedroom wall."

"It's a piece of paper," he repeated. "If I were working for a corporation, I'd never even see my name on it."

But her concerns fed his doubts. Would he be able to walk away from the completed project and hand it over to strangers? What if they revised the program or messed it up? Would he feel like he'd given away his child for adoption? He fingered the earpieces of his glasses and pushed them farther back on his face.

"That's the fourteenth time you've done that since I got here." Paige put down her soda and held out her hand. "Why don't you fix those glasses?"

"I don't have a screwdriver small enough."

"I do." She scooted over to her camp satchel and foraged through the folds, digging out an eyeglass repair kit. "Give them to me."

He stared at the kit. "Do you carry the kitchen sink in that bag? How is it you just happen to have--?"

"My dad's an ophthalmologist. I always carry this for emergencies at camp or whatever." She held out her hand.

Feeling like Superman handing over his cape, he slipped off his glasses.

"Don't be nervous." She lifted them delicately by the wire rims. "I've been adjusting glasses most of my life."

Paige held up his lenses to the light and stared at the thick plastic. "No wonder you heard me sneak up on you. You've probably developed acute hearing to compensate for poor vision."

She studied the side of the frames. "Particularly in your right eye."

She wiggled the screwdriver into tiny frame screws he could barely see. "Good grief, it's a wonder these earpieces are still hanging on." She bent them down and then raised the glasses to his face. "You have really nice eyes."

He blinked. "Except that I can't see worth crap."

She smiled. "'It is only with the heart that one can see rightly. What is essential is invisible to the eye.'"

*"The Little Prince."*

Her mouth dropped open. "You know it?"

*As well as Winnie the Pooh and Batman.* "My mother used to

read it to me when I was a kid."

"Mine too." Paige fitted his glasses back on his nose. Her fingers stroked his temples and behind his ears in an almost-caress. "Better?"

He let out his breath and tried not to steam up the lenses. "They're a little tight."

"You're just used to them falling off your face." But she obligingly took them off, brushing her fingers over his cheeks, and adjusted them. "Okay now?"

The glasses were still snug, but he didn't think he could handle her touching his face again. And without his glasses he felt not only sightless, but vulnerable. "They're fine. Thanks."

"Except for being filthy." She pulled them off again and dug in her bottomless satchel. She found a small spray bottle and a soft cloth. Gently she cleaned and dried each lens. "What happened to your right eye?"

He flinched.

"I'm sorry. Am I getting too personal?"

*Getting?* She'd passed that point thirty minutes ago.

She softened her voice. "An injury?"

And she just kept going. He held out a hand for his glasses. Paige ignored it and continued rubbing and polishing.

"An accident," he said. "When I was in the Air Force."

She kept polishing his lenses, holding them captive. The world beyond her face was hazy, a cloud of weaving shapes and flowing colors like some weed-induced vision. The only things in his focus were the cornflower blue eyes watching him expectantly, as if she had no place to go and all the time in the world to wait. Kind eyes. Concerned. Caring.

He swallowed. Damned socialite had not only gotten under his skin, now she was in his face, and if he let her, she'd burrow her way inside his heart. *Well, would that be so terrible?* Would the earth shrivel up and cease to exist if a hard-ass loner let someone get close to him?

"It happened during a test flight," he said finally. "We were doing a war exercise. I had to dive through flames and missiles."

Paige gasped.

The hazy shapes in the lab's reception area became the clouds of dark smoke he'd had to maneuver through. Fire crackled through shrubs and trees. The smell of smoke filled his lungs. "I must have hit something on the way down."

"Oh, my God!"

"I landed the plane safely." By keeping both eyes on the target. "But something exploded as I was exiting the cockpit. Zapped my right cornea."

The room was silent except for the sounds of labored breathing. And dark, like that day. Had he blacked out? No, he'd closed his eyes. He opened them to see a teardrop squiggle down Paige's cheek.

She brushed it aside. "You could have lost your eye. Thank God they were able to save it."

"Yeah."

They sat quietly together, not touching, not looking at each other. Finally Paige said, "That disqualified you from flying, didn't it?"

Ten years later, those words still knocked the air out of his lungs. "Spent the rest of my military career in the second seat. Flight navigation and instrumentation. Programming the sound system is what got me interested in voice activation response."

A warm hand grasped his wrist. "Well, at least your misfortune had a silver lining."

Silver lining? Since he was three years old all he'd ever wanted to be was a pilot. When he woke up in the military hospital and realized he'd never fly again, it had almost broken his will to live. He shook off her hand. "Can I have my glasses back, or do you plan to ransom them until I've told you my whole life story?"

Paige jumped. "Oh. Sorry." She'd forgotten she was still holding his lenses, unaware she'd been caressing them like a security blanket, staving off the raw pain. She felt as if her own eye had been slashed, her own dreams shattered.

After sliding the glasses over Brian's ears, she brushed away a long, loose hair that had fallen into his face.

"You're a real touchy-feely type, aren't you?"

"I guess." She drew back her hand. She'd pushed him farther than he'd wanted to go. But she didn't regret coaxing him to talk. "I work with blind kids. They can't see smiles or read expressions. They understand pats and hugs." She plastered her hands to her sides. "I'm sorry it bothers you."

"I didn't say it bothered me."

His mouth could be as expressive as his eyes. She'd assumed his dour expressions were all frowns. Now she noticed a subtle twitch in his lips that hinted at enjoyment or amusement. It made her wonder what else he could do with those lips.

A shudder of awareness rocked her. Brian McKay wasn't like any of the boys she'd grown up with. He was a man. Not just because he was older. She sensed he'd been a man all his life.

The air between them crackled with intensity. Paige jerked herself to her feet. "I really appreciate your taking on this project," she said, circling Victor's platform. "It's going to mean so much to the kids. Especially Elena."

His gaze followed her. "You shouldn't build your hopes up too high about reaching that little girl. It's not good for her. Or you."

"What do you mean?"

He stood and brushed off his jeans. "What if you do connect with her, and she reaches out and confides in you? What happens after camp is over? You raise her up to believe somebody cares about her and then you disappear from her life."

"But I won't. I'll keep in touch."

"How? Send her a Christmas card?"

It sounded so cold and unfeeling, and she didn't want to admit Brian had a point. She sighed. "You always see your glass as half empty."

"I see my glass the way it is."

Paige dropped the argument. She could hardly ask Brian to believe life was rosy when he'd suffered such disappointment. But he didn't have a monopoly on regret. Her mother always said you had to take the bad with the good, and just believe the sunshine would come back.

She fought a pang of grief and guilt. Mom had just stopped believing too soon. But Brian had so much going for him. The sunshine was out there for him if he'd just open himself up and let it in.

*Right, Pollyanna, all you have to do is think lovely thoughts.* Or maybe that was Tinkerbelle. She sighed. She'd never met anyone as self-protective as Brian McKay. Or as intriguing. How ironic that the inventor of a product which could help draw out her shy campers could benefit from the same encouragement.

Paige turned back to the robot, envisioning him with a round, lifelike head, equipped with appropriate facial features. "Victor, you are going to be one handsome devil once we get you fixed up."

Behind her, Brian typed something into the computer. "Thanks, doll," the robot said in his scratchy voice. "You're pretty hot yourself."

Now *that* was something she never expected to hear out of Brian McKay's mouth. But of course it wasn't his mouth. Not exactly.

"Victor, you're such a flirt." Kiss-kissing the air in front of her, she squeezed the wiring that would become the robot's hand. "I'll bet you've got all the little girl robots lined up for miles."

"I only have eyes for you, doll," Victor said/Brian typed. "That is, I would if I had eyes."

Paige giggled. "Tell your creator to make you some. Pinocchio became a real live boy. Maybe there's hope for you and me."

She didn't hear any typing. No sound at all except her own breathing. Finally the keyboard behind her started clicking again. The robot spoke. "Do you want a boy or a man?"

Paige felt a hand on her waist. She whirled around. Brian tugged her hard against his body and cupped the back of her head with his other hand. His lips descended onto hers with perfect accuracy, capturing her mouth, making her forget to breathe.

He kissed her with unerring confidence, parting her lips with his tongue. His breath flowed into her like a conquering wind. Her mouth opened for him willingly, eagerly. She felt powerless to deny him, helpless against his invading touch. His natural, masculine scent, unmasked by fancy cologne, seduced her more than the most expensive fragrance.

She curled her fingers around his neck. He grabbed her bottom and wedged her between his legs. Paige gasped. His chest wasn't the only thing that was lean and hard.

Her lips locked on his, aflame with desire. Her body squirmed against him, begging and demanding with equal intensity. Every rational thought escaped her except one single-minded craving.

This wasn't like her. Paige Anderson didn't get herself into situations she hadn't thoroughly evaluated first. She summoned her usual reserve, but need overpowered her. She couldn't get enough of Brian's scent, of his skin, of his touch.

But just as she gave herself up to desire, he pulled back, leaving her panting and hungry for more. "That wasn't Victor," he snarled.

Paige wiped a finger across her lip as her breath slowly returned. "What...what's wrong?"

Brian's dark brown eyes were as hard as his body. "You should leave," he growled. "I'm sure you must have some social obligation."

He picked up her bag and tossed it at her. In thirty seconds she found herself on the outer side of the closed door.

Paige held onto the stair railing to support her wobbly legs. What had just happened? She felt like an engine revved from zero to sixty--then slammed into neutral. That was some serious, take-no-prisoners kiss. She'd never been so swiftly and thoroughly aroused by a man she barely knew.

By any man.

Why had he stopped? What had provoked his cold fury?

She stumbled down the steps to her car, her heart pounding. She couldn't remember ever feeling so out of control. The sensation frightened her. And thrilled her. Like that ride on the motorcycle. Or the California Screamin' roller coaster she'd watched in awe, but been afraid to ride.

Paige had always been a merry-go-round girl, sticking to the predictably calm ride with no surprises. But suddenly that roller coaster held a whole new appeal.

\* \* \*

*Stupid schmuck.* Brian shoved the frozen dinner into the microwave and slammed the door. What the hell was wrong with him? He was jealous of a goddamned robot?

He nuked the macaroni and cheese until it screamed for mercy, then slapped the half-melted container onto the particleboard over cable spool that served as his dining table.

She shouldn't have kept touching him like that.

*Right, make it her fault.*

55

He forked a macaroni curl and dangled it over his mouth until the steam dissipated, then snapped it with his teeth like a fish with a worm. *You're the worm, McKay.*

He let the cheese sauce cool, then shoveled in a mouthful of pasta and swallowed it with a scoop of guilt. What kind of backstabbing lowlife makes a move on another guy's girl? Even a sleaze like Connor deserved better treatment. And Paige? He'd attacked her like a rabid, irrational animal.

But she hadn't pushed him away.

His phone vibrated in his pocket. Brian's heart thudded involuntarily against his rib cage. *She doesn't know your number and she wouldn't call if she did.* He reached into his pocket as the programmed tune 'I Hope You Dance' chimed. He flipped the phone open. "Hi, Mom."

"Hi. How did things go in Chicago?"

He frowned. "Don't know. Connor's not back yet." And he hadn't called. Not a good sign unless his brother had gotten so drunk celebrating he couldn't find his phone.

"You didn't go with him? Wouldn't the company want to meet the inventor?"

Her too? Brian clenched his fist. "When you take your car into the auto shop," he snapped, "do you meet the mechanic? No. The good-looking, smooth-talking service tech dazzles you with the few buzz words he knows. The guy who actually works on your car has greasy hands, dirty fingernails, and holes in his coveralls."

"And a fistful of attitude." His mother sounded tired. "How many times have I told you: You're as good as anyone and better than most. When are you going to believe that?"

"I believe it now. I just don't think anyone else does." And it would take more than one torrid kiss to alter that perception.

He dabbed at a string of cheese with a paper towel. "But soon, we can look those people in the eye and tell 'em all to go to hell. You're gonna have your dream house on Easy Street, with a swimming pool and a hot tub and a servant for every room."

"That would be *your* dream house, Hon. I'd be tripping over all those servants. All I want is for you to be happy."

"I'm happy."

"Um hum." She sounded as convinced as he felt. "If you do land the contract, you should buy yourself that plane you've always wanted. Then you could fly up and see me more often."

Her guilt-edged arrow found its mark. He hadn't been home since Christmas.

"There's a spectacular fireworks display over Lake Tahoe for the Fourth of July," she hinted.

He stalled. "When is that?"

"Math genius. The day after the third."

He grinned. "Okay, okay, I'll come."

"What's keeping you so busy? Friends?" Her voice brightened hopefully. "Maybe a girlfriend?"

"Work," he answered too quickly.

"You know what they say about all work and no play."

Brian shut his eyes and braced himself for the lecture.

"I promised I wouldn't nag you until you were thirty," Mom teased. "Time's up. You should get a social life, maybe think about settling down. Most of my friends have grandbabies by now."

"Which they'll probably have to help support after the babies' fathers ditch them." His stomach soured. "At least I won't do that to you."

"Not all relationships fail." She cleared her throat. "You're not like him, Brian."

"Damn straight. If I were, I'd have to shoot myself."

Her sigh was as poignant as it was exasperated. "Son, you have to get over your anger. He was what he was. Charming, impetuous, and irresponsible."

She was still in love with the prick, even after his death. "What I can't get over is how he treated you."

"I took a chance on love and I don't regret it. I guess I'm a one-man woman. And I've got news for you. You have more of my genes than his. If you ever do meet the right woman, you're going to fall fast and hard."

"Never gonna happen." He said it jovially but something in his chest felt like he'd just lied. "Love you, Mom."

After clicking off, he chucked the burned, dried out macaroni into the garbage. A glob of pasta floweret and yellow-orange goo clung to his black T-shirt. He pulled the shirt over his head, sniffing the still pungent scent of pine and cologne and shampoo. Eau de Paige triumphed over Aroma de microwave.

He shoved the T-shirt into a small duffel bag, and inspected the square plastic laundry basket where he kept his clean clothes. He was down to his last pair of underwear. Sighing, he tugged off his jeans and stuffed them into the laundry bag, then stripped off his briefs and socks and tied the drawstring. Quik-Wash Laundromat tomorrow.

Naked, he switched on the portable TV and flipped channels. Nothing but reality shows and asinine sitcoms. And porn.

What was so alluring about silicone-enhanced freaks of nature? Brian clicked off the television and closed his eyes, visualizing a normal-proportioned female with golden, flawless skin and sparkling blue eyes. Breasts that fit into a man's hands. Hips made for mounting. And a sexy tattoo on a firm, pale butt cheek.

Damn. He was hopeless.

## Chapter Four

**B**rian was puttering with the specs for Victor's new program the next evening when Connor straggled in and plopped down his overnight bag. "Still playing with your toys, I see."

A half dozen retorts sprang to mind but he let them go. "So?"

Connor tossed his suit jacket over Brian's desk chair. "Get me a beer, would you?"

"I'm not your freaking servant."

Connor strolled to the back of the lab in slow motion, and took so damn long returning Brian almost wished he *had* gone for the damn beer. So he could empty the bottle over his brother's head.

"Well?" he said, after Connor had settled in his chair and propped a leg on his desk.

His brother took a long, slow sip, purposely prolonging the torture. "They're on board, pending a complete demo of Suite Smart."

Yes! "Ten million for the hardware, software licenses, initial installation and training, like we agreed?"

Connor stared into the long neck of his beer bottle. "I'm still negotiating that." He fixed his eyes on Brian's. "An Allied finance exec and their lead programmer agreed to come for a site tour July seventeenth."

Brian's heart raced, then skidded to a stop. "That's in three weeks."

"So? Is that a problem?"

He sucked in his gut. "No problem. It'll be ready." If he could resolve that one programming hitch in the bed module. Which might mean putting in twenty-hour days from now until the visit. He wiped his palms on his jeans. That meant no time to work on Victor. How was he going to tell Paige?

Maybe he wouldn't have to. Maybe she was so disgusted with the way he'd behaved yesterday she'd never show up again.

The front door jingled and fruity cologne filled his senses. "Hi, guys, anybody home?"

He just couldn't catch a break.

Paige whooshed through door to the lab like a warm Santa Ana wind, wearing a long black crinkly skirt with white designs and a black silky top. Not typical camp attire.

"Oh, good, you're both here." Her gaze lit on Brian, then quickly darted away. She sidled up to Connor. "How did the meeting go?"

Her eyes sparkled, entranced, as Connor filled her in, using all the drama of his birthright. The way he told it, the president of Allied had practically declared Connor and *his* product the savior of their company. "We just have to wow them with a dog and pony show."

"That's wonderful," Paige effervesced in her champagne-bubbly voice. "Let's celebrate." Her gaze swept over Brian and back to Connor. "Dinner at the club. My treat."

"Great." Connor grabbed his suit jacket and Paige's arm. "Let's go."

"Both of you." She focused on Brian for the first time.

She was just being polite. Brian looked down at his work jeans and wrinkled t-shirt. "I'm not dressed."

"Right," Connor agreed without hesitation. "Some other time." He nudged Paige toward the door but she didn't move.

"You're fine. But the restaurant can probably lend you a jacket and tie if you'd feel more comfortable."

Brian flexed his fingers. He'd feel more comfortable tied up and tossed in a hog pen. But if he didn't go, he'd lose any chance he might have with Paige. And she could end up in Connor's bed tonight.

"Brian wouldn't enjoy the club." Connor tried again for the exit. "He'd be uncomfortable and out of place--"

"Just give me a minute to wash up," Brian blurted out before Paige changed her mind.

\*  \*  \*

Paige loved dinners at the club. By day the restaurant smelled like sunscreen and freshly laundered towels. But after sunset, with sculpted candles shimmering on white linen tablecloths and a three piece combo playing light jazz, it exuded an air of quiet, simple elegance.

"Miss Anderson. Mr. McKay. How nice to see you again." The maitre d' bowed. Glancing behind them at Brian lurking in the doorway, he raised a brow. "Three this evening?"

"Yes, Charles, thanks." The maitre d' led the way to a table in the back. The place was busy for a week night. Paige knew at least half the people here. She weaved between tables, waving at an older couple she recognized from church, shaking hands with one of Daddy's colleagues, and exchanging hugs with a girl she'd known at UCLA. Connor stopped every few feet to shake a hand or slap a back.

Paige turned to check on Brian. He trailed silently behind, looking as if he were about to be executed by lethal injection.

He'd hardly said a word on the ride over, but she'd felt his stormy presence behind her. He was still sulking, apparently, about yesterday. Why was he angry with *her*? *He* had initiated the kiss, and *he* had slammed on the brakes.

Connor pulled out her chair and seated himself beside her.

61

Brian took the chair opposite, his eyes cold and guarded. The evening hadn't even started yet, and the brothers were already revving up the testosterone. Paige sighed. It was going to take more than a civilized meal together to heal the rift between these two.

When the waiter poured the champagne, she raised her glass to toast her companions. "Here's to Suite Smart."

Brian sat quietly nursing his drink as Connor took center stage, starting with anecdotes about his trip to Chicago, then dragging out old stories from their high school glory days. Paige tried to focus her attention on his lighthearted monologue but her gaze kept drifting across the table to Brian.

He'd cleaned up well. Somewhere in that cavernous laboratory he'd found a clean black dress shirt and khaki slacks. His hair was combed and his glasses straight. As Connor had predicted, he did seem out of place here. But he looked neither nervous nor intimidated. Brian's condescending eyes wore an expression of practiced boredom, as if his heart and mind were somewhere else. Despite Paige's attempts to draw him into the conversation, he either answered in two-word sentences, or didn't respond at all.

"Remember junior year when we rowed against that public high school that dumped our whole crew in the drink?" Connor leaned against her and brushed a hair away from her ear. "When our boat overturned, you laughed so hard you dropped your cheerleader megaphone into the water."

Because Connor had looked so astounded to be bested by a public school. She edged away. "I'm sure we're boring Brian."

Brian made a show of stifling a wide-mouthed yawn. "No, really, I'm fascinated. Tell me more about Muffy and Sissy and Biff."

Oblivious to the sarcasm, Connor continued his monologue. Paige made polite eye contact but her gaze kept returning to Brian. His dark eyes barely flickered. What was it about him that was so arresting? His silent presence charged the air with a dark sexuality that radiated across the room.

Or maybe it was just her. Paige sipped her champagne, ignoring the flush of heat spreading over her face and body.

A singer joined the pianist, and began warbling show tunes.

Connor downed his drink and poured another. "Look, Jon and Liz Van Allen just came in," he said, swiveling in his chair. He turned back to Paige. "We should stop over and say hello."

Liz's father was a stage director at NBC studios in Burbank and had been good friends with Connor's dad. "You go ahead. We'll be fine here." She smiled sweetly at Brian as Connor stood and waltzed off to network.

Brian shot her a daggered look, his eyes as hard and intense as yesterday.

Paige set her glass down and glared back. "Will you tell me why you're so mad? What did I do?"

He lowered his gaze. His harsh expression softened. "It wasn't you." He swirled his glass around the tablecloth. "I stepped over the line."

The line? Aaah. *The code.* "It's a guy thing, right? The first commandment of the Universal Guy code: *Thou shalt not hit on thy brother's girl.*"

"Something like that."

"Okay, I can respect that. There's just one thing: I'm not Connor's girl. I'm not anybody's girl."

His expression was unreadable. But his eyes burned into her.

She touched his hand. "It was just a kiss, Brian. If you feel uncomfortable, or guilty, or whatever, we can just forget it happened."

He pulled his hand away. "I've already forgotten it."

That makes one of us. That kiss was so demanding, almost desperate. She wondered where all that emotion had come from.

Unrequited love? A painful breakup? Or pent-up passions he'd never expressed? "Can I ask you a personal question?"

"Could I stop you?"

She chuckled. "Were you ever married?"

"Nope."

"Engaged?"

"No."

"Ever had a serious girlfriend?"

He pressed his elbows to the table and leaned forward. "I'm not a virgin, Paige."

"That's not what I..." She swallowed. "I didn't mean to imply..."

"You look nice in red."

Paige glanced down at her black and white dress. "I'm not wearing--oh." She patted her flushed cheeks, which burned even hotter under his stare.

How did he manage to make her feel so...out of control? She was used to men flirting with her. Men more adept than Brian McKay. Paige had always directed the mating game, thwarting the advances that didn't interest her, subtly encouraging those that did. But all Brian had to do was look at her and she felt as helpless--and as hungry--as she had locked in his embrace.

She struggled to regain her composure. "I was just guessing you've never been in a long-term relationship."

"Dated the same girl all through college." He leaned back in his chair. "That long-term enough for you?"

Longer than any relationship she'd ever been in. Six months seemed to be her limit. The point when men often got bored with a woman. Paige usually broke it off before they could get there. "What was her name?" she asked, ready to catch him in a lie.

"Mandy."

He wasn't lying, she could tell by his eyes. Mandy. She tried to picture Brian as a student, with a girl on his arm, walking her to class, meeting her for lunch in the cafeteria, snuggling with her in her dorm room at night. She imagined the kind of girl Brian would date. A straight A student. Almost pretty, but hid her attractiveness behind thick glasses just as he did. Probably wore knee socks in the winter instead of shaving her legs. "Why did you two break up?"

"She wanted to get married."

The waiter arrived with their salads. Paige glanced at the table across the room. Connor had taken a seat, and was apparently regaling his friends with some amusing story.

When the waiter left, she turned back to Brian. "What do you have against marriage?"

"Nothing. It's divorce I'm not fond of."

Ouch. Sometimes she failed to appreciate how lucky she was. Her parent's marriage had been shaky at times, but deep down there'd been bedrock of mutual love. "I guess it must have been difficult for you as a child, knowing your parents didn't love each other."

His eyes narrowed. "Why would you say that?"

Oops. "I mean, I would guess that--"

"My mother never remarried. She loved my father until the day he died." Brian swigged down his champagne as if it were a two-dollar beer. "Unfortunately, that asshole Dr. Mike that the TV world adored didn't give a shit about anyone but himself in real life. The bastard let Mom support him until he got his break, and then it was goodbye family and hello Hollywood."

Paige's throat tightened. Brian's cold resentment revealed more pain than an angry outburst. "How old were you?"

"Four."

A long time to hold a grudge. Especially against a father. Gil McKay had always seemed so nice, even taking Paige and her sisters to his studio once to watch him shoot an episode for his series. She shuddered. The man she thought she'd known was only an actor. How could a man be kinder to neighbors than to his own flesh and blood?

She wanted to reach out to Brian, help him past his anger, but the glare in his dark eyes warned against it. *Give him his space, Paige.* Maybe someday he'd trust her enough to share more.

She drizzled her on-the-side cup of vinaigrette dressing over her salad. "I talked to the camp director today about our project," she said in a lighter tone. "She was excited and thought it was a great idea to bring Victor to the camp."

Brian set down his glass.

"She wanted us to do a program for the entire camp, but--"

"Paige, about Victor..."

"--but I told her it might ruin the point of the project if children who could see experienced the program at the same time as the sightless ones. I want my kids to really believe in their new friend. Oh, and I bought some patterns today for Victor's clothes. I'll bring them tomorrow and you can pick out the one you like. I'm partial to the overalls myself but--" She realized she was rambling. "I'm sorry. What were you going to say?"

"Nothing." He stabbed a fork into his salad and took a crunchy bite.

Had she said something to offend him? Or was he still dwelling on his bitter feelings for his father? The man was as moody as he was unpredictable. Yet, the more he hid, the more she wanted to uncover.

Connor ambled back to their table and plopped down beside her just as the entrees were served. "Why is everybody so quiet and serious? This is supposed to be a celebration. More champagne?"

He ordered another bottle, topped off their glasses, and clinked his against hers. "To lots and lots of green glorious money."

Paige touched her glass to Brian's. "To good friends."

Connor downed his drink, then leaned back and curled his arm around Paige's shoulder. His lips brushed her cheek. As he nibbled at her earlobe, his fingers walked down her arm and detoured to her breast.

"Connor!" She nudged his hand away. It wasn't like him to behave so inappropriately, especially at the club where everyone knew him. And in front of Brian. *Oh.*

Brian didn't utter a sound, but when she dared a glance at his eyes, they were seething.

Paige looked away. His kiss didn't constitute ownership any more than Connor's clumsy groping. Why were men so possessive?

Undaunted by her rebuff, Connor turned his attention to his rib eye steak and baked potato. And to three more glasses of champagne. Before he could pour the fourth, Paige palmed her hand over his glass. Smiling, but with a gray glare in his eyes, Connor pried her fingers away, sucked one between his lips, and then placed her hand onto her lap.

Paige stole a glance at Brian. He lifted a brow but said nothing.

Connor forked the rest of his steak into his mouth. "This place knows how to prepare meat," he said a little too loudly. He pointed to Brian's T- Bone. "Better than that gristle you get at Bubba's Bull Pit, huh?"

Brian defiantly poured half a bottle of A-1 sauce on his steak. "The food's no better here than anywhere else. They just wrap little panties around the lamb chops, call it 'cuisine,' and up the price twenty dollars." Venom dripped from his mouth. "Private clubs are just an excuse for some people to convince themselves they're better than others."

Paige folded her arms. "If you hate this place so much, why did you agree to come?"

"I didn't want to be rude."

"And this is you being polite?"

"Told you he wouldn't fit in here." Connor poured himself yet another drink, emptying the second bottle. He dumped it into the ice bucket and snapped his fingers at a passing waiter. "Another bottle of the same."

"You don't need another one," Paige said quietly, waving the waiter away. She'd had one glass, Brian two. Connor had finished off the rest.

The glare in Connor's eyes was almost frightening. "I'm not one of your charity projects," he hissed. "You don't tell me what I need and don't need." He grabbed her wrist and squeezed.

Brian's dark eyes blazed. Paige's stomach muscles tightened as he stood and faced his brother. But instead of taking a swing, he stepped over to Paige's chair and held out his hand. "Dance?"

*Dance?* She placed her hand in his and let out her breath as he led her to the wood floor. "Great counter. I was afraid you were going to hit him."

"He's not worth the trouble." Brian's fingers were tight against her palm, his jaw clenched. "I'm sorry I embarrassed you. The shitface is right. I don't belong here."

"You're my guest. You have as much right to be here as Connor does. And he's the one who's embarrassing."

The singer, a Bonnie Raitt look-alike, stepped up the tempo with one of Bonnie's signature songs. In a fluid motion, Brian drew Paige into his arms. His fingers splayed against her back. His other hand, still holding hers, kept them a respectable distance apart. But she was close enough to inhale the scent of Irish Spring soap over the sweat of a hard day's work. She placed one hand on his shoulder and grasped his waist with the other, resisting the urge to slide her fingers under his shirt.

He twirled her in a wide circle, rolling her along his arm and then reeling her in again, tighter this time. Paige caught Liz's curious stare as they danced past the Van Allen's table. Brian seemed to see only Paige and hear only the music.

*Something to Talk About.* She recognized the classic song now. Smiling, Paige rested her head on Brian's chest and tugged him closer. *All right, let's give them something to talk about.*

The buttons on his cotton shirt caressed her cheek. His stubbled chin grazed the top of her head. She felt safe in his arms, comfortable with his lead. Forgetting Connor, social politeness, and the obligation to make everyone get along, she let go, for an idyllic moment, of the self-imposed responsibility she'd carried since Mom died.

"You dance very well," she said as Brian led her through turns and twirls. His hand brushed across her bottom. At her ragged gasp, he caught her in his arms and pressed his body against her. Hard. The heat of his thighs burned a path up the inside of hers.

"Mandy was a dance and drama major."

When the music faded out, he braced his arm against her back and dipped her so low her hair almost touched the floor. Only his arm and his other hand supporting her neck kept her from falling. His upper body lay horizontal above her and his lips hovered close to hers, almost touching. The suggestion of intimacy overpowered her. She could see herself, feel herself, making love with him.

She grabbed his shoulders, and he slowly pulled her up.

"Wow," she breathed.

"It was just a dance," he said modestly. But a seductive twinkle flashed across his dark eyes.

As he took her elbow and led her off the floor, guarded stares and hushed mumblings followed them to their table. Paige blushed like a teenager caught making out in the back seat. For a minute she'd forgotten they weren't alone in the room.

The Van Allens had settled in at their table, Liz in the empty chair across from Paige's, and Jon in Brian's.

Connor pulled out her chair. "Paige, you know Liz and Jon."

69

Brian stood awkwardly.

"Oh, sorry, did I take your chair?" Jon jumped up and grabbed one from an unoccupied table, setting it at the edge of theirs directly in the path of waiters and diners. Then he sat back down in Brian's seat.

Face frozen, eyes iced, Brian took the fifth chair.

Paige introduced him to the Van Allens. When Jon's eyebrows shot up at Brian's last name, Connor said quickly, "A distant relative."

He wouldn't even acknowledge Brian as his brother? The hostility went deeper than Paige had thought. Not that her sultry dance with Brian had helped that tense rivalry.

"So you're not one of the Hollywood McKays?" Jon asked Brian, trying to ascertain, apparently, if he was someone he should be nice to.

"Reno," Brian said, and that ended that conversation.

Liz Van Allen turned to Paige. "You and Connor must come over tonight to see our new place. We hired that decorator everyone's raving about and he's just done wonders with the east patio. We could go for a swim. But don't worry about bringing suits." She winked. "Swim attire is optional."

"And I just got a new stash of candy," Jon said to Connor.

"I'm in," Connor said.

They all seemed to have forgotten Brian was even at the table. Paige did a slow burn. He'd probably rather count wallpaper patterns than spend the evening with her obscenely rich Beverly Hills friends, but he should have at least been offered the chance to refuse. She turned to him as if Liz had merely overlooked mentioning his name in her invitation. "Are you up for a midnight swim?"

Liz Van Allen raised her brows at Paige as if she'd committed the social faux pas of the season.

"Gee, so sorry," Brian said. "I have to feng-shui the country house tonight. You two go on. I'll catch a cab back."

Liz's taut features relaxed. "So nice meeting you, Mr. McKay," she said with finality, then turned to Connor. "You can follow us. We'll wait for you at the parking lot entrance."

Paige took out her credit card, silently steaming. She couldn't decide who took the prize for rudeness, her snobby friends, or an intellectual elitist who thought that possession of social graces should be made a capital crime.

She didn't want to spend the evening baby-sitting Connor and his coke-snorting friends any more than Brian did. But if she let Connor go off alone with the Van Allens, in his condition, she'd feel responsible for whatever happened to him.

She paid the bill, avoiding Brian's eyes, knowing he was judging her by her friends. She'd always been embarrassed by the arrogance so many of her friends seemed to think was their birthright, but she'd tolerated it. Accepting others in your social group, not making waves, was the price of belonging. She'd learned that lesson in eighth grade and wasn't inclined to repeat the course.

They walked outside into a light mist. "Feng shui?" she asked Brian as they stepped away from the awning.

"Country house?" Connor sneered.

Brian shrugged. She started to insist on driving him back to his motorcycle, but the glare in his eyes stopped her. *Leave it alone.*

The valet brought the Infiniti and Connor got into the passenger seat. Paige tipped the young man and settled in, fastening her belt. Brian stood outside her car door and spoke quietly into her ear. "Don't let Connor drive tonight."

As if she would even consider that in his state. "It's nice to know you do care about your brother."

His eyes met hers. "I'm not worried about *him*."

Involuntarily, she melted under his gaze like warm chocolate.

71

Her heart hurt. How had she messed things up so badly? She'd only wanted to take him out to celebrate his achievement, in a place where she felt accepted and comfortable.  But he wanted no part of her world and apparently thought her as vain and shallow as her snooty friends. She told herself she didn't care what Brian thought of her, but the lie fell far short of believable.

She wished she had his courage. He didn't care if people liked him. He was just himself. She'd spent so much of her life trying to fit in, trying to be what everybody else expected of her, she wasn't sure who the 'real' Paige was.

As he walked away toward the cab stand, she fought the urge to leap out of the car and run after him. To go back with him to his motorcycle, jump on behind him, wrap her legs around his thighs and ride off to whatever cave he called home. Just once, she wanted to say to hell with social expectations and her own personal code of behavior and do something wild and crazy.

Instead, she turned the keys and started the car.

## Chapter Five

*I* *t was just a kiss.*

As he waved away the valet's attempt to call a cab and walked out to the sidewalk, Brian mentally dissected Paige's statement. 'Just a kiss' was the obligatory lip-brush you gave a date at the end of a not-so-stellar evening. Or to your mother's friend's daughter who 'just happened' to visit the weekend you were in town.

What he and Paige had shared the other day was not, in his book, 'just a kiss.' Her tongue had been all the way down his throat and her hands had been as eager as his. When he'd come to his senses and pulled away, they were probably sixty seconds from naked and writhing on the floor.

Yet she acted as if it were nothing more than a handshake.

A light breeze sang through the palm trees, dropping cool, welcome moisture onto his hot brow. His body still burned from the contact with hers. His heart pounded as if her cheek still pressed against his chest.

*She probably dances that way with everybody.*

Darkness descended around him like a cloak as he trudged down Santa Monica Boulevard toward the ocean. His feet already felt like pounded mush and he had three more miles to go. But after two income-less years working on the Suite, his meager savings was almost gone. He wasn't about to spend money on a cab he might need for next week's groceries.

At least the weather was perfect. In Reno it was either hotter than hell or colder than a witch's tit. But that was the only thing he liked about this town.

*California girls.* He'd never understand them.

*      *      *

The next morning, his feet burned as if a blowtorch had scorched his soles, and his head ached from a short but sleepless night. Brian saved the latest changes to the Suite Smart program and moved to the keyboard next to the robot's platform. "I don't get it, Victor. How could she flirt with me, dance close with me, and then leave with Connor?"

"She's a tease," the robot responded before Brian realized his fingers were typing.

"The worst kind of tease." She hadn't just touched his body, she'd seduced him into opening his heart, then reached inside, and twisted it.

"Still talking to that robot?" Connor trudged into the office, carrying a fast food bag and holding a can of soda against his temple. "Let me know when he talks back."

Brian typed onto the keyboard. "Connor is an ass," the robot's voice chirped.

Connor rolled his eyes.

Brian glanced pointedly at the clock. Ten past noon. "A little late, even for you."

Connor groaned. "I got so wasted last night. Liz and Jon had some quality coke..." He winced as he rolled the cold drink over his forehead. "Doesn't usually affect me this much. I guess I was already a little buzzed from the champagne."

"I think you passed 'a little' with the second bottle."

"You think you hold your booze better than me?"

"I hold everything better than you."

Connor fixed his bloodshot blue eyes on Brian. "If I were in your position, I'd think twice about biting the hand that feeds me."

"You don't even feed yourself." He wasn't in the mood for Connor's crap today. "You let your girlfriend buy dinner."

"It was Paige's idea to pay. And she's not my girlfriend."

"So I keep hearing." But what he kept seeing was Connor's hands all over her. He strode into the lab.

Connor followed him. "You bowed out too early. Things heated up later and Paige got really friendly."

*Don't turn around. Don't let him see he got to you.*

"In the back seat of her car," Connor drawled, "Ms. Goody Two Shoes was all over me. Couldn't even wait until we got back to my place."

Brian clenched his fists. *Not your business.* Paige could bed whatever jerk she wanted. He couldn't care less.

Connor unwrapped his lunch and spread it over Brian's desk. "Paige said you're working on some project for her campers."

"Just writing a little code."

He pulled out Brian's chair and plopped his butt in it. "Unless she's paying you more than the Allied Hotels proposal, you don't have time for that shit."

"The more you talk, the longer it's gonna take me." Brian's stomach growled as he watched Connor chomp down his burger. He'd been working on the Suite since seven a.m. without a break, following a schedule he'd set for himself to keep on track. If he met his daily goals, he figured he could steal a few hours to work on Victor and still make the site visit deadline.

Connor flipped the top off his drink and washed down his food. "So how much is Ms. Goody Two Shoes paying you?"

Brian tightened an Ethernet cable that had come loose from the fileserver.

Connor swiveled his head. "She *is* paying you?"

"It's for the kids, Connor."

"Yeah?" Connor's bleary eyes tried to glare. "Well charity begins at home. I've got a hell of a lot invested in Suite Smart, and if it's not ready on time, your ass won't be worth that one measly dollar."

Brian fought the urge to knock Connor's ass out of his chair. Silently he recited his mantra. *The smart triumph over the strong.*

"You're being played for a sucker, Bro. All she has to do is wiggle her butt and she's got you just where she wants you. And you're never going to get any."

Brian clamped his back teeth. "Drop it, Connor."

"You are so whipped," he sneered. "Straight talk isn't working so let me give it to you in a metaphor." Connor paused dramatically. "Paige is like a butterfly. Pretty to look at, flits around sucking the nectar from a lot of men--er, flowers. But she never lights on one. And if she ever does, you can be damn sure it'll be someone with a lot more money and class than you!"

Brian's jaw hurt from grinding his teeth. "Like you?"

Connor stuffed food wrappings into the paper sack. "I'm not interested in Sweet and Sexless. The babe *I'm* spending the weekend with knows how to make a man feel like a man." He dropped the mustard-smelling trash into Brian's waste container. "I'm just trying to stop you from making a damn fool of yourself."

When his brother headed out front, Brian slammed his fist against his desk, bouncing burger bun crumbs to the floor. Just because Connor was an idiot didn't mean he couldn't make sense once in a while. Law of averages.

Still, Brian had made a commitment to Paige and her campers, and he'd keep his promise. All he had to do was work smarter and harder, and he'd been doing that all his life.

A stale granola bar from his desk drawer quieted his stomach's rumblings. No time to take a lunch. He'd planned to re-program Victor's script today after Connor left, but the jerk hung around all afternoon. For no apparent purpose.

If he'd hoped to keep Brian from being alone with Paige, the tactic was a bust. She never showed. Brian didn't hear from her until she bounced into the lab late Friday afternoon, wearing a green tank top, cut-off jean shorts, and the California sunshine in her hair.

"Sorry I didn't make it yesterday." She plopped her canvas satchel on Connor's empty desk. "My sister's nanny was sick so I had to pick up Phillip at Bible camp and stay with him until Helene got home."

"You could have called to let me know," he said, more gruffly than he'd intended.

"I did call." She raised a surprised brow. "Didn't Connor tell you?"

Brian gritted his teeth. "He must have forgotten to give me the message."

Paige lit in Connor's chair and pulled her legs up, hugging her knees. "I can't stay long. I've got to start preparing side dishes for the barbecue."

"Barbecue?"

"The Anderson family's traditional Fourth of July barbecue. I hope you can come."

He recalled the promise to his mother. "I have plans."

Her smile cratered into a pout. "I wanted my family to meet you."

"Why?"

She blinked an incredulous look. "Because you're my friend."

Like Connor was her 'friend'? "Nobody's a stranger to you, are they?" Everyone she met was somehow connected to somebody else. Paige linked them all together and drew the whole chain into her world.

She crossed her legs. "You say that like it's a bad thing."

It was hard not to be seduced by her openness. But Brian wasn't doing any more threesomes with her and Connor.

"Connor's not coming," she said as if she'd read his mind. "He has other plans."

*A cool weekend with a hot babe.* Brian sucked air into his lungs. "So do I."

Thankfully, she dropped the subject. "I brought the patterns." Paige pulled two packages out of her bag and laid them out on Connor's desk. "Which do you like? Sailor suit? Or overalls?"

"Paige, I really don't care--"

"Overalls, then." She dug into her bag again. "What fabric do you like for the shirt?" She held up a red cotton swatch with some kind of western pattern and a blue and yellow floral something.

He pointed to the red. "Not that it matters. The kids can't see."

"Well, at least Victor won't be naked." She giggled.

"Which is more than I can say for you and your friends." Damn, had he said that out loud?

Her blue eyes flashed indignantly. "Excuse me?"

Too late to back down. "The nude swimming party?"

She shoved the fabrics into her bag before glaring back at him. "*I* didn't swim, nude or otherwise. But they were all so stoned, *somebody* had to keep an eye on them."

"Responsible Paige, always looking after everybody else."

"What's wrong with that?"

"Nothing, if you're Mother Teresa." She'd kept her clothes on. Stupid relief fanned his gut. "Why do you hang out with those people if you don't like them?"

She narrowed her eyes. "Who says I don't like them?"

Could she not hear the uncertainty in her own voice? "Do you?"

Sitting back, she crossed her arms over her chest. "They're my friends."

God, she couldn't discriminate at all. It was physically impossible for Pollyanna Paige to voice a negative thought about anybody. "Do you hear yourself?"

Her arms fell into her lap. "I grew up with them. We know the same people. Go to the same parties. I'm comfortable with them."

"So it doesn't matter if they're the most self-indulgent assholes in the world? As long as you've got the right pedigree, you can be Paige's friend."

She glared at him for several seconds before she spoke. "Not all rich people are assholes, Brian." Her stare intensified. "And not all assholes are rich."

Okay, he deserved that. But he was done letting her jerk him around like a goddamned puppet. "Look, I don't give a flip who you do or how you do it. You can sell raffle tickets to The Paige Show for all I care. Just leave me out of your game."

She propped her hands on her hips. "What did I do to you?"

"You kissed me."

"*You* kissed *me!*"

"You didn't kiss me back? That wasn't your tongue playing house with my tonsils?"

Her eyes lost their fire and her lips slowly curled. "For somebody who's forgotten that kiss, you seem to have an awfully vivid memory."

"I got a temporary flashback."

"Careful, Brian, you almost smiled." She got out of the chair and walked over to him. "Maybe if I helped it along..."

She placed a finger on either side of his mouth and gently tugged his lips in an upward curve. Her breasts brushed his chest. It took all his self-control not to grab those fingers, suck them into his mouth, and pull the rest of her body after them.

She smoothed caressing hands over his cheeks. He flinched. "Sorry. I forgot you don't like to be touched."

"Not unless you mean it," he muttered.

Paige stood on her toes, raising her face to his. Her hands still held his cheeks. Her blue eyes stared into his. Her lips were inches from his mouth, enticing, inviting. The scent of pine and Chanel dizzied his senses. He reached out to crush her against his smoldering body.

*Butterfly.* He pulled back just as she set her heels down. "Are we working on Victor or not?" he asked hoarsely.

She held his gaze for an instant before she picked up her satchel and followed him to the robot's platform.

*Close call.* Struggling to refocus, he sat at the computer keyboard.

Paige pulled a chair up beside him, too close beside him. "You don't really have plans for the Fourth, do you? Except to sit in that dreary lab and work all day."

He bit down on his anger. "You don't give up, do you?"

"Okay, okay, you have plans. End of subject." Here came that killer smile. "But if you change your mind..."

Brian tried not to let her voice seduce him as she rattled off details of time and place. With anyone else, an invitation like this would mean she liked him and wanted to be with him.

But last night she'd been with Connor. Played nursemaid to him, driven him safely home, maybe tucked him into bed. Sure, that didn't mean she'd crawled in beside him. But in all her pretty protestations, she'd never said she hadn't.

## Chapter Six

"Paige, the potato salad is to die for. Exactly like your mother made it."

"Thanks, Aunt Ella. I used her recipe." Paige took the empty bowl and exchanged it for another batch of potato salad from the fridge. There was no recipe. The salad tasted the same because Paige had made it last year, as she had the year before and the year before that. Mom had loved entertaining, and in her good moments, had planned grandiose parties. But when the depressions hit, somebody had to pick up the pieces. That somebody had always been Paige.

Aunt Ella carried the fresh bowl outside. Paige took the pies out of the refrigerator and lined them up on the kitchen counter. This was the first Fourth of July without Mom. And Paige would have given anything to have her mother serve the salads and take credit for making them, anything to see her sitting in her favorite chair blowing kisses at Daddy. Anything to have her back again.

"Hey, Paige, where's the beer?" Her cousin Denny scavenged the kitchen.

She swallowed her guilt in one gulp. "Ice chests. Red is beer, blue is soft drinks."

"Great party." Denny disappeared in the same motion as he'd entered.

"Let me help you with the pies." Helene waddled into the kitchen, holding one hand flat against her back. She'd gotten a lot bigger with this pregnancy, much earlier, than she had with Phillip.

Paige frankly wondered how she was going to get through the next two months.

"You sit and take it easy." Paige slipped the pies carefully into the oven to warm, then closed the oven door and dabbed a dish towel at the perspiration on her brow. The air-conditioning was cranked up to max, but with two ovens going, and thirty people wandering in and out of the house, it was struggling to keep up.

"If you didn't insist on being a martyr, you could be out there right now enjoying Uncle Joe whistling the Star Spangled Banner while crushing beer cans on his forehead."

"Gee, sorry to miss that." Paige winked.

Helene hugged her. "Great to have you home, Sis." Holding onto the back of the chair, she helped herself up. "Where's Shelly? She should be in here helping you."

"She went with Nick to get more ice."

"Well, that'll take an hour. And we're almost out of Margaritas."

Paige banged the last few cubes of ice out of the refrigerator door dispenser and dropped them in a tray.

Helene grabbed it out of her hand and crushed the ice in the blender. "I'm pregnant, not helpless. Go take a break."

How could she when there was work to be done? Paige salted a cold glass, and when the pitcher of Margaritas was ready, followed Helene out to the yard to a large table occupied by Daddy's golf buddies and their wives.

"Now there's a pretty sight. Two lovely ladies and a full Margarita pitcher." Dr. Royce took the pitcher and sloshed some into an empty glass. "Coming your way, Neil." He waved to her father. Flushed from the heat of the grill, Daddy mopped his brow with a pot holder and waved back.

Paige bent over the little girl clutching Mrs. Royce's hand. "Hi, Katie, it's Miss Paige. Want to go play in the sandbox?"

No response from the child.

"Maybe later," her mother said, holding Katie close. "Say hello to Miss Paige, sweetie."

Katie curled up in her mother's lap, as shy as Paige had ever seen her. All these unfamiliar voices must be overwhelming.

Paige crossed the yard to the barbecue pit. "Hi, Princess." Daddy took the cold glass from her and held it against his cheek. "Aah, that feels good. I think we picked the hottest day of the year to have this shindig."

"Next year maybe we should do Fourth of July in October." She sniffed the smoke curling up from the grill. "Brisket smells wonderful."

"Well, grab a plate."

"In a bit. I just want to check on a few things."

She pulled a beer from the ice chest and sauntered across the lawn, dodging a Frisbee thrown awry by her cousin. A slight breeze ruffled her hair. Paige kicked off her flip-flops and dug her toes into the cool grass. Despite the heat and all the work, she loved the Fourth. Cold beer and juicy watermelon. Granny Anderson trying to con suckers into a game of poker. All the aunts and uncles from Daddy's side, Mom's three sisters and all their children and grandchildren, the whole family together. Except...

She sank into a lawn chair. It wasn't just Mom she was missing. Something else niggled at her. She'd put out all the salads, plastic plates, cutlery and napkins. Double-checked the drinks in the cooler. But she still sensed something was missing.

The roar of an approaching motorcycle surged over the sounds of clinking glasses and laughing children.

*That.*

Paige caught her breath as the engine noise grew louder and closer. She hadn't wanted to admit, even to herself, how much she'd hoped Brian would come.

When the bike sputtered to a stop out front, she jumped to her feet and raced upstairs to freshen up, her heart flipping over like a hormonal teen.

She rushed out of the bathroom and peered over the catwalk railing just as the doorbell rang. Brian stood outside the glass door, balancing a case of beer on his hip. She started down the stairs but her brother-in-law got to the door first.

Ted unlatched the door and held it open with his back. Brian stepped inside just as five-year-old Phillip charged across the living room with his toy train. If Brian hadn't swerved, her nephew would have crashed into the case of beer.

"Whoa, fella." Ted stooped and caught his son in his arms, his ginger hair two shades darker than Phillip's bright red mane. "You almost had a train wreck. What did Mommy tell you about running in the house?"

Paige watched unobserved from the landing as Brian set the cardboard case on the floor and rubbed Phillips's unruly carrot top. "My mama always said touching red hair brings you good luck."

"Worked for me." Ted grinned. "I got lucky when I married his mother." He shook hands with Brian. "I'm Ted Bennett. Helene's husband."

"Brian McKay." He bent to pick up the beer.

"I'll take that off your hands. Come on in." Ted grabbed the case out of Brian's arms.

Paige scrambled down the stairs.

"Paige, your friend brought liquid refreshments. Keep this one on the invite list, would ya?"

She motioned for Ted to put the beer in the utility room fridge. "Hi, Brian, I'm so glad you came." She led him into the kitchen and kissed him on the cheek. One cheek. Two would probably be too Beverly Hills for him.

Linking an arm through his, she followed his gaze. He was

studying the cabinetry that went all the way to the ceiling, the double ovens, shiny metallic appliances, and the assorted built-ins.

"Nice place," he said. "I've seen hotel kitchens that weren't as big as this."

"I'll give you a tour of the house after you've met everybody." She moved outside to the patio and started to step onto the lawn, but Brian hung back.

"You said 'a small family gathering,'" he said. "There must be a hundred people here."

"Only forty-two and that's counting the babies." She eyed his blue striped polo shirt and jeans. Maybe he was wearing a swimsuit underneath? Paige pictured him in a bright red Speedo and nothing else. No, Brian would never wear a Speedo. But she was okay with the 'nothing else.'

Flushed from more than the heat, she stepped out to the yard and took two beers from the ice chest. She steered Brian toward her father. "Daddy, this is Brian McKay."

Dr. Neil Anderson wiped his hands on his Kiss-the-Cook apron and extended one to Brian. "Welcome to the Anderson Family's Twenty-first and Last Fourth of July Barbecue."

Brian's brows raised the question but he didn't ask.

"The first year my parents gave this party, Daddy swore it would be the last," Paige explained. "He says the same thing every year. It's part of the tradition,"

Dr. Anderson grinned. "You're Gil McKay's son?"

Brian's expression darkened. "No. Well, yes. But..."

"I know who you are." The ridge above her father's nose puckered. "It's been a long time. Last time we saw you, you were off to join the Air Force." He turned to Paige. "He was at Gil and Vonda's celebrity golf tournament. You must have been about thirteen."

86

*The uniform guy.* Paige swallowed as the memory took shape. She'd been gawky and clueless. Brian had looked so impressive in his Airman's dress outfit, complete with buzz haircut and a super-serious expression. She'd thought he was hot.

"Paige says you're in business with your brother now. Voice activated systems?"

"Yes, sir." Brian sounded wary.

Daddy sipped his Margarita. "The latest technology, I guess. Connor was optimistic your product would be a big hit."

"I hope so, sir."

"What's with the 'sir'? Call me Neil." He turned to the platters piled high with meat and began shoveling chicken and ribs onto a Styrofoam plate. "Paige fixed all the sides and desserts from scratch and they are delicious." He winked and hooked his thumbs behind the bib of his apron to display the wording. "But I don't let her wear this."

After they loaded their plates, Paige searched for a place to sit, waylaid three times by old friends. She introduced Brian around, then finally found two empty chairs at the end of the golf buddy table. "This is great," Brian said, taking bites of brisket and potato salad. "Sure beats fast food and microwave meals."

"My friend!" From the other end of the table, Katie Royce broke away from her mother and ran toward Brian's voice.

Mrs. Royce followed her. "Sweetie, you know you're not supposed to talk to strangers."

"He's my friend," Katie insisted.

Brian stood and pushed back his chair. "Hi, Katie." He hunkered down to let the little girl feel his face. "Are you having a good time?"

When Brian called her daughter by name, Mrs. Royce furrowed her brows at Paige. Dr. Royce broke off his conversation with the other docs.

"Brian--Mr. McKay--visited the camp last week." Taking the Royces aside, Paige quietly explained the planned program with the robot.

"Great idea." Dr. Royce strode to the barbecue pit and clapped her father on the back. "Gotta head out, Neil. Picking up Kyle from a pool party. See you on the driving range."

Katie reluctantly surrendered Brian's hand and took up her mother's again. Why was she so obsessed with Brian? Apparently he just had a way with kids.

*And why are you obsessed with him?*

The breeze picked up slightly, making eating dinner *al fresco* more enjoyable. Paige held her hair off her neck to catch the cool air and tucked it into a scrunchie.

"Paige, great to see you." Hale Donovan sauntered up to the table, his wife Sara and twin toddlers trailing behind.

Paige introduced the family to Brian. "Hale and I went to high school together."

"She was the first girl to break my heart," Hale said dramatically, clamping his hand over his chest as his wife looked on.

"Your heart's never been in better shape," Paige teased, with a nod to Sara.

"Yeah, you're right." Hale put one arm around his wife's shoulder and patted her belly. "Did you know we're expecting again?"

"No. That's wonderful!"

The twins took off in opposite directions, Sara and Hale chasing after them across the yard.

"Hale and Paige," Brian said with a half smirk. "King and queen of the prom, right? I'll bet he was the quarterback and you were captain of the cheerleading squad."

Paige traced her finger around the rough stubble on his jaw. "Jealous?"

"No. Just curious why you would invite an old boyfriend to a 'family' party."

"He's still my friend. And he's not the only one. A few minutes ago I introduced you to two others."

Brian looked incredulous.

"Don't you keep up with any of your old girlfriends? What's Mandy doing these days?"

"I have no idea."

"You don't hear from her?"

He shook his head. "Why would I?"

Wow. Four years of intimacy and then nothing. "You're a strange one, Brian McKay."

"Because I don't keep my old girlfriends' pictures in my cell phone? No, you do one better. You keep the actual guys around."

She bristled. "Just because we don't date anymore, can't we still like each other?"

"Of course, what was I thinking? Everybody loves Paige."

"Except you, apparently." Why had she ever thought she could reach this man? He was so determined to defend his glass-half-empty view of the world he attacked anyone who saw things differently. "I've got to see about dessert." She stood and gave his cheek a playful pinch. "Try not to alienate anyone while I'm gone, okay?"

\* \* \*

*Butterfly,* Brian thought, as Paige flitted around her guests, serving pies and conversation. An exquisite creature, to be admired and enjoyed. But never caught or caged.

He foraged through the ice chest and dug out another beer to wash down his apple pie. The afternoon heat plastered his hair to his head. He settled at a small vacant table in the corner of the yard and propped a foot on an empty chair, grateful for the solitude.

His face was tired from smiling. Whoever said it took fewer muscles to smile than to frown had never spent an afternoon with Paige's family. In the last hour, he'd met her older sister Helene, her cousins, uncles, various aunts, and her card shark grandmother.

Blue-haired Granny Anderson played poker like it was her last day on earth and she needed money for the trip. Smelling fresh meat, she'd charmed Brian into a game of five-card stud. When her eyes lit up as she swept his quarters into her suitcase-sized purse, it brought back childhood memories of playing Go Fish with his own grandmother. He'd let her win, too.

Sweat trickled down his jaw and his shirt stuck to the lawn chair's webbed back. Sipping his beer, he watched Paige flounce around in her bikini top and wrap-around skirt, doing her hostess thing. She'd asked him to stick around, and he didn't have any place to go, anyway, except back to the lab. When he'd canceled his trip home, Mom had peppered him with questions he didn't have answers for, but at least she believed he wasn't permanently chained to his computer and was getting out to meet 'some nice girls.'

"Hey." The little boy he'd almost collided with at the front door skidded to a stop in front of him, grinned, and rubbed his fire-red hair. "Did you get lucky?"

Brian chuckled. Not much chance of that, not with Paige's whole family and a string of ex-boyfriends as chaperones. "Not yet, Phillip."

The little boy high-fived him and darted across the lawn.

Brian turned back to enjoy The Paige Show. God, she was beautiful. The perfect hostess, a smile for everyone. Just like Reno's dazzling casino lights, beckoning in hapless gamblers and then taking them for all they were worth. He watched her charm one of her father's golf buddies, then grace her smile on a beefy-armed guy tossing a Frisbee. Brian's chest tightened. The odds were better at the roulette table.

If he left now, she probably wouldn't even miss him. Crushing his empty beer can into a twisted aluminum lump, he stood.

"Go, get her, Tiger."

He blinked. A beautiful girl in white jeans and a bright orange halter top appeared like a Cheshire cat, smile first. Her bright blue eyes, the same shade as Paige's, held a mischievous glint. Had to be the younger sister.

"I'm Shelly."

"Brian McKay." He extended a hand. She shook it and propped her left hand against her hip. Probably to support the weight of a huge diamond ring that would cost a working stiff a year's salary. "Nice rock."

She giggled. "Thanks. It was Nick's grandmother's." Settling into the chair beside his, she gave Brian the once over, starting at his glasses and roving down farther than he felt comfortable with. "You're here with Paige, aren't you? Why aren't you over there?"

"I'm not exactly--"

"But you like her?"

"Everybody likes Paige." He cast another glance toward the circle of guys surrounding her and sat back down. "Besides, she's dating my brother."

"Connor?" Shelly rolled her eyes. "What's he got over you?"

Was she kidding? "Looks. Charm. Money."

She waved an airy hand. "Standard equipment on most of the guys Paige knows. Maybe she's looking for something different."

He tried not to presume too much from that. "You think she'd go for average-looking, socially inept and poorer than dirt?"

Shelly giggled. "I think she goes for brains."

He supposed she meant that as encouragement, but it didn't exactly summon images of passion between the sheets.

"Smile for the camera, Brian." Shelly leaned in close to him and wrapped an arm around his shoulder just as her father snapped a photo. Brian looked past the photographer and caught Paige's gaze taking in the scene.

"You'll have an opportunity to purchase that on the way out," Shelly said with a wink. She sipped her Margarita. "Paige talks about you all the time," she said. "She goes on and on about that robot and how you two are going to present it to her campers. And her face lights up every time."

Victor was his competition. How bad did that suck?

Shelly must have read his face. "I don't think it's the robot Paige lights up over," she said, covering his hand with hers. "Hang in there."

If he'd learned nothing else from life, Brian knew how to wait for what he wanted. He rose from the chair, his body heating as Paige swept among the guests in that sexy sarong and bikini top. "Patience is my strong suit."

Shelly winked. "I'll bet."

\* \* \*

After tossing out the watermelon rinds, covering the pies, and organizing the leftover salads into the fridge, Paige finally left the kitchen and returned to the backyard barbecue. The crowd at the tables had thinned. Most of the families with small children had left or were gathering their clans for departure. The younger guys--and a few macho older ones--were playing volleyball in the pool. Cozy groups of women idled away the afternoon dishing gossip.

She didn't see Brian anywhere. Had he left without saying good-bye?

"Point to server!" The yell came from the pool. "Three to two. Unh. Unh." Denny grunted like a seal, flapping his arms.

Paige turned toward the game to watch a masterful serve barely skim over the net and drop to the other side in a splash that soaked two opposing players. She returned her focus to the server's powerful arm. And muscular, winter white chest. She should have recognized Brian immediately. He was three shades lighter than everybody else.

She pulled up a chair and watched him rack up four more points before his side lost the serve. "Way to go, Brian!" Paige cheered with his teammates. He caught her gaze and winked.

The other side served and won a point or two, but Paige lost track of the score. Her eyes were on Brian. His concentration was so intense. When he leaped to return a volley, his abdominal muscles tightened and he looked like a long, lean rocket ready to launch. A wild zigzag of chest hair surrounded his nipples and streamed enticingly down to his stomach. And beyond.

He wasn't wearing a Speedo, of course. Brian's dark navy swim trunks extended halfway down his thighs. But they clung to his wet skin. Paige involuntarily licked her lips.

"Shopping?" Shelly pulled up a chair and joined her.

Paige tried to laugh off her absorption. "Hardly. Practically everyone in that pool is related to me."

"One isn't." Shelly kicked off her sandals.

So much for playing it cool. "I don't get me, Shelly. He's not sexy. He wears his glasses in the pool, for God's sake. He lives in southern California and looks like he's never seen a beach."

"And you're so hot for him you could jump his bones right now."

Paige sighed. "God, am I that obvious?" She turned to her sister. "You two seemed to be getting along well earlier."

"Just checking him out for you. You know my heart belongs to Nicky."

"And if it didn't?"

Shelly studied Brian's physique. "In the dark, it doesn't matter if his body's white or golden tan." She winked. "Just what he does with it."

Paige blushed. "I wouldn't know about that." She turned to her sister. "But I'll say this: the man kisses like the world is going to end tomorrow."

Shelly grinned. "So why haven't you slept with him?"

"Um...he hasn't asked me?"

"Has any man ever refused when you offered?"

"Brian's...different." She recalled his cold rebuff after their high-intensity kiss. "I'm not sure he's interested."

Shelly's brows lifted and she opened her mouth in fake shock. "Not interested in you? Is he breathing? Does he have red blood in his veins?"

Paige giggled. "Most guys think of me as the girl next door. *You're* the type men pant over."

Shelly hiked up the shoulder on her halter top. "Not this one. The whole time I was talking to him, he never took his eyes off you."

Paige turned back to the pool, unable to take her eyes off *him*. Brian played more like an athlete than a computer geek. Despite the balls skimming over the water and splashing his glasses, he never missed a shot.

"What say we join the game?"

She turned back to her sister. "Not me, thanks." Paige's skin heated at the vision of herself in her bikini reaching for the ball and crashing into Brian's bare chest. "I am getting warm, though. Let's bring out the ice cream."

In the kitchen, they scooped the homemade ice cream into plastic bowls. "Shelly, am I a snob?"

"You?" Her sister chortled. "You're the least stuck-up person in Beverly Hills."

"Which isn't saying much."

Shelly met her eyes. "Did Mr. White Chest call you that?"

94

No point in pretending that was a generic question. "Not in those words. But..."

"He's really got you stirred up."

Paige sighed. "He criticizes everything I say and do. He makes me so mad sometimes I want to slap him."

"Normal couple behavior. Nick and I fight all the time." Shelly winked. "And the making up is wonderful."

"It doesn't feel normal." Normal was being polite and considerate. Normal was getting along, being comfortable with someone, not alternating between the twin sensations of wanting to scratch a man's eyes out or tear his clothes off.

"Well, maybe you've had too much normal." Her sister's eyes glinted. "Maybe what you need is wild and crazy. Intense, fire-breathing, high highs, low lows, and the thrill of bouncing in between."

Roller coaster. Brian's kiss. Paige fought against the sensations that could be her undoing. She'd long ago vowed to forego those emotional peaks to protect herself from the dark, depressive valleys. Anything to avoid ending up like her mother. "Come on, let's take this ice cream out before it melts."

When they returned outside, the volleyball game had ended. Armed with two bowls of ice cream, Paige found Brian sitting on a lawn chaise, chatting with--or more precisely listening to--Granny Anderson.

*Females under seven and over seventy.* Paige smiled as she approached her grandmother's chair. "I see you've met Brian."

"Met him?" Her grandmother winked, adjusting the large straw sunhat tied beneath her chin. "I won three dollars off him earlier."

Paige shrugged at Brian in mock sympathy. "I warned you." She looked to pull up a chair.

"There's room here." Brian slid to the edge of the chaise and patted the space beside him.

There was, but just barely. Paige had to prop half a butt cheek against Brian's hip to keep from toppling the chair to one side. He didn't seem to mind. He hooked an arm around her waist to anchor her.

"Strawberry or chocolate?"

"Chocolate."

She handed over a bowl of ice cream and offered the other to her grandmother. Granny waved it away. Paige spooned the strawberry flavor into her mouth and clutched her neck as the ice cream froze her throat and chest on its way down.

When Granny got up to hustle another card game, Paige tried to move to the chair, but Brian tightened his hold. *O-kay.* She snuggled against him, drinking in the scent of chlorine on his skin.

"So," she asked, "has this afternoon been as tedious and uncomfortable as you expected?"

"How do you know what I expected?"

"You're not that hard to read."

He chuckled. "Actually, I'm having fun. I like your family."

*Call a press conference. Brian McKay said something positive.* "They like you too. Shelly thinks you're hot. What's going on between you two?"

His face never changed expression but his eyes twinkled. Eyes flecked with red, irritated, no doubt, from the chlorine. "We're irresistibly attracted to each other. She's dumping Nick and we're running away to Vegas at dawn."

Paige grinned. "Not until you've finished the Victor project, you're not."

"Oh, I see how it is. For a minute, I thought you might be jealous. But you were just cracking that whip."

A weird image crossed her mind of herself in black garters and leather boots, cracking a whip at Brian's feet. Where on earth did that come from? Paige blinked it away but summoned it back momentarily to check out what Brian was wearing in the image. *Nothing.*

"I'm actually glad you and Shelly are getting along, but I'm surprised. I thought it more likely you'd hit it off with Helene."

"Why?"

"Because you're both serious, and hardworking, and have IQs off the charts."

He frowned. "I'll cop to the first two, but..."

"Quit being modest. When I first met you at Suite Smart, I thought you were some kind of genius."

"That's only because I was standing next to Connor."

She laughed out loud.

"My IQ is only slightly north of normal, Paige. I just use what I have."

She almost passed that by as an offhand remark, before she realized Brian didn't make offhand remarks. "You've had to work harder than most people for everything, haven't you?" She stroked his hand.

He rubbed her fingers with his thumb. "Nothing wrong with working for what you want."

Did that include her? She angled her body toward his. He braced his hand against her back. His skin was warm and damp. She hungered to taste him. His wet, straggly hair brushed against her cheek as he covered her mouth with his.

His kiss was gentle, easy, sipping her lips like sweet wine. The taste of chocolate ice cream mingled with strawberry as she savored his tongue. Paige forked her fingers into his hair and twisted a damp curl.

"You two look cozy." Shelly strolled over with Nick in tow.

"We're economizing on chairs," Paige answered, breaking the kiss. "What are you guys up to?"

"We're going to set up the media room and watch some DVDs. You two interested?"

Paige looked at Brian.

"You're not going to see fireworks?" he asked.

"No, we usually stay here and set out chairs on the front lawn." Paige pointed to the ladder leaning against the garage. "The guys like to watch from the roof."

"You'd get a much better view from the hill," Brian said.

"Yeah, but you'd have to park ten miles away, so what's the point?"

"I can park the bike right at the base of the hill." He scanned her face. "Why don't we go?"

Paige hadn't watched fireworks up close since she was a kid. Her heart pounded with delight at the thought of riding his motorcycle with the wind in her hair and seeing the skies light up all around her. "I can't. I have guests."

"Most of them have already left," Brian pointed out. "Those that are still here aren't going to miss you."

She glanced at the dirty tables, the trash still needing to be picked up, serving dishes to be washed, chairs to be folded and put away. "I'm the hostess. I can't just leave."

"Sure you can," Shelly said. "Nick and I will clean up."

*Right. Sometime next week.* She bit her lip. "I'd really love to, but... Maybe some other ti--" Some other time? There wouldn't be Fourth of July fireworks for another year. And then there would be another party to host.

"Yeah. Sure." Brian reached under the chaise for his shirt and jeans, then got up and went into the house.

She started after him, but was stopped on the way by a request for a tissue and a child looking for the bathroom. When she finally caught up with Brian, he'd dressed and put on his shoes, and was headed to the front door.

"You don't have to leave."

"Yeah, I do."

"Why? To finish feng-shui-ing the country house?"

"Does it matter?" His eyes, so vulnerable earlier, were hard and cold again.

She turned to hide embarrassing tears. If he wanted to leave, let him leave.

He spun her around to face him. His hot breath fanned her face. Pressing his hand against the small of her back, he pulled her hard against him. "Are you scared to ride the bike?" He teased the catch on the back of her bikini top, a flicker away from unfastening it. "Or afraid of being alone with me?"

Her nipples peaked against his chest. "Neither," she lied.

She wasn't afraid of physical intimacy. She wanted that. Since coming home, she'd subordinated her own desires to her family's needs. She missed the sensation of rough skin against soft, of losing herself in a man's scent. But if she got involved with Brian, she feared he'd burrow past her usual defenses to the deep, ugly places in her heart. And she might let him in.

Her arms ached from exertion. She dropped them to her sides, realizing she'd been clutching his waist like a panicked child clinging to a security blanket. She couldn't risk a summer romance, not with this man. Because when the time came, as it always did, to walk away, she was afraid she wouldn't be able to let him go.

"Paige!" Her father's voice boomed from the kitchen. "Do we have any corkscrews in this house that work?"

She shot Brian a helpless look. "Coming, Daddy."

As she walked to the kitchen, the glass door slammed.

"Never mind," her father said when she came to his aid. "I found one." He popped the cork on a 1997 bottle of Merlot and joined his buddies at the kitchen table.

Paige glanced at Nick and Shelly, kissing and teasing as they chased each other up the stairs. In the living room, young couples cuddled close, laughing and talking. Paige fought a dull ache in her heart. Surrounded by family and friends, she'd never felt so alone.

Outside, a motorcycle engine roared to life.

Paige dashed to the front of the house. "Brian, wait!" She threw open the front door. "I changed my mi--"

The deafening roar drowned out her words as the motorcycle sped away.

*  *  *

He was done. Finished. Permanently hanging up his butterfly net.

Brian gripped the handlebars as the wind lashed his cheeks and forehead, sealing a second layer of pain over his fresh sunburn. He should have listened to his mother and used sunscreen. Better yet, he should have gone home to Reno where he belonged, instead of chasing a dream he could never own.

He parked the bike, unlocked the door to the lab, and chunked his helmet on Connor's desk. "The strong defeat the weak," he said aloud. "The smart triumph over the strong." But a sweet-smelling, sensuous woman could make mincemeat out of all of them.

"Hey, Brian," Victor said in recognition of his voice.

Brian turned to the robot. Had he left it activated? He scanned the warehouse. "Connor?"

"Yo." His brother emerged from the bowels of the lab, wiping his hands.

Strange. Connor rarely ventured beyond Brian's desk or the bathroom, and Brian had never seen his hands dirty. "What's up?"

"Nothing. Just checking inventory." Connor's gaze lit on Brian's sun flushed face. "You went to the Andersons' barbecue?"

"I stopped by."

"So?" Connor grinned lasciviously. "Did you get any?"

*You son of a bitch.* "Should I have plowed her in the potato salad? Poked her in the pool? It was a family party."

His brother chuckled knowingly. "I warned you."

"What about you?" His best defense was an offense. "Why are you back so early? You couldn't keep up with your hot babe?"

"Don't worry about me. I managed fine." Connor headed out front to his office. "Just needed to look over some invoices, run a few numbers."

"We're not behind on our vendor payments?"

"No, we're good." Connor closed out the spreadsheet he'd been working on before Brian could catch a glimpse of the screen, and shut down his computer. "I'm out of here."

After he left, Brian rebooted the PC. Connor had password protected it, but since Brian had set up the computer, he just logged in as administrator. Opening up Excel, he selected the most recent spreadsheet off the list and brought it up.

Connor kept pretty detailed records. The next vendor payments weren't due for another week and all had been paid timely, at least with the minimum required amounts. R.T. Dunaway? He didn't recognize that vendor. An invoice for eight hundred dollars, no other detail.

Scrolling back, he found two more payments to the same name, one in April and one in March, for a thousand dollars, and five hundred. What had they bought for twenty-three hundred dollars?

He wandered to the back of the lab and examined the salvage items stored there. No new acquisitions. Mostly old computer monitors, keyboards, patch cables, and a couple of motherboards. Stuff he'd thought he might need for the Suite but which he'd probably end up selling for scrap.

Maybe he could use another keyboard, though, for the program at Paige's camp. If the kids did get wise and figured out Victor's words came out of a computer, he could at least show them how he worked, let them type words and make him talk.

He dug out a keyboard and blew off the dust.

White dust.

He sniffed the powder that had settled between the keys. What the hell? Reaching back into the shelf, he shuffled the other salvage items. Hidden among the parts he found four cellophane bags of white powder. His muscles tensed. Cocaine?

# Chapter Seven

When Paige parked outside the Suite Smart lab the next afternoon, Connor's Mercedes screeched into the next space.

"Slumming?" he said as he fell in step beside her. His gaze lowered to her daffodil yellow tank top and lingered on the cleavage revealed by her open camp shirt. "I'm guessing you're not here to see me."

"I'm here to work." She held the edges of her blouse together and showed him the bag containing the robot's clothes.

"Work," Connor repeated dully. "Work is what people get paid for."

As if Gil McKay's trust-funded son would know much about that.

He dug his keys out of the pocket of his gray Calvin Kleins. "It's great that you have all this free time to give to the downtrodden masses, but Brian doesn't. The dollar man has a deadline. And you're distracting him." He unlocked the front door and stooped to pick up the mail from the floor just inside.

Distracting? Paige set down her stuff. Had her project been taking up too much of Brian's time? He *had* looked tired yesterday. Maybe his bloodshot eyes weren't just from the chlorine. "Why do you call him that?"

"'Dollar man?'" Connor grinned. "Why do you think?"

"He's worth more than you to this project," she said hotly. "Without Brian, you wouldn't even have a business."

"Wrong, Ms. Bleeding Heart. *I'm* the business. Without me, your favorite geek would just be playing all day with gadgets and robots." He flipped through the mail and tossed most of it onto his desk, stashing two thin envelopes in his shirt pocket. He faced her, casting another lurid glance down her tank top. "Don't do anything I wouldn't."

*That leaves a wide margin.*

After Connor left, she moved inside the lab. The afternoon was hot, and with only a lone ceiling fan swishing the warm air around, the genius's playground was stifling. She slipped off her white cotton shirt and stuffed it into her satchel, then smoothed down her tank top to reveal a provocative glimpse of bosom. "Hello?"

"Hi, Doll face," a robotic voice answered. "Wanna play with my hard drive?"

She swiveled to Victor's platform, expecting to see Brian at the keyboard. Keyboard. But no Brian.

"Victor!" Assuming Brian was watching from somewhere, she thrust out her hip. "You're awfully cheeky today--for a guy who doesn't have cheeks."

No deep, masculine laugh. And no keyboard clicking a smart response. She was talking to a robot nobody was operating as if that was perfectly normal. Moving away from the platform, she stepped deeper into the electrical jungle, hopscotching over cords and wires. "Brian?"

"Here." He emerged from behind a curtain in the back. "How did you get in?"

"Connor. Came, sorted through the mail, and left."

He grunted as if that didn't surprise him, wiping his hands on his shirt. He wore the same faded black T-shirt as the first day she'd met him. That day she'd thought him the poster boy of brainy nerds. This afternoon she visualized the muscles beneath that shirt and the swirls of chest hair her fingers itched to play with.

He was staring at her chest as well. And frowning. "Is that what you wore to camp?"

She edged a finger under the strap of her yellow camisole top. "I had a blouse over it. It's stuffy in here without air-conditioning." She held her damp hair off her neck. "But if it makes you uncomfortable--"

"Not at all." His tone suggested she could strip naked without it affecting him, but his eyes told a different story. She glanced quickly downward. His body agreed with his eyes.

She lifted her gaze. "I brought Victor's clothes."

"Great," he said with less enthusiasm than a dog for a bath. "Let's get started." He threaded his way through metal and wires toward the front of the lab.

Paige followed. "You still mad at me?"

"I wasn't mad." He sat at Victor's keyboard, avoiding her eyes.

"Well, you gave a good impression of it. You tore away from my house yesterday like your pants were on fire."

He shrugged. "It's a fast bike."

Still mad. Maybe he had a right to be. Or he might be just tired and overworked. *Thanks to you, Paige.*

She pulled the child-sized farmer's shirt and overalls out of her bag and began to dress the robot. "He talked to me when I walked in. You need to teach him some manners."

Brian grunted.

"Were you operating him remotely?"

"Nope."

She glared at him. "He flirts that way with everybody? What if you had a client come in, and--"

"I programmed him to recognize voices," he explained grudgingly. "And to respond with a greeting the first time a person speaks."

*The chip.* "You had my voice print from the day you set me up to use Suite Smart."

He nodded.

And *that* was the greeting he'd programmed Victor to say to her? She didn't know whether to be flattered or insulted. "Could you do that with my campers? If I brought you a tape recording of their voices?"

"P-robably." His dark eyes squinted. "But it would take time and--"

"Then never mind. I don't want to *distract* you any more than necessary."

He lifted a brow.

"Connor told me you're pushing hard for the Suite Smart deadline."

Brian frowned. "Connor should mind his own business." He pushed his glasses farther up on his nose. "Suite Smart will be fine. Site visit's not for ten more days. After this week I'll be able to devote all my attention to it."

"You're that close to finishing Victor's programming?"

He nodded. "We'll go through the script today, I'll make any changes you want, and then he's ready to roll. I won't disappoint your campers."

"Thank you." It sounded so final. Today was the last day they'd need to work together. Next week, the camp program. And then there'd be no reason ever to have to see Brian again. A sharp twinge zinged her chest. "So let's get started."

Brian stepped to Victor's keyboard and pushed a single key.

"Hello," the robot squeaked. "I'm. Victor O-O-One. What's your name?"

"Paige." She tried to put herself into the dialogue as one of her campers would. "What does the O O One stand for?"

"It. Means. I'm. One. Of. A. Kind. Are. You. One. Of. A. Kind?"

Wow, a great way to get the children to realize that each one was special. "This is good." She turned and smiled at Brian. "What should I ask him next?"

He handed her a typed script.

She read the first question. "How old are you?"

"Eight. Years. Old. My. Birthday. Is. July. Twenty. Five."

She smiled at Brian. "You've made him the same age as some of the kids. And given him a birthday."

"The birthday isn't hard coded," he said, looking pleased despite his obvious attempts to act aloof. "I'll make it whatever day we do the program."

"So we'll have a birthday party for him." She felt as excited as she knew the kids would be.

"I'm getting a fire truck that sprays water," the robot said. "And a Carrie Underwood CD. She's hot."

Paige giggled. If Brian would inject the same flirtatious charm into his own personality that he gave to that robot... "What flavor ice cream do you like?"

"Chocolate," the robot responded. "With nuts."

Perfect. She turned to Brian. "The birthday party is a great idea. You're a genius."

"It was your idea."

"You're still a genius."

"Not even close. But thanks."

"You're being modest."

"Just a realist."

Glass half empty. Brian had undoubtedly been a realist since he came out of the womb. "It's good dialogue. Nice ice breaker. But how can Victor get the kids to talk?"

He pointed to the stool opposite the robot. "Check it out."

She sat, trying to put herself into the mind of a seven-year-old.

"What's your favorite color?" Victor asked.

"Yellow." She stole a self-conscious glance at Brian. His fingers were typing, but his eyes were on her camisole.

"What's your favorite food?"

She stretched her brain for an answer the robot's programming wouldn't have predicted. "Chateaubriand and Grand Marnier soufflé."

Victor didn't miss a beat. "Sounds yummy," he said. "I like pizza and hamburgers and hot dogs, and, of course, ice cream and cake."

Not bad, he was prepared for any response.

"What's your favorite song?" Victor asked.

She thought a minute. "I Hope You Dance."

"That's mine, too." The robot said the words but Paige heard them coming from Brian. She tingled with hope. Could a realist still possess a sense of wonder? Dare to risk? She thought of motorcycles and roller coasters. And dancing in Brian's arms.

*Don't be stupid, Paige. That's Victor's standard answer. Every song is his favorite.*

She swiveled her chair to face Brian. "I like that you're trying to create a special connection with the child, but each one will have a different answer. If Victor claims each song as his favorite, he loses his credibility."

"You see this as an entertainment program, with all the kids listening to each other's answers?"

"Sure. Don't you?"

He shook his head. "I thought it would be an individual thing. You wanted the kids to open up. I don't see them sharing their feelings with everyone else listening."

He would definitely know about that.

"And if the conversation does get personal, I'll need to key specialized questions and responses."

"I guess I could ask Jenna to keep the rest of the group while you and I work with the kids individually." Paige refocused to visualize the one-on-ones. "This is going to require good communication and timing. Since I know the kids, I'll jot notes for you to key Victor's responses. How fast can you type?"

"How fast can you write?"

A good point. Her spirits deflated like a popped balloon. "This isn't going to work, is it? I won't be able to write fast enough or talk soft enough. Most of my kids have extra-sensitive hearing." She sighed. "I'll just have to write up some specific notes about each child. Then you can work up a script--"

"Let's do it now."

Paige dragged her stool next to his chair, inhaling the scent of Irish Spring soap. The air got warmer. "How about a question about what they enjoy doing, or what they want to be when they grow up, or..."

"One at a time."

She leaned in close, watching the computer screen as he typed her questions into the programming format. They worked well

109

together, her voice and his fingers flowing together in easy rhythm. Brian had lightning fingers. And sexy ears. She'd never been turned on before by ear lobes but Paige had to fight the urge to nibble and to swirl her tongue inside his ear. She didn't even want to think about what he could do with those fingers.

"We're a good team," Brian said. "Feed me something else."

"What did you have in mind?" She turned to him. His eyes glowed like dark embers. Her heart pounded like a bass drum as he scooted his chair closer. Not touching her. But near enough for Paige's skin to heat and her breath to falter. Her mouth moved silently. Her body ached and tingled. *Kiss me.*

He let out a deep groan. His five o'clock stubble scraped her cheek. His lips covered hers.

Paige closed her eyes and breathed him in. His kisses were all different: one rough and demanding, yesterday's soft and gentle. But always intense. His mouth was the focus of the universe, compelling her, controlling her, sending shivers of delight to cool her hot skin.

He pulled her onto his lap and deepened the kiss. Her lips parted for his tongue. She straddled him, eager to feel his hardness between her thighs, her mouth hungry for more than his tongue.

He teased her mouth, then his lips blazed a trail of heat down her throat. Paige lowered her camisole strap, encouraging his mouth lower. He nuzzled the swell of her breast. When his tongue flicked against her hard nipple, she whimpered and grabbed his hair. "Brian..."

Suddenly she found herself on her back on the hard floor, her breasts exposed. Brian stood over her panting heavily, unzipping his jeans.

This was happening too fast. She pushed herself up to a sitting position and smoothed her camisole back down to her waist. "Wait," she gasped. "Slow down."

"Wait for what?" He drew a condom packet out of the pocket of his jeans.

Obviously, he was prepared. But Paige wasn't. Not for this, not right now, not this way. "That's not what I meant. I just...wasn't expecting..."

His eyes filled with confusion. "Did I miss something? You waltz in here half naked and you expect me not to react?"

"I wasn't--I didn't. It was hot and I..." *Don't lie, Paige.* She'd expected him--wanted him--to react exactly as he had. But she hadn't thought it all the way through. "It's just a little soon, that's all. We've barely know each other a week. Most of the men I've...been with, I've known much longer."

"Like twenty years? I won't wait that long." He yanked his tee shirt over his head. His jeans dropped to his ankles, revealing a full erection barely restrained inside his black briefs.

He advanced toward her. Paige scooted backward on the dusty cement floor. "What the hell is wrong with you? I said No."

Brian stared at her a full minute, dark eyes blazing. Then he yanked his jeans back up over his hips, fastened them, and reached for his shirt. "You know what my Air Force buddies called girls like you?"

She could guess. She helped herself up off the floor and glared into his eyes. "And what about you? You kiss me like your heart's on fire. Then you want to pretend it never happened. You practically make love to me on the dance floor, and then you stomp off and leave. I never know where I stand with you."

"That makes two of us."

Paige blinked. How obvious did she have to be? "I took you to dinner at the club. I asked you to my home, to meet my family."

"You took me *and Connor* to the club. I met your family and every guy you've dated since sixth grade."

"I have a lot of friends, okay. But you were the only person I practically begged to come. When have you ever invited me to anything?"

"The fireworks?" he said quietly.

"That wasn't a date. That was a booty call."

She regretted the retort as soon as she made it. Even more when Brian's face darkened. Paige's anger fizzled into frustration. She sank onto a stool. "I'm sorry. I wanted to go, but I had no choice."

"Yeah, you did."

"Maybe," she admitted. "But so did you. You could have stayed."

"And taken a number to talk with you? No thanks."

This was going nowhere. The man didn't want a relationship, he wanted an ownership patent. She scooped up her satchel and headed to the front.

"You know what you are?" His angry voice taunted after her.

She turned. "I know what you think I am."

"You're a goddamned butterfly," he spat out between rabid lips. "Today you're with me, next month it'll be some jock you went to high school with." His dark eyes burned, a fiery contrast to his cold, hard expression. "I don't like sharing. And I'll be damned if you'll introduce me at next year's family barbecue as Mr. Last Summer!"

"Not to worry." She fished her blouse out of her satchel and struggled to fasten the buttons, paying no attention to whether they matched the right holes or not. "Because you're permanently off my guest list." She stomped to the door and twisted the knob, her sweaty palms barely able to catch a grip.

*Don't let him see you cry.* Blinking furiously, Paige slammed the door behind her and stormed out to the parking lot.

Blurry-eyed, she nearly tripped over Brian's huge Harley. *Fragile, stubborn male ego.* She kicked the rear tire until her big toe throbbed in pain, then limped to her car.

Her fingers trembled as she snatched her key out of her bag and shoved it into the Infiniti's lock. The stupid key wouldn't fit. She rammed it again and again, scratching a sliver of paint off her door, before she realized she was holding her house key.

*Aargh.* The key dropped to the ground. She stooped to dig it out of the gravel, then raised slowly, her gaze moving up a pair of well-worn boots, faded jeans, and a snug black tee shirt.

"This one might work better." Brian held her car key in his palm. It must have slipped out of her bag when she dashed down the stairs.

There was no point in asking how long he'd been standing there and invite his snarky *Long enough.* Paige went for the key, but he jerked his hand out of her reach.

Her five-year-old campers acted more mature. She lunged for the key, scraping his palm as she snatched it from his hand. She kneed him in what would have been his groin but he shimmied away from the blow at just the right instant. Her knee connected with air. "Fuck you, Brian McKay! And the bike you rode in on." She unlocked the Infiniti and hurled open the driver door.

"Paige."

She closed her eyes. The way he said her name made her feel like her bones were melting inside her skin. He stood behind her, his breath hot on her neck. Though she couldn't see his hands, she sensed them at her sides, struggling to keep their distance.

"I'm sorry. I shouldn't have come on so strong. I thought you wanted the same thing I did."

"I...did." She might as well be honest. Slowly she turned to face him, keeping her body halfway inside the car so as not to touch him. "Just..."

"Not with a caveman dragging you by the hair to his cave," he finished for her. "You wanted to be courted."

Courted? "May-be."

"My bad. I've never been particularly smooth with women." He backed away, leaving her more space to breathe.

She sighed, relaxing her tight shoulders. "I'm sorry, too. For losing my temper. I haven't been that angry in...in a long time." Not since that last argument with her mother. "You bring out the worst in me."

To her amazement, Brian chuckled. "That was losing your temper? Saying 'what the hell' instead of 'heck' or 'what in the world'?"

"I said 'fuck you' too!" she said adamantly, although her anger was losing its edge.

"Yeah, but you didn't mean it." He grinned. "I'm kind of glad you lost your temper. It was a nice change from Pollyanna Paige. Perfectly groomed, not a hair out of place." He glanced at her blouse, the buttons of which were misaligned. "Never a raised voice or an unkind word. Nice, nice, maddeningly nice."

"I try."

He cocked his head. "Maybe you try too hard." He walked away, toward his bike, then turned back. "I haven't eaten since this morning. Want to go for a burger and fries?"

The words *Not even if we were on a deserted island and the only available food was in your tent* sprang to her lips, but she stifled them. Then it hit her: he'd just asked her out. On an actual date.

She grabbed the helmet out of his hand and stuffed it on her head. "You're buying."

\* \* \*

Brian drummed his fingers in rhythm with the Fifties song on the juke box and watched Paige chomp down her Johnny Rockets Original hamburger as if she hadn't eaten for a week.

"This is to die for!" she exclaimed between bites. "I was totally starved. The kids were so wild today I didn't get five minutes to eat."

"I'm glad you're enjoying it." And he enjoyed watching her. She ate, as she did everything, with gusto. "Sorry it can't be chateaubriand and grand whatever, but..."

She wrinkled her brow. "Chateau--? Oh." She wiped a mustard dribble from her chin. "Those aren't my favorite foods. I was just trying to come up with something to challenge Victor."

He pointed to a mustard spatter she'd missed, now staining her pristine, buttoned-up-to-her-neck-but-still-with-the-wrong-buttons white blouse.

"Damn." She grinned. "I mean 'darn.'" She tanked a napkin into her water glass and scrubbed unsuccessfully at the stain.

She was a mess. Helmet hair, blouse mis-buttoned and mustard-stained, and another dollop of mustard dribbling down her cheek. A sensuous, beautiful mess. "So what *are* your favorite foods?"

A lazy smile teased her mouth. Her tongue darted out and innocently licked her upper lip. "Burger and fries."

Oh hell, he was a goner. He tried to tell himself that all he needed was one night to possess her and then put her out of his mind, but his heart knew better. He'd fallen fast and hard.

Damn, he hated when his mother was right.

Paige slurped her milk shake and set it on the chrome table. "Brian."

Even the way she said his name made him feel warm and mushy inside. And hard on the outside. "Yeah?"

"You really think I'm too nice? 'Maddeningly' nice?"

She'd remembered and repeated his exact words. "Maybe I was a little too harsh."

She bent her straw and flipped a glob of milk shake onto his nose. "You prefer naughty?"

115

How could she look so childlike and so damn sexy in the same moment? He wiped off his nose. "If I said yes, would it do me any good?"

Paige pushed her fingers into her cheeks and wrinkled her face. "I. Am. Here. To. Please," she said in a dead-on imitation of Victor.

Brian laughed until he thought he'd split his sides—or his pants. He'd never seen this silly side of Paige, not even after a couple of Margaritas. But he liked it.

He plopped a nickel into the tabletop jukebox, stood and held out his hand. "Please me."

They danced and rocked to Little Richard's *Tutti Frutti*. Paige easily followed his lead, twirling under his arm and jitterbugging like a Fifties teenager in a poodle skirt. They followed that with Bill Haley's *Rock around the Clock*, until Paige dropped exhausted into the red leather booth, pulling him down beside her onto the bench seat.

He ordered another cherry coke. Paige downed her entire glass of water and asked for another. Looking disheveled but happy, she leaned against the wall of the booth, and drew up her knees between them. "Brian."

"Paige."

She scrutinized his face as if it held the answer to all questions. "Have you ever been in love?"

But not that question. "No," he answered a little too quickly. "Have you?"

"No." She rubbed her hands along her knees. "At least I don't think so. I mean, I thought I was, every time, but I guess I was wrong." She searched his eyes. "You weren't in love with Mandy?"

He shook his head.

"But you dated four years! She wanted to marry you. How can you be so sure?"

*Because in four years I never once felt the way I do tonight.* He swigged his cherry coke. "Mandy and I were convenient. We both worked the late shift at the school cafeteria. I walked her home one night, she invited me in, one thing led to another..."

"You used her. For sex."

"No." But pretty damned close, he was ashamed to admit. Though they'd lived together, he and Mandy had hardly seen each other. She'd had her life and friends. He'd had his life and--well, he'd had his life. When either of them wanted sex it had been easy to turn over and find a willing, available partner. They got along well, never fought, and could have lived together forever if she hadn't played the marriage card. "I guess we used each other."

Paige stared reflectively into her empty milk shake glass. "Maybe the whole concept of love is just something Hollywood dreamed up. Young girls fall for it, and guys use it to get those same impressionable girls into bed. But real love, aching and wanting and caring-so-much-you-hurt love, doesn't exist."

"Yes, it does." He could have kicked himself for letting those words loose without engaging his brain. And for encouraging her innocent, hopeful eyes to fasten on his. "Not that I'd actually know what it's like," he hedged. "But it's not just about sex."

He waited for the usual Paige protest, comment, analysis-- anything to get him off this hook. But she remained silent.

He rolled his coke glass between his hands. "Look, a guy can get off on sex with anybody: fat or skinny, pretty or ugly, good girl or slut. But being in love changes all the rules. When you're in love-- at least I guess this is how it is--it's not about sex, it's about *her*." He forced himself not to look away from her eyes. "When you're in love, it's her or nobody."

She kept staring at him. He concentrated on fondling his coke glass and listening to himself breathe.

"Brian."

His stomach rolled over and tied itself into knots.

"I know you need to work on Suite Smart. But you're not working Saturday night, are you?"

He should be working Saturday night. As he should be working every night. If he was going to have the Suite ready in time for the demo. "What do you have in mind?"

"My sister's engagement party." She swiveled her legs off the bench and dropped them to the floor. "I'd like you to come with me if you can spare the time. As my date."

His heart skipped. And sank.

Her voice rushed on like a motorbike with a tailwind. "It's black tie but if you don't have a tux you can wear a suit--"

"Who bailed?"

"Excuse me?"

Did she think he'd come in from Reno on a turnip truck? "You wouldn't ask somebody to a formal affair only two days in advance. You'd have nailed down an escort at least three months ago."

"I only got back into town three *weeks* ago. I just figured I'd go alone." She tore her napkin into strips and then shredded each one. "Then that day I ran into Connor at the club--"

"You asked him, but then he bailed on you."

She shook her head. "I never asked him."

"Why not?"

"Because I met you!"

His breath caught in his throat.

"That is...I mean..." Paige blinked furiously as if her thoughts were racing to catch up with her words. "I didn't know then that I..."

He touched her quivering chin, hoping she couldn't hear his heart pounding. Why did he do these things? Go out of his way to hurt the person he wanted so much to like him? "I'd be honored to take you to the party. What time should I pick you up?"

"I'll pick *you* up." She smiled. "No offense, but with a long dress and heels and a fresh hairstyle under that helmet..."

"I'll get a car. And I'll dress appropriately." He ran his finger over her lower lip. "I promise not to embarrass you in front of your rich friends."

Her lips and teeth teased his finger. "I'm not worried about your appearance. But you might consider ditching your holier-than-thou-I-hate-everyone-who-drives-a-decent-car-and-has-a-nice-house attitude."

"I'll be my usual charming self."

"That's what I'm afraid of." She took his hand before he could draw it back and squeezed it. "Brian, you don't have to impress me. But you have a luxury business catering to high-priced clientele. It wouldn't hurt you to make the effort to network. Learn to schmooze."

He paid the tab with a couple of twenties, waving off the waitress's attempt to bring back change. "That's what I have Connor for."

"Do you trust him?"

The lady had a point. "I thought Miss Glass Half Full thought the best of everybody."

"I try to." She slid out of the booth, weaving her fingers between his as they strolled out of the retro diner. "But I don't like to see people I lo--like---get hurt."

He swallowed. *Don't make too much of that, McKay*

Though dusk had not yet fallen, the crescent moon had already risen in the sky, so perfectly shaped it looked like a cardboard cutout dangling over the parking lot. He crooked his arm around Paige's waist and guided her toward the dark and empty stalls of the Farmer's Market, drinking in the scent of Chanel and ocean breeze. "I'll dress up," he promised. "I'll smile. I'll schmooze. Any other requirements for an official date with Paige?"

She turned to him, lifting her hand to his neck, and ran her fingers through the ends of his collar-length hair. "A goodnight kiss."

Fire arched through his loins. "I may need some practice. What exactly did you have in mind? A sweet kiss?" He brushed his mouth lightly over hers, his tongue barely teasing her lips, then drew back. "Or--?"

Before he could move in for the next demonstration, she gripped his hair and pulled his face down to hers. Her tongue probed his lips apart and delved inside. He captured it with gentle teeth and drew her in deeper, tasting every surface of her mouth.

He tried to hold his body back but when she dipped her hands inside the waistband of his jeans and pressed herself against him, he couldn't pull away. Her fingers slipped inside his briefs, heating his bare skin. Her nails dug into his buttocks. He enveloped her in his arms, oblivious to everything except her hair and face and skin, absorbing the feel and fragrance of Paige.

Slowly she pulled back, her eyes dreamy and sensuous. "I can't make up my mind." She winked. "I think we need more practice." She turned, sashaying her cute little ass across the parking lot toward the Harley.

He grabbed her around the waist and pulled her back. Inhaling her scent, he buried his face in her hair and kissed the nape of her neck. He caressed her stomach over the thin cotton material, then slid his hands upward to cup her breasts.

When his thumbs flicked her nipples, she gasped. He stilled. Had he gone too far? So soon after his big mistake? Paige covered his hands with hers and pulled them down to her stomach.

Then pushed them under her top and repositioned his hands on her bare breasts.

God in heaven, he'd never touched skin so soft. Or nipples so hard. The peaks pushed into his palms as he rubbed and caressed, hardening him to full arousal. He strained and thrust against her. She moaned, leaning into him to feel him closer. Her arms reached up and grabbed his neck.

"Get a room!"

*Shit.* He tore himself away from near-bliss, dismayed he hadn't even heard the bikers as they slowed, laughed, and cruised on. He was definitely losing his edge.

She faced him, laughing. "Mmm, I guess we both could use a cold shower."

"Or a dip in the ocean," he agreed, trying to steady his breathing. He was damn near gone. Every part of his body ached to touch every part of hers.

Paige smoothed his hair away from his forehead. "Saturday." Her smile teased but her body promised.

\* \* \*

Paige clutched Brian's stomach as he steered the Harley through the Santa Monica streets and down the beach roads. The wind in her face felt like heaven. And the majestic view of the pink and orange sun setting over the Pacific Ocean would make a confirmed atheist believe in God.

He wasn't joking about the dip in the ocean. She hung on for dear life as the bike veered off the pavement, maneuvered around a row of posts, and skidded onto the beach, spitting sand behind it. Her heart pounded in her chest. Was this even legal? Part of her hoped not. The defiant, risk-taking part, so long inhibited by the cautious persona that kept her from feeling too much joy--or too much pain.

Cold shower! The bike leaped through the icy tide, washing them both with salt-water spray, soaking Paige's clothes to her skin. Squealing like a child on her first roller coaster ride, she clung to Brian in delight and exhilaration. Whatever the price of this thrill, she wanted it to go on forever.

How had the mild-mannered computer geek she'd reached out to in friendship managed to touch the depths of her secret heart, and make it quiver? She just didn't get it. But at last she understood why she hadn't wanted to ask anyone else to Shelly's party.

Because it had to be him or nobody.

# Chapter Eight

*Three o'clock in the freaking morning.* Brian tossed the phone onto the bed and willed himself awake. He'd averaged four hours of sleep a night for the past week. The additional script changes to Victor's program had put him another day behind schedule for Suite Smart. A schedule which did *not* include driving two hours into the desert to bail Connor out of some Podunk county jail.

Of all his friends and family, why the hell had Connor called *him*?

Ten minutes later, the bike roared to life in the early morning darkness. Brian patted the canvas pouch beside him with the set of clothes Connor had asked him to bring. Including underwear. Had to be a hell of story.

Brian blinked to keep his eyes focused on the road. That problem with the Suite Smart mattress had turned out to be a bigger issue than anticipated. He'd hoped to work on it at least a few hours this morning. He'd already written off the rest of the day--this afternoon to get a haircut and pick up the tux, and then tonight for...entertainment. His jeans tightened in anticipation. Oh, yeah he was looking forward to tonight. As soon as he was able to pull Paige away from that party.

He skidded the bike to a stop in front of their bank's ATM machine. Eyes half closed, he slid in his plastic card, typed the account's PIN number, and selected Withdrawal. Connor had whined that the jail wouldn't take credit cards, and promised to replace the money into the Suite Smart account at the end of the month when he got his trust fund check. He'd damned well better. Their cash reserves were getting awfully low.

But not this low. Brian stared in disbelief as the screen blinked, "Transaction denied. Insufficient funds." Not possible. Just the other day they'd had over nineteen hundred dollars in the account.

Maybe he'd inadvertently keyed the wrong PIN? He slammed the screen with the flat of his hand, as if that would jar the machine's memory, and tried again. Same response. He checked the balance. Twenty-nine dollars and sixteen cents.

"Connor!" Brian's fists shook. His worthless brother was lucky to be safe in jail now, instead of here. If he'd taken their business money to buy booze and dope, Brian should let him rot in that cell.

It was tempting. Connor had already racked up a couple of DUI's this year. This one could mean his license. But when he did get out, guess which sap would get stuck driving him around?

Resignedly, Brian turned back to the ATM and withdrew five hundred dollars from his personal account, leaving it emptier than Suite Smart's. So much for renting a car tonight.

Steaming despite the early morning chill, he got back on the bike and burned rubber. By the time he reached Bend-in-the-Road, California, population 12, the sun was rising. And promising a hot, dry day. Brian parked the bike in front of the Sheriff's office, shrugged out of his jacket and dusted off his jeans.

"Connor McKay?" he asked the weary-looking deputy.

The man shuffled out the paperwork with the speed of a tired tortoise. He eyed Brian's bundle. "Those his clothes?"

"Yeah." While the deputy carried them to the back, Brian signed the forms and read the charges. "Vagrancy and indecency?"

The returning deputy swished a toothpick in his mouth. "Found him passed out on the side of the road, naked as a jaybird."

Connor came out wearing Brian's clothes, looking like hell. He was going to look a lot worse before Brian was done with him.

124

"Thanks, Bro." Connor grinned sheepishly as he staggered outside, nearly tripping over his own feet. "This Wyatt Earp clown wouldn't take my plastic, even when I told him who I was."

Brian shoved him toward the bike. Connor winced as the sun hit his half-closed eyes. Brian stared at his brother's bloodied face. "What the hell happened?"

"I got rolled." Connor grabbed the Harley's handlebars for support. The snug tee shirt rolled up to reveal a pasty paunch dotted by red raised welts. "That girl I've been seeing, the hot blonde?"

"We haven't exactly met."

"We were out drinking last and she ashhhed me to drive her to her mom's place in the country." Connor's slurred speech intensified his foul breath. "I stopped at the ATM before we left L.A. I dropped Tracy off at some farm house about two o'clock this morning. The next thing I remember is waking up beshide the highway." He scrubbed the side of his face and flinched. "I think the bitch drugged me. One of her Farmer Brown friends must have knocked me out and drove me to the middle of nowhere."

"And stole your clothes and cash." Suite Smart's cash.

"Yeah." Connor tried a grin. "Don'sha just hate it when a woman you thought was after your body was only insherested in your money?"

"I'll let you know if it ever happens."

Connor coughed and his face turned yellow. His throat gurgled.

"Not on the bike." Brian nudged him aside and Connor fell like a weak tree limb. And puked all over his just-washed shirt and pants. *Brian's* shirt and pants.

Brian dug a bottle of water out of his saddlebag and poured it over Connor. It didn't do much to alleviate the smell. "You took the money out of the business account? Why the hell did you need nineteen hundred dollars?"

Connor planted both hands on the ground and started to push

himself up. "You don't know this girl. She--"

Brian knocked him back down with the side of his boot, sending him sprawling in the dirt. "There was no girl, was there? You went out to meet your dealer."

Connor's mouth opened for another protest, then settled into resignation. He brushed his hand across his pale forehead. "I owed him twenty-five hundred dollars. I borrowed the money from Shweet Smart, hoping I could talk Artie into taking nineteen hundred now, and waiting till next week for the rest."

Artie. R.T. "R.T. Dunaway?" The mystery name on the books. That would explain the unexplained twenty-three hundred dollars.

Connor blinked and managed a confused nod. "And friends."

Brian scrutinized the cuts and bruises on Connor's face. Lifting the hem of the tee shirt with two fingers, he inspected the welts on his stomach, side and back. And grimaced. "What did they hit you with?"

"A tire chain, I think." Connor groaned and lay back on the ground.

"Stupid fuck," Brian muttered, helping him to his feet. "You drained the account. Where the hell did you expect to come up with the rest of the money by next week?"

"I figured I'd get an advance from Allied Corp. After we wow them with the demo, as sort of a sign of good faith before they go home and get the hotshots to approve the deal."

"One problem, butthead. The site visit isn't until a week from Tuesday."

"Axshully, it's this coming Tuesday."

In three days? Brian's head felt light, his body unsteady. If he'd eaten any breakfast it would have joined the contents of Connor's stomach on the ground.

Connor grinned like a cartoon character. "I called Allied and

126

moved it up. The sooner they come, the faster we get our money..."

"And you didn't even ask me?" Bile filled his throat.

"Oh, yeah, I meant to tell you. What's the big deal? Why wouldn't you want to go ahead and get it over with?"

"Because the Suite's not fucking ready!"

Connor blinked as if the sun had blinded him. "You said it was." His pale cheeks reddened and his dull eyes found a focus. Brian.

"I said it *would* be. There's a problem with the mattress wiring and--"

"You fucking lied to me!" Connor hurled his fist and took a swing at Brian, missing him by a foot when he stepped aside.

"*I* lied? I'm busting my butt to make this happen, and you sabotage us by stealing money to support your coke habit?" He landed a punch to Connor's mid-section. Connor swayed unsteadily and righted himself, a doped-up drunk feeling no pain. Why had he ever taken this piece-of-shit on as a partner?

*Because you couldn't get the money for Suite Smart anywhere else.*

He took deep, full breaths, mentally reciting his calming mantra. The desert air filled his lungs with desolation. And fortitude. He couldn't give up. Not now. Not yet. He still had three days.

Something rattled inside his head. Where had that naïve optimism come from? He must have drunk from Paige's half-full glass.

He plunged a helmet over Connor's head. "Where's your car?"

"Hell if I know. Bastards probably stole it too." Connor struggled to pull off the helmet. "I'm not riding that damn bike."

"Suit yourself. There's bound to be a bus coming through within the next eight or ten hours." Brian started the Harley's engine and roared off, spraying gravel.

"Hey!" From his mirror, he watched Connor running after him, dragging the too-long pant legs. He looked as panicked as a three-year-old left by his mother in day care.

Oh hell. He stopped and waited. Connor hoisted himself up behind him and Brian gunned the bike. He was afraid the asshole might fall off, but instead he held on and leaned in, a dead weight with a heavy helmet against Brian's back.

*Time to get the ass sober.*

He pulled into a truck stop half a mile out of town and grabbed two stools at the counter. After a pot of coffee between them, Connor showed signs of life. "Shit, that was something out of Midnight Express," he said, digging into a three-egg omelet. "If you hadn't showed up when you did, I was going to claw my way out under the walls."

"Why'd you call me?"

"I didn't want to bother my mother at that hour." Connor chomped on a piece of toast. "Not that she would have showed up until afternoon, anyway, after her aerobics class and her manicure."

"What about your friends?"

"I saw them earlier at the bar playing pool with a couple of hot, willing babes. No way they'd have left that action to drive out to the boonies to bail my ass out."

Connor's friends were as egotistical and self-absorbed as he was. What an ironic twist. Despite his popularity, the only person Connor could count on when he was down was the guy whose guts he most hated. That must really suck.

"I'll have to tell Mom I got carjacked on the highway." Connor glared at Brian. "And *you* won't say anything different."

"Connor, I haven't spoken to your mother in twelve years."

"Yeah. Well." He pushed aside his coffee and reached for his wallet. "You think this place takes cards?"

Brian pulled out his last twenty and slapped it on the counter. "Let's get the hell out of here."

Maneuvering the motorcycle with Connor hanging on his back brought back a memory of piggybacking him on his ten-speed when they were kids. Brian recalled the first time he'd laid eyes on his brother, or even knew he had one. Connor must have been about three. Cute. And sweet. Brian had loved playing with him.

In succeeding summers, though, the cute kid had turned into a first-class brat. Breaking things and blaming his misdeeds on Brian. Once he'd even slammed his own face against the wall and told his parents Brian had hit him.

It wasn't just that Connor couldn't share. He'd seemed to resent Brian just breathing the same air.

And he hadn't changed. Connor might act self-assured, the swaggering, confident heir to power. But on the inside he was still that spoiled, insecure little boy who refused to take responsibility for his own actions and tried to manipulate his parents--and everyone else--into liking him.

Damn, his brother's life sucked worse than his.

Off the highway, about half mile ahead, something silver metallic glinted. "What's that?"

Connor straightened. "Shit," he said as they got closer. "It's the Mercedes. They must have just taken it for a joy ride and dumped it."

Brian pulled over to the shoulder. "Well, let's see if they left any moving parts."

The Mercedes was almost intact. The dashboard was busted, the radio and CD player ripped out, and a long scratch ran along the driver's side. Letters were carved into the paint. NEXT WEEK. OR EISE.

But the keys were in the floor board and the engine started on the first try.

Connor got in, rolled down the driver side window and held out his hand. "Thanks, man." His smile actually looked genuine. "I owe you."

"Damn straight," Brian said, but he didn't shake Connor's hand.

"I'm done with the coke," Connor said. "Once I've settled with Artie, I'm off the stuff for good."

"Sure you are."

"I mean it." Connor's bloodshot eyes brimmed with Gil McKay sincerity. "I'm a businessman now and I can't be a good manager if I'm stoned out of my mind."

"Right. You're turning your life around." Brian strode back to his bike. Like he'd believe this bird could ever change.

* * *

How had he let himself get roped into this? As he escorted Paige to the Mercedes, Brian felt like an imposter. Crashing someone else's party. Wearing somebody else's clothes. The rented tux, designed for someone shorter, chafed his crotch. The cuff links twisted into his wrists. Even his buffed and polished shoes felt stifling on feet that were used to open sandals.

"Nice touch." Paige admired the 'Congratulations Nick and Shelly' sign on the door panel and checked out the Mercedes. "Connor's car?"

Brian opened the door for her and settled her in against the white leather seat before she could take a closer look at the hand painted sign and the threatening message it covered. "Yeah."

"How'd you manage that?"

He started the engine, affecting an innocent look. "Charm."

She lifted a perfectly arched brow. "No offense, Hon, but if you got Connor to give up his car on a Saturday night, you had more than charm going for you."

*Hon?* Did she realize what she'd called him? *Don't take it to heart, McKay.* Sweet endearments were probably de rigueur with Paige's crowd at fancy society occasions like this. Maybe he should have brushed up on air kissing.

Paige touched his arm. Her glistening blue eyes, the same color as her sparkly dress, roved over him. "Do you know how sexy you look tonight?"

He ran nervous fingers through his slick backed hair. "If I do, it's only a reflection of your aura." God, had he really said that embarrassingly corny line?

Miraculously, she bought it. "You see, you don't need Victor to speak for you. You can be charismatic and charming when you want to. I know you'll have a wonderful time tonight."

He was definitely planning on that. But first he had to survive this social ordeal.

As he pulled up at the country club and handed the Mercedes keys to the valet, Brian puffed out his chest with confidence, hoping not to give himself away as a Clueless Outsider. He couldn't help imagine that the other arriving guests were all staring at him, wondering what Cinderella's mouse coachman was doing escorting the princess to the ball.

Paige waited at the curb for him to reach her side. In her strapless, periwinkle gown, she looked like an ethereal goddess, exquisite as fragile blue glass. Almost too dainty to touch. Tentatively he laid his fingers on her arm. Soft as velvet. She faced him and smiled. Girl-next-door-innocence shared a face with sultry temptress, sending warm waves all over his body.

Linking her elbow with his, she stepped through the oak paneled doorway as if making a royal entrance.

The Club's ballroom was decorated, fittingly, in green and gold. Every table reeked with the smell of money. As soon as they entered, Shelly dropped her fiancé's hand and ran to greet her sister.

"Paige, thank God." Shelly looked like a sweet southern girl in her Georgia peach dress, but her voice was harsh and frantic. "We have a disaster. A wreck on the freeway caused the bakery's delivery truck to stop short, and the cake got smushed."

Paige took it in stride. "I wouldn't cry over smushed cake. Just slice it up ahead of time and nobody will know the difference."

A half dozen other women pounced on Paige before they got halfway into the room, kiss-kissing her on both cheeks and babbling nonsense Brian couldn't care less about. Paige, the perfect hostess, dutifully introduced every one. Not that he'd remember any of their names. Or even what they looked like. His gaze was fixed only on her.

God, she was beautiful. And competent. And caring. Her sister Shelly was the star of this show, but Paige was the producer, director, and set designer. Brian examined the elegant table linens, perfectly matched to the floral arrangements. The decorations, the catering, the music--Paige was responsible for everything that happened behind the scene. And he'd guess, not appreciated nearly enough for her efforts.

He moved out of her glow, searching for a quiet place to escape the crowd, but she came after him. "No, you don't. No hiding. You're going to schmooze, remember?"

He couldn't think of anything he'd enjoy less.

"And dance," she said with a flirtatious wink.

He tried a teasing protest. "Dancing wasn't part of our deal."

She pouted. "You danced at Johnny Rocket's. And here at the club, only last week."

He still dreamed about the warm sensation of her arms around his neck, the arousing fragrance of her perfume. "The alternative was sitting at a table with Connor."

She giggled that sweet, light titter he'd come to look forward to more than his next meal, and brushed an incentive kiss against his cheek. "I'm the hostess. If I don't get this party started, no one else will." She laid a warm hand on his back and nudged him toward the dance floor.

"Paige!" A tall, handsome, bodybuilder type with glossy platinum hair appeared through a hole in the crowd and touched Paige's elbow. "You are a vision tonight. May I have the first dance?"

Brian grabbed her other arm. "Sorry, bud, this one's taken." He attempted a caveman-style drag to the dance floor but Paige slid her hand down his arm and clasped his hand in a light but firm vise.

"Nice to see you, too, Evan. Brian, this is--"

"Evan Shore, Shore Photography." He extended his hand.

*Schmooze.* Brian grasped Mr. America's hand in a firm shake. "Brian McKay, Suite Smart Corporation." *Network.* "Voice activation technology."

"Good to meet you, McKay." Shore raised a brow. "Any kin to Gil McKay?"

"Distant relation. He was my father."

Evan Shore was unfazed. "I know your mother. She used to pose for me in her modeling days."

*I don't think so.*

"Vonda's a lovely lady. Please tell her I said hello."

He gritted his back teeth. "Vonda McKay is not my mother. Nor is she--" A sharp elbow nudged his rib. "I'll tell her I saw you." Grabbing the offending elbow, he wheeled Paige with one motion onto the dance floor.

"You didn't have to be rude." She held herself slightly away from him, one hand fingering his shoulder, the other a tentative touch at his waist. "Even if your stepmother is a witch spelled with a B, it wasn't necessary to transfer your hostility to Evan."

"Do you want to psychoanalyze me or dance?" Brian splayed his fingers against her back and tugged her closer. She didn't fight him. Her perfume filled his nostrils when she leaned into him, cheek to cheek, molding her body to his.

The DJ had chosen a slow, haunting song. Something about the course of true love, or the love of true course, whatever. It didn't matter. Nor did the people staring at them as they moved to the center of the floor. He couldn't see anyone but Paige. She felt light in his arms and her body moved with him wherever he took her.

Her hair smelled like fruit and flowers. He pressed her tighter against his chest, imagining touching her and holding her against his body, horizontally positioned. Sweet and slow and all night long.

*Tonight.* Blood pumped in his veins and other places. Tonight he'd make love to her like he'd been aching to since the moment he saw her pull her panties over that delicious butt cheek.

He brushed his lips over the nape of her neck, almost forgetting the people watching. And then, suddenly, they weren't alone. Shelly and her fiancé waltzed beside them, and then two more couples. Ten minutes later, half the party was dancing. Including Paige's father, twirling around with Shelly to a brisk country song, then handing her back to Nick and reeling in two other ladies in turn.

"Careful, Daddy, don't hurt your back," Paige said as he boogied beside them. "Remember Helene's wedding?"

"I was fifty pounds heavier then. I'm in much better shape now," her father retorted. He whirled past them to a round of applause.

Brian smiled to himself and drew Paige in close. "You do know how to get a party started."

She grinned. "We can sit down now, if you want."

Another song started. A slow one. Her body felt soft and warm and fit perfectly in his arms. "No, let's stay here."

After half a dozen more dances, dinner was announced. People swarmed to the buffet lines as if they couldn't afford to buy their own meal. Maybe that was how rich people came to be rich.

After they'd filled their plates, Paige directed him to a round table with six other people, all strangers to him. Paige had apparently seated members of the family at different tables, so each could be sure the conversation didn't lag. An obligation Paige performed well. Except for jumping up every three or four minutes to check on this, take care of that, say hello to someone she'd missed earlier.

While she was gone, Brian ate in silence. The other couples spoke among themselves. But eventually, the conversation lulled and curious eyes turned to him.

He swallowed. *Schmooze, McKay.* He took a deep breath and introduced himself. Nobody shot him down. In fact, they asked questions. What did he do? How did he know the Andersons? Having nowhere to escape, he told them about his business, explaining in layman's language the highlights of the Suite Technology.

"We should stay at a hotel like that next time we go down to the Caribbean," one woman said to her husband, then turned back to Brian. "You'll let us know which chain you sell it to, won't you? Charlie books a lot of conventions in the islands. Do you have a card?"

So that's all it took. He produced a business card from his wallet, and wrote his above Connor's. Networking. It was just talking to people. Most of the time a wasted flapping of gums, but you never knew when you might meet someone influential.

"Hi." Paige paused behind his chair and wrapped her arms around his neck. "What you been up to?"

"Schmoozing."

Smiling as if she didn't believe him, she sat and finished her entrée. And almost made it to dessert before Shelly appeared to drag her away. "I'll be right back," Paige promised.

He doubted that. After Hostess Paige resolved the crisis of the moment, there would be another needing her attention.

He glanced at the clock on the gold-papered wall. Ten-thirty. The party was scheduled to go until twelve. If he knew Paige, she'd

135

stay to the bitter end, until every guest was tucked away in their vehicle.

But then, he'd have her to himself.

Brian ambled to the nearest bar station and refreshed his drink, admiring Paige's finesse as she soothed hurt feelings and turned frowns into smiles.

She was magnificent. And breathtaking. Her hair, piled on her head with a few tempting curls hanging loose, caught the glint of the chandeliers and sparkled like spun gold. She was charm. Grace. And a touch of innocence.

But not too innocent. The strapless gown skimmed across the upper swells of her breasts, dipping, when she exhaled, to reveal an extra hint of delicious cleavage. Not that his imagination needed any help going there. Just watching her raised his temperature several degrees, heating him from his neck to his feet. And all points in between.

He downed his drink and ordered another, eyeing the clock hands twitching too-slowly forward. To fill the time he imagined he was caressing Paige's bare skin. Cupping her bottom. Burying his face in her. Covering her with his body and thrusting inside her. Being one with her.

Just as his fantasy climaxed, Paige appeared beside him in real time and led him wordlessly to the dance floor, her hands moving under his jacket and over his sweat-crumpled shirt. He splayed a hand against her bare back. Her skin was hot. Desire played in her eyes. Barely aware of the rhythm or music, he lowered his head and kissed her.

His body hardened the instant her lips scorched his mouth. Their tongues met and mated as if nothing could keep them apart. She clung to him, swaying in time to the music, intensifying his torture with every motion.

The music ended abruptly. Paige broke their desperate kiss, staring at him with dewy eyes. Her breath was ragged and her cheeks were pink. Her eyes said, *I want you.* But the sound from her lips was, "I guess we'd better mingle."

Mingle? He wanted to mingle his body and soul with hers, crushing her in his passion. But there wasn't a damned thing he could do about it now except suffer the torment of desire.

He braced himself for an endless evening of 'schmoozing.' But shortly after eleven, the party started winding down. Couples began to leave. Even the guest of honor begged off with a headache from the excitement, saying she and Nick were going to his place to chill out with an old movie. Brian wasn't fooled, nor, apparently, was Paige. Shelly had that look in her eye. The engaged couple were dying to have at each other.

He fought to manage his own body's frustration as Paige's older sister came up to say goodbye.

"Baby-sitter's got to be home by midnight," Helene said to her husband, sounding wistful.

"I told you we should have hired that college girl," Ted replied with an edge in his voice.

Paige heard it too. "What's up, guys?" she asked.

"It's nothing." Helene shouldered her evening bag. "The band that was playing when Ted and I met is at the Black Cat Club tonight. The last show starts at 11:30. Our babysitter has an early curfew..."

Brian sensed the wheels turning in Paige's head before she ever opened her mouth. No!

"I'd be glad to watch Phillip while you guys go out," she said brightly. She turned to him. "You wouldn't mind dropping me off there, would you Brian?"

# Chapter Nine

S ilence steeped the Mercedes like a cloud of noxious gas.
*Big mistake, Paige.* She'd realized it the second she'd seen the hurt and disappointment in Brian's face.

"Thanks for driving me to Helene's," she said tentatively.

He grunted without even a glance.

So, he wasn't going to talk. Paige folded her hands in her lap, almost wishing for one of his cutting remarks. Even a cursing fit. Anything was better than this cold politeness.

She studied Brian's hands as he deftly handled the Mercedes from freeway to freeway. Imagining those masterful hands and competent fingers touching her body.

Everywhere.

She folded her arms across her breasts to hide her unsteady breathing, but he never looked at her. Just stared straight ahead with his knuckles white on the steering wheel, as if he were gripping someone's neck.

Didn't he think she shared his frustration? Every move, every touch, every look tonight had been foreplay. Her body ached with desire, anticipating being in his arms. Making passionate love to him as she'd wanted to since that first fiery kiss. But she'd ignored her yearnings--and his--when she'd opened her mouth without engaging her brain. Or her heart.

"Helene needed my help," she offered lamely.

He barely aimed a steely glare at her.

*You could have said 'No,' Paige.* Or nothing at all. But she just couldn't help herself. Why had she carelessly sabotaged this evening?

And then it hit her. It wasn't careless at all. Subconscious, maybe. But she'd screwed up their evening on purpose. Because her rampant desire for Brian scared her all the way down to her tingling center.

"It's the next exit," she directed.

No response. The only way she knew he'd heard her was the quiet clicking turn signal.

He took the suburban streets with almost the same speed as the freeways, careening around corners, jolting but never out of control. At Helene's house she half expected him to roll to a California stop while she jumped out. Instead, he parked at the curb, turned off the engine, and got out of the car.

"You don't have to come in with me. Ted will take me home after."

"I picked you up. I'll take you home." He hooked his arm through her elbow to keep her from tottering on the steps, the perfect, polite, steaming-under-the-collar gentleman. "Besides, how are you going to get the babysitter home?"

He had a point. It was too late for the girl to walk home by herself. Paige let herself in the front door with her key, introduced herself and Brian to the sleepy teenager, and went in to check on her nephew while Brian drove the girl home.

Philip was fine. Paige, on the other hand, was having a self-analysis attack. What was wrong with her? Why couldn't she handle this relationship as smoothly as all her others?

Because this was the first time she hadn't been in control. She'd managed all those other affairs, guiding, nurturing, and eventually ending them when their time was due. Clean, neat, with no hard feelings. None of those bland vanilla relationships had grabbed her by the gut, slammed her against a wall and blotted out every thought except being with that person.

She picked up a book Helene had left on the coffee table and skimmed through two hundred pages in fifteen minutes. Brian had said he'd be back in five. She threw the book on the couch, unable to recall even the names of the main characters.

Maybe he'd decided not to come back. He was fed up with her teasing and wavering. He'd pegged her the moment he saw her as a flighty, shallow socialite who didn't care about anything except the next party, and she was doing an excellent job of proving him right.

There was a knock on the door. "This is cul-de-sac city," Brian said as she let him in. "I got lost in the maze."

"It is tricky." She motioned him into the living room.

He'd taken off his jacket and tie in the car. His shirt was open at the throat. His dark wavy chest hair was as wild and unrestrained as Paige's emotions. She couldn't keep her eyes off him.

The male version of the shy librarian who hides under shapeless clothes, Brian covered his sexual appeal with faded tee shirts and wrinkled flannel. But Paige had seen the passion in his dark eyes, without the shield of those thick glasses he hid behind. She'd felt his hot lips burning out of control. Her mouth watered at the thought of tangling her fingers in his tufts of dark chest hair, tasting his bare skin and...

She checked her lust in mid-fantasy as another image intervened, that of five-year-old Philip wandering in and finding his aunt ravenously attacking a naked man on his family sofa.

Brian sat beside her, leaving several inches between them. As if this were an awkward first date. And probably their last.

Their eyes met silently. Paige swallowed. "It's just a couple of hours. They'll be back by two."

He grunted and reached for the television remote control.

"No." She took it out of his hand. "Philip's a light sleeper and once he wakes up, he can't fall back to sleep."

His brows rose and knitted but he made no comment.

Paige fumbled in the end table drawer. "We could play cards." She retrieved a deck from the back of the drawer.

"You mean, like, gin rummy?" His eyes laughed at her.

"Or poker."

That caught his interest. "Strip poker?" His gaze raked over her.

The thought of undressing in front of him appealed far too much. "How about we try an interesting variation? Instead of taking off our clothes, the person who wins each hand gets to ask the other a personal question. And the loser has to answer it. Honestly and completely."

He frowned. "I fail to see that as an improvement over the original."

She sighed. "Okay, how's this? If I lose, I'll take something off. If you lose, you have to answer my question. Honestly."

His slow smile fed equal parts of desire and uneasiness.

She let him cut the deck, and then dealt the cards, hiding a smile. Daddy had taught her to play poker at age six, and by the time she was twelve, she could beat everyone in the family except Granny Anderson, who flew to Vegas every month for a regular tournament and kicked the other seniors' butts. And had separated Brian from three dollars on July fourth.

She lost the first hand.

Brian cleared his throat expectantly.

It was just one hand, the luck of the draw. Paige pulled off one diamond studded earring.

"Jewelry doesn't count," he said.

She raised a brow. "Who made that rule?"

"I did."

She guessed he was imagining her naked except for her earrings and her diamond pendant. A fantasy that aroused Paige as much as she hoped it did Brian. But fantasy was all he'd get out of this game because she was going to beat the pants--er, secrets--out of him.

And she did have two shoes. After clipping her earring back into place, she slipped out of one high heeled sandal and presented it to Brian with a little erotic fanfare, humming "The Stripper."

He took the shoe with dry amusement, and set it on the table. Okay, so he didn't have a foot fetish.

Brian won the second hand as well, with three of a kind.

Barefoot now, she was a *little* worried. But her poker face didn't let it show. In fact, this was a good strategy. He'd think she was a rube, and get cocky and careless on the next round.

He did exactly that. Paige exchanged only one card and got the card she needed for two pair, and he had nothing.

As she swept up the cards, Brian folded his arms and leaned back into the sofa cushions. His expression was tense and wary.

"I'll make this first question an easy one," she said. No point in scaring him off. "What did you have to do to get Connor to lend you his car?"

He chuckled low in his throat. "I helped him out of a jam this morning."

"What kind of jam?"

He grinned. "That's another question." He picked up the cards and shuffled the deck. "Next hand."

Typical cagy Brian, doling out answers as if they were pearls. He was going to make her work for every one. Paige focused on the game. She thought he had him with a two pair, aces and tens, but Brian opened his hand to reveal a straight. He licked his lips.

"Pantyhose," she said. "Turn your back."

"No way."

*Suit yourself.* Facing him, she stood and lifted her dress above her knees. The full skirt bounced on her hips as she tugged at the waistband and slowly slid the pantyhose down. Unhurried. Deliberate. A seductive striptease intended to torture him.

As she rolled the stockings down over each thigh and leg, a thought tormented *her*. She wasn't wearing a bra. She had two articles of clothing left. The dress. And her lace blue, thong panties.

She let him catch a peek at the panties as stretched out each leg to remove the hosiery. Signaling the show was over, she stood, smoothed down her dress, and laid the pantyhose on the table next to her two shoes.

Brian's eyes were hot with desire but his voice was steady. "Ready to quit?"

"No way." She shuffled an extra time, then dealt the next hand, summoning every ounce of concentration. Brian smirked when she asked for two cards, and he only needed one. But when he revealed his three of a kind, she bested him with a full house.

Showering him with a triumphant grin, she started to follow up on the Connor/Mercedes story, then changed her mind. Brian was a better poker player than she'd reckoned on. She shouldn't be wasting her questions on insignificant issues. This was her chance to learn about his past, his family, his beliefs. What were his dreams and desires? What was he thinking right now? She looked into his tense, tired eyes. And guessed.

"Will you be able to make the deadline for the Suite Smart site visit?"

"Absolutely." He picked up the cards to shuffle them, then, as if remembering he'd promised to tell the whole truth, laid them down again. "Maybe not."

His poker face was gone. Paige saw worry that bordered on panic.

She leaned toward him. "Having a problem?"

He let out a deep sigh. Bowing his head, he rattled off in a monotone, "I've had to reprogram the mattress several times and it's still not right. And Connor moved up the site visit. Allied is coming on Tuesday."

"*This* Tuesday? Omigod, is there anything I can do?"

He glared at her. "Sure, you can start up the Visual Studio .NET debugger and tell me why I am getting a memory dump when I try to use 64 bit processing instead of the normal 32 bit processing."

She drew back her hand that had been about to touch his. "You don't have to be nasty. I just wanted to help."

"Sorry." He lifted her hand from her side and kissed it, sucking one finger into his mouth. "I didn't mean to take it out on you. I just...I didn't figure how much time I'd need."

Oh, God, it was her fault. She'd stolen critical days, working on Victor. He'd been burning the candle at both ends to ready the Suite and yet not disappoint her. She ran her finger over his lips. "You should go home. Get a good night's sleep. Maybe in the morning you'll feel fresher and--"

"Deal the cards, Paige."

She shuffled and dealt the next hand in tense silence. He wasn't going to quit, apparently, until he saw her naked.

And she wasn't giving up until she got him emotionally naked, stripped of his cynical defenses. She yearned to touch the man inside as much as she craved his body.

He didn't ask for any cards this round, but she couldn't tell if he was bluffing. Finally, after getting the exact three cards she needed, Paige laid her ace high straight triumphantly on the table.

He showed her his four sevens with a wicked grin.

She didn't ask him to turn his back this time. And she didn't do a strip show for him. Without fanfare, she reached under her dress, pulled the panties down and quickly stepped out of them. Scooping up the thong, she set the scrap of lace on the table next to his other trophies. "My deal?"

He swallowed so hard she heard him gulp. "Paige, we don't have to play anymore."

"Why not? I'm having a great time. Aren't you?" He had to know she didn't have anything else on under the dress. But she wasn't about to wimp out. She'd finish what she'd started. "Cut the cards."

Paige had dealt herself a terrible hand this time. And exchanging three didn't help a bit. Heat flushed her face and neck. What if Helene and Ted walked in and saw her stark naked on the couch...

"Okay, Paige, that's enough. You've got nothing. I know you've got nothing."

*I've got my pride.*

"Give it up. Let's see your hand." He pried her fingers off her cards.

She only had a pair of threes. But he had scratch. Zippo.

She stared into his eyes, but if he'd thrown away a better hand, he wasn't telling.

He smoothed his fingers over her cheek, sending warmth through her body. "I will answer one more question. And that's the end of the game."

She nodded, mellowed as much by his gesture as by his tender expression. "Why does Connor call you his dollar partner?"

*Shit.* Brian clenched his fingers. He should have expected she'd ask that. Hell, he was surprised she'd waited this long. He sucked in a breath. "That's how much I have invested in the business."

She smiled. Not a superior, looking-down-her-nose-at-him smile, but a wide eyed, awed grin. "And I thought Connor was a good businessman. How did you parlay that into a half interest?"

"Desperation." Feeling a weight slowly slip off his shoulders, he hooked his arm around her waist and settled her at his side. "I've had the idea of a voice-activated hotel suite since the Air Force, but I had no money, no collateral for a developmental loan, and no interested investors."

Paige leaned into his shoulder as if he were telling her a bedtime story.

"After my discharge, I worked a couple years for a technology firm in Reno. Saved a little money. But not enough." He squinted at a smudge on his glasses and pulled a handkerchief out of his pocket. Wiping the lens made the blur worse.

"Then two years ago I got a letter from the attorney for my father's estate." He pulled off his glasses and set them on the coffee table. "Nobody had even called me to tell me the bastard had died. But then they discovered I was mentioned in the will. So I came to Los Angeles for the reading."

His stomach soured at the memory of his humiliation. "I thought maybe, finally, the old man had chosen to make up to me in death what he never gave me in life. I sat in that room for an hour while the executors read off every piece of art donated, every little item from his script collection and his wardrobe. And then, finally, they came to me." The pain had never left him. "One dollar. He left me one fucking dollar."

Paige gasped and pulled back to look into his face.

"Gives new meaning to the term 'Favorite Son,' doesn't it?"

Her sea blue eyes blinked furiously as if wavering between anger and tears. "Why would anybody do such a heartless, cruel thing? If he didn't want you to have anything, why not just leave you out entirely?"

"Because he didn't want me to contest the will. If he left me out, I could take it to court, say it was an oversight, or he wasn't of sound mind, or whatever. This way it was clear: the bastard just hated me."

"I'm so sorry." Paige's arms were suddenly around his neck, filling his senses with the sweet fragrance of lavender.

He pressed his hands against the waist of her blue sequined dress, trying not to think of what she was or was not wearing underneath. "Connor got half a million dollars. More than even he could run through in a year." And not counting the millions already earning interest in his trust fund.

"So you convinced him to put up the money for Suite Smart."

"I was out of options. I wasn't leaving that room without something for my trouble and my mother's suffering. I would have groveled on the floor if he'd asked me to. Fortunately, all I had to do was convince him he could make a killing in a startup business without doing any work."

Tears welled in Paige's eyes. Pity or caring?

"Sometimes I feel guilty for conning him into it," he admitted. "If I can't make this fly, he's out half a million dollars. I haven't lost anything."

"Except two years of your life." She cupped his cheek with one small hand. It was soft but steady with warm strength. "You will make it happen. And you haven't done Connor any disservice. This business is his first venture away from Mommy and Daddy's checkbook. He gets to wear a suit and carry a business card and be somebody in his own right, not just 'Gil McKay's boy.' If he lost every penny, it'd be worth it for him."

"I doubt he'd see it your way."

She sat back, eyes wide. "What if--I'm just saying *If*--you don't finish in time? You can just schedule another meeting. Or sell it to another buyer."

He shook his head. "There's a clause in our contract. I was so anxious for the investment money, I signed away my rights to the profits if I don't present a saleable product by the end of this month. After that, I'd just be working to make Connor rich. Richer," he amended.

She gazed up at him in horror. "He wouldn't hold you to the contract. Surely he'd share whatever profits with you, whenever they happen."

She looked so convinced. So naïve. "You really believe that, don't you?"

"Connor put in half a million dollars! Why would he throw that away?"

"To screw me over." He glared. "And don't give me one of your Pollyanna looks. Connor would gladly lose half a mil in Suite Smart to keep me from getting a dime."

Tears spilled over onto her cheeks.

"I know. You can't believe that dear sweet Connor--"

"I don't know that! I'm crying because *you* believe it." She swiped at a tear, searching his face with those big blues that saw the best in everybody. "Why do you hate him so much?"

Wasn't it obvious? He dried her face with his handkerchief. "Connor's never had to work a day in his life. He got a brand new Jaguar on his sixteenth birthday, just for breathing. My mother was a night auditor in a two star Reno hotel and I worked there too, every day after school since I was twelve. Making beds, carrying room service trays, hauling luggage. I bought my bike with the money I earned. Nobody gave me a damn thing." He caught his breath, letting his thoughts catch up with his words. "You don't think I have reason to hate him?"

She ran her fingers through his hair and kissed him on the eyes. "You don't hate Connor. You resent him, because your father loved him and not you."

*Pollyanna dribble.*

"Isn't that true?"

He shot her a daggered glare. "Is that a question? Are you willing to take that dress off for it?"

She didn't respond to his challenge, just stared at him with eyes so warm with compassion they threatened to melt him from the outside in. "That's it, isn't it? Your pain and distrust comes from not having your father's love, not the money he denied you."

He clenched his fists around her skirt. "I don't need the bastard's love."

"No, you don't. You're a strong and capable man with personal resources Connor will never have. But the hurt little boy inside you is still wallowing in self-pity."

"That's a bunch of psycho-babble," he mumbled, all out of cutting, smartass remarks. He just didn't have the heart to fight it anymore.

"Oh, Brian." She wrapped her arms around his neck, taking no heed that the front of her dress dipped down to reveal hard pink nipples. Her lips found his and he relished her, savoring her sweet breath and eager tongue. And her comforting, believing-in-him, warmth. He wanted her strength, her innocent confidence, her childlike belief that goodness prevails. His heart ached for her touch. His body needed her skin against his, her legs wrapped around him.

He hoisted her across his lap. She dug her knees into the leather cushions, straddling him. He slipped his fingers under her gown, cupped her bare, soft bottom, and pulled her hard against his erection. The room disappeared. The rest of the evening became a blur. Nothing else existed except the intense, driving need to be inside her.

Until he heard the sound of the garage door opening.

# Chapter Ten

Paige grabbed her panties and hose from the table and looked for her purse, but she must have left her tiny evening bag in the car.

"Gimme." Brian reached for the evidence and shoved them into his jacket pockets just as her sister and brother-in-law entered the room.

"Hi." Paige hugged Helene in greeting. "How was the band?"

"Still good." Ted slipped out of his tux jacket and laid it over an armchair. "But they've gotten so old. Amazing how everyone ages except us." He grinned at his wife.

Helen pecked Paige on the cheek. "Thanks for doing this. You too, Brian." She held her hand out to him for a shake. "Did Philip give you much trouble?"

"Didn't wake up once." *Not that you'd have noticed,* Paige thought guiltily. She'd been completely focused on Brian.

Ted looked at the cards on the coffee table. "Who won?"

"Um, I think we both did." She assembled the deck and put the cards back in the drawer. "Glad you had a nice evening." She slipped her feet into her shoes and took Brian's arm. "Guess we'd better shove off."

Brian opened the passenger door of the Mercedes for her, then settled into the driver's seat and started the engine. "Where to now, Madam?"

Not back to her house. Not with Daddy probably still up and Shelly liable to walk in any minute. "How about your place," she suggested with a seductive smile. "I've been dying to see your etchings."

Brian wouldn't play. "Don't have any etchings."

"No?" She trailed a finger across his lips. "Well, then, we should make some. Why don't we put a big piece of paper on the floor, and you lie down on it, naked, and I'll trace around you." She ran a teasing hand from the top of his head across his temple, down his cheek, and over his neck and shoulder.

If that shocked him, his poker face didn't show it. And if it turned him on, the only clue was in his eyes.

"I'll take my panties now, please."

He extracted a tangled wisp of blue lace and nylon from his pocket and dangled it over her head. When Paige grabbed for the panties, he yanked them out of her reach. "Not so fast. You can win these back in a poker game."

"Oh no. No more poker." She lunged, but he waved her underwear behind him like a flag.

"No kissee, no panties."

She'd never seen Brian playful. But she was enjoying every second of the tease. "You want a kiss?" She sank her mouth onto his, forcing his lips open, ravishing him with her tongue. Pulling his shirt loose from his slacks, she slipped her hand under the suspenders and tweaked his hard nipple.

He groaned, took control of the tongue play, and forked his fingers through her carefully assembled hairdo. She fumbled for the buttons on his shirt, eager to taste him.

"Hold on." He nudged her away. "If we're going to act like hormonal teenagers, let's at least find a parking spot not directly in front of your sister's house."

He put the Mercedes in gear and was starting to pull away from

151

the curb when the double door of the three car garage creaked open. A black BMW backed down the drive. The taillights flashed as it stopped behind them.

Paige rolled down the steamed-up window.

Ted pulled alongside and lowered his window. "I didn't know you were still here. Your Dad's been trying to call you but you didn't answer your cell."

She felt in the floor board for her evening bag, pulled her phone out of the bag and read four missed calls. "Is anything wrong?"

"He threw his back out."

"Oh, no!" She'd warned him but the stubborn man wouldn't listen. She reached for the door lock, then froze. Part of her was already hurrying home, worried and guilty for not being there when Daddy needed her. The other part thought of Brian and cried out in frustration. She couldn't do this to him again.

Ted looked from her disheveled hair to Brian's lipstick-smeared mouth. His face crinkled into an embarrassed grimace. "No need for you to go. I'll take care of it." He straightened. "You two go ahead and do...uh...whatever."

Brian put the car back in gear. "Thanks, man, but we've got it covered." Before Paige could comment or protest, he waved to Ted and sped away from the house.

God, what could she say to him now? "I'm sorry," she mumbled as he turned onto her street, trying not to break down.

"Not your fault."

"But we didn't have to go. Ted would have handled it."

"Your father asked for you."

Of course. Daddy would never think of asking for Helene. Or Shelly. It was always her.

"He relies on you," Brian said as if he'd read her thoughts. "He loves you." When he looped his arm around her, she recognized the unspoken longing in his eyes. *If I had a father who loved me...*

"Brian..." She leaned her head against his shoulder and slipped her hand over his chest. For once she had no words. He'd had every right to be angry with her tonight. She couldn't have blamed him if he'd ditched her at the club and never looked back. But he'd stuck it out. And he was still here. She breathed in the deep scent of woodsy cologne, wondering how long it would be before she disappointed him again.

\* \* \*

Finally. Brian keyed in the last string of code for the Suite Smart mattress, and then rubbed his tired eyes. He couldn't remember the last time he'd slept. He hadn't eaten real food since the eggs Paige had cooked at five a.m. yesterday, after they'd gotten her dad settled inn bed. But it would all be worth it if the damn program worked.

He clicked on the demo and tested the program commands. Responding to his voice, the computer image bed raised and lowered in twelve different combinations, including undulating from side to side like a hammock. Everything worked perfectly.

In the demo.

He went to the back of the lab and tugged on the mattress. He'd forgotten how much weight the servos, gear boxes, and moveable framing added. "Connor! I need your help."

His brother appeared at the doorway between the office and the lab. "Moi?" Connor sank his teeth into an apple. "The mad scientist actually needs my help?"

"Do you want to make this sale? Get your ass in here and help me move the mattress."

Connor crunched his apple. "You're pretty cranky for a man who's about to become a millionaire." His face twisted into a knowing smirk. "Aaah. You didn't get any, did you? You sprang for a tux and flowers but the butterfly didn't put out."

Suppressing the seething inside, Brian stared him down. One day to financial independence and he'd be damned if he'd lose it in a pissing match with Connor. "Pick up the damn mattress."

With Brian pulling and Connor pushing, they got the mattress to the Suite and hefted it onto the bed platform. While Connor caught his breath, Brian hooked up the wiring.

"So that's it?" Connor asked when he'd finished. "Everything's ready?"

"Yep." He just had to copy the developmental program over to the production server.

Connor grinned. "You just barely saved your ass, Bro'."

"And yours." If the sale came through, Connor could pay off his debts without having his legs broken, or worse.

Connor surveyed the entire Suite model, inspecting each item. Like he'd know if something was wrong. "You're going to wear a suit tomorrow, right?" He frowned. "You do have a suit?"

"Yeah." He'd bought one to attend the reading of their father's will. What a negative return on investment that was.

"The team from Allied will be here at nine," Connor said, as if the running time clock wasn't stamped in Brian's mind. "I'll be in at eight. With doughnuts and coffee." Looking pleased with his contribution, Connor started for the door.

"Connor." He should probably say something supportive, like 'Let's get 'em,' 'or Way to go Bro', but all that came out was, "Schmooze and charm these guys all you want in the pre-game small talk, but when they come in here for the demo, keep your trap shut unless you know what you're talking about."

\* \* \*

Paige clicked off her cell phone and set Daddy's lunch on a bed tray, wishing she could be in two places at once. Her campers would be fine without her; Jenna Carroll had agreed to combine their two groups for the day. But if she could clone herself, she'd send one Paige to the Suite Smart lab, helping Brian however she could to prepare for tomorrow's site visit. Even if only to bring him coffee or rub his back.

Rubbing his back. Waves of lust cascaded through her. Probably a good thing she wasn't a clone. She'd probably distract more than help.

At least she had his cell number in her phone now. Though he'd been working nonstop on the Suite, he'd phoned three times since he left yesterday to ask how her father was doing.

Adding napkins and a white carnation to the tray, she carried it upstairs to Daddy's bedroom. "How would you like Lobster Thermidor and rice pilaf?"

"Not particularly." Her father inspected the tray. "What have you got?"

"Tomato soup and a grilled cheese sandwich."

"Wonderful." He propped himself against his pillows and picked up a quarter sandwich. "That was Brian on the phone?"

"Yes. He called to see how you were."

"You told him how much I appreciated his help?"

"Twice."

When they'd arrived at the house Saturday night they'd found Daddy sprawled on the foyer floor, leaning against the bottom step where he'd tried to drag himself up the stairs. His immobility added fifty pounds to his weight and she never could have budged him alone. But Brian had lifted Daddy easily, walked him slowly up the stairs, undressed him, and helped him into bed. He'd even escorted the older man to the bathroom several times during the night. He hadn't left until six the next morning.

"He's a good man, that Brian. You should invite him over."

"He's working on a deadline." Paige pulled the vanity chair next to the bed, wondering if Brian had gotten any sleep at all in the last couple of days. "Daddy, how well did you know Gil McKay?"

He sipped his soup. "As well as most neighbors know each other, I guess. We spoke about the weather, the Lakers, family and kids."

"Did he ever talk about Brian?"

He dabbed at his chin with a napkin. "Not much. Just once that I recall." He stared into the dresser mirror as if searching his memory. "You and Connor were about nine, I think. You and Shelly were giggling over your dolls and Connor stood there watching like he wanted to play but didn't want to ask. Gil remarked that he wished he'd had another child so Connor wouldn't be so lonely."

"Another child?"

Her father shrugged. "When I mentioned his son in Reno, Gil said, 'He's not my son. He's my ex-wife's mistake.'"

"Like he had nothing to do with it." Paige clenched her fists. Brian never had a chance. His father had hated him even before he was born.

"Some people shouldn't be allowed to have children." Daddy moved the bed tray aside. "Most parents want the best for their kids, but even the most well-meaning ones mess up."

"You didn't." She leaned over and kissed his cheek.

"Sure I did. I spent so much time at my practice and when I was home, your mother's problems required most of my attention. I didn't give enough time to you girls. Especially you."

"I'm not complaining."

"Exactly. Helene was always winning awards to be celebrated, and Shelly had her own ways of getting attention, but you were never the squeaky wheel. You've always been the peacemaker and the nurturer, and we've taken you for granted."

"I don't mind." Not most of the time, anyway.

"You're the strong one," he said as she fluffed the pillows around him. "I just want you to know how much I appreciate everything you did for your mother when she was out of sorts. This family couldn't have managed without you. You made Mom's last years bearable."

Paige's hands tightened into guilty fists. "I don't think you want to go there, Dad."

His eyes locked with hers. "Princess, it wasn't your fault."

Rationally, she knew that. She'd been three thousand miles away when Mom died. Which was exactly the point. Logic aside, Paige still felt as responsible for her mother's death as if she'd taken a knife and stabbed her in the heart.

*  *  *

At seven-forty-five the next morning, Site Visit morning, The First Day of the Rest of Brian's Life morning, Paige showed up at the lab, looking clean and pressed and glowing in her khaki camp shorts and white shirt. She carried a bouquet of fresh spring flowers in a small crystal vase.

"I thought these would look nice in the Suite," she said. Her gaze took in Brian's navy suit. "*You* look nice."

"Thanks." He led her through the warehouse to the model Suite.

The clean warehouse. Brian had spent half the night boxing the unused wires and components that littered the floor and tossing them out in the dumpster. He'd mopped the concrete floor until it gleamed.

His effort was not lost on Paige. "The place looks great." She reached up and gently lifted his glasses to reveal his bloodshot eyes. "And I'm guessing Connor had nothing to do with it." She lowered his glasses into place and fussed with adjusting the eyepieces. "I would have come over and helped if you'd asked."

"You needed to be with your Dad." He hadn't even considered

asking her. He was so used to carrying his own weight--and often the weight of others--he couldn't even wrap his mind around the concept of somebody wanting to help *him*.

Paige arranged the flowers on the nightstand and inspected the room approvingly. "Good luck this morning. I'm sure everything will go well."

She rose up on her toes and pecked him on the lips. "I know you're busy, but I thought I'd load Victor in my car for tomorrow's presentation. I don't think he'll ride on the back of your motorcycle."

"Good idea." He packed up the robot, components and accessories, and loaded them into the trunk of Paige's Infiniti. Of course he'd just finished when Connor arrived, bearing a box of doughnuts. Brian's stomach growled. The smell of powdered sugar made him realize how hungry he was.

Paige smiled at Connor. "Just came by to wish you boys luck." Maneuvering around the cardboard box, she pecked Connor's cheek, then turned again to Brian. "Go get 'em, Tiger."

As if she wanted to make sure Connor didn't miss it, she wrapped her arms around him and kissed him full on the mouth, including tongue. "Gotta run. Late for camp." She slid into her car and drove off.

Connor raised a brow but didn't say a word. Meek and mild this morning, he played his role of schmoozing salesman to the men from Allied Corporation well. They lapped up his jokes and stories with their coffee and doughnuts. As the gracious host, the pre-show warm up act, Connor smiled and charmed and entertained. But when Brian led the visitors to the Suite, Connor zipped it exactly as Brian had ordered.

"The Suite is activated totally by voice recognition," Brian explained to the awed visitors as the paneled doors opened at his command. They nodded and inspected the room. As Connor pointed out the room's amenities as if he were presenting game show prizes, Brian recorded their voice imprints into the computer.

Josh, the tech guy, took off his suit jacket and laid it over the desk chair.

"Is it too warm in here?" Brian spoke into the computer. "Mavis, please adjust the temperature to sixty-eight degrees."

"Mavis?" Josh grinned as the air-conditioner fan kicked on. "I assume that's an acronym?"

"Multiple Application Voice Initiated System." Since Paige had reacted so positively to his naming the robot, Brian had decided to apply the same personalization to the Suite Smart controller. He turned to the thirty-something tech guy. "What kind of music do you like?"

"Huh? Oh." Josh faced the computer, then deliberately turned away from it. "Mavis, how about some alternative rock?"

The stereo system ramped up The Killers' *Mr. Brightside*.

Ray, the finance guy, had a couple of decades on Josh. "What? No Springsteen?"

"Springsteen." A robotic voice crackled through the room. "Please make a selection. *Born in the USA. Dancing in the Dark. Born to Run.*"

"*Born in the USA*," Ray said, and smiled when the music changed.

"The application includes a playlist," Brian explained. "But the guests can also plug in their personal Ipods or MP3 players and interface to the stereo system."

Ray got the biggest kick out of making coffee. He fixed three cups, one with cream, one with sugar, and one with both, while Josh adjusted the room lighting, opened and closed the drapes, and played with the TV, all by voice command.

"What channel does Los Angeles get CNN on?" Josh searched for a TV guide, then blinked when the screen flashed and the channel switched to the cable news network.

"You don't need to know," Brian explained. "Just ask for the station by name."

Ray whistled. "Pretty cool for a hotel system. Mr. World Traveler can be in Phoenix today and Montreal tomorrow, but he can always find the channels he wants."

Yes! Brian tried not to show his excitement. He'd been about to say the same thing, but the message was much more effective with Allied's finance representative realizing it himself.

Ray ordered another cup of coffee, this one black, and sipped it. "How about a chocolate brownie to go with this coffee, Mavis?"

*How about manna from heaven? And while you're at it, a windstorm blowing in hundred dollar bills?* Brian forced a smile. "If this were installed in one of your hotels, you would have just commanded Mavis to activate a room service order."

Josh walked around the room like a kid in a video arcade trying to decide which game to play next. "Does this all run off one server?"

Brian nodded.

"What AI language is it written in?"

"Lisp," he replied.

"You used Open source code?"

"For the basics. Minimal customization so it'll be easy to upgrade to future versions."

The finance guy looked bored with the technical discussion. "So what does the bed do? Sing Brahms's Lullaby?"

Connor spoke for the first time since they'd entered the suite. "Check it out."

Ray lay down on the bed and tested the massage. "Shoulders," he commanded. The head of mattress undulated. "Legs." The foot of the bed responded. "Wow, this is great."

Brian shot a look at Connor, who returned it with an almost

imperceptible nod. For the first time in two years, he felt like they were truly partners. The mattress demo was the last item on their agenda. In a matter of minutes, their baby was as good as delivered.

"Back," Ray commanded, and smiled as the bed massage complied. "Feet. Whole body."

Josh turned to Brian and fired off more questions. "Does the system interface using hard wire or wireless?"

"Wireless."

"How much redundancy?"

"Triple."

Connor glanced at Brian with a worried frown, like a teammate asking if his partner knew the right answers. Brian shot him a subtle wink.

Ray propped himself on his elbows and glanced at his digital watch. "I could do this all day, but we should be heading out." Reluctantly he spoke the "Off" command.

The mattress continued its massage as if he hadn't spoken.

Brian's heart stopped.

Ray swung his legs off the bed. "Off." Still nothing happened.

*Shit.* "Speak a little louder," Brian said coolly, as he edged toward the manual shutoff control.

"Off," Ray said again.

Brian tapped the manual control switch under the bed with his foot. The massage stopped.

"Minor audio modification," he said as the man stood. "Simple adjustment." Thankfully, neither Ray nor Josh had noticed Brian's fancy footwork. Nor had Connor.

"How long will that take?"

"Couple of hours," Brian lied, casually swiping his hand across his moist upper lip. "Come back after lunch and--"

"We've got a plane to catch," Ray said, just as Brian had counted on. "But we're favorably impressed. If the committee agrees, we're prepared to come back with our offer, say, next Tuesday afternoon?"

"Fine," Brian agreed, forcing a smile despite the hard knots twisting his gut.

Josh shook Brian's hand. "So what can we expect in the way of service and maintenance?"

Before he could speak, Connor angled up to Josh and patted him on the back. "We'll send our team out to do the installation and training as soon as the leasing agreement is signed. Six months of setup. Then we can offer a two-year service contract including updates and on call trouble shooting."

Leasing agreement? Service contract? Brian turned to Connor but his brother ignored his glare, launching a megawatt smile as he accompanied the guests out the door and to their rental car.

Brian seethed. As soon as Connor walked back in, he jumped on him. "What the hell did you tell them? I thought we agreed to sell, not lease."

"Calm down, Bro." Connor took off his suit jacket and tossed it over his desk. "Leasing makes more sense. We sell them the hardware but lease the software licenses. Two years, two million dollars."

"If we sell the Suite outright, we can make at least ten."

"And then we're out of business," Connor said, showing more intelligence than Brian had given him credit for. "But this way, once the lease is up, we can lease it again to Allied, and then to its competitors, year after year."

"But then we have to support it." Brian bit down hard on his back teeth. "I would have to support it." If they sold the patent as well as the hardware and software, it would be up to Allied's programmers to do the product upgrades and maintenance. "Ten million dollars, Conner. That'll buy a lot of coke."

Connor brought himself up to his full height and peered down at Brian's head. "I'm done with that. I'm not Gil McKay's spoiled kid any more. I have a business to run."

Damn, Paige had been right. Connor did get off on wearing a suit and tie and playing the businessman. Brian tried another tack. "And what if in the meantime somebody else patents a similar product and puts it out there for less?"

"If we sell Allied a maintenance agreement and charge them a monthly service fee for support and software upgrades, they've invested a fortune in our product and it's much harder to switch."

Another good point. Brian had been so focused on the technical side he hadn't considered the marketing aspects.

"Why are you so anxious to sell?" Connor challenged. "Is there a problem with the Suite I don't know about?"

"That's ludicrous," Brian lied. Well, it was only half a lie. The mattress problem wasn't the reason he wanted to sell. He pressed his palms against his brother's desk. "I want out, Connor."

He had to get away from this stifling laboratory, from this oppressive town. He refused to stay handcuffed to his spoiled half-brother for the rest of his life. "We had an agreement. Two years to get the product ready, six months to install it and train the hotel's programmers, and then I'm out of here."

Connor pouted. "And what about me?"

"Frankly, Scarlett, I don't give a damn." Brian tore off his tie, wadded it into a ball, and stalked toward the lab. "You just go back to Allied and tell them we'll sell the whole Suite, patent and all for ten mil."

But first he had to fix it. Brian strained against a ten pound vise pressing against his forehead. He'd spouted the first believable explanation he could come up with, but it didn't seem like an audio problem. The mattress had responded to all the other commands.

Maybe he'd been so damned tired last night when he'd copied the program into production, he'd left out a line of code with the various shutoff commands.

For once, he prayed he'd been that careless.

# Chapter Eleven

What could have caused the malfunction? Everything worked except for the shutoff. It had to be an error in the last string of code.

Brian paced to the front office to make sure Connor hadn't returned, then stalked back to the Suite. At least the dope head wouldn't be breathing down his neck anymore, now that he thought the deal was done.

After testing every series of commands, Brian concluded that when all massage units were simultaneously activated, the noise of the motor interfered with the voice. Unless he shouted directly into the sensors, the program couldn't recognize the command.

But a honeymoon couple wouldn't know where the sensors were. And they weren't likely to care.

He took off his glasses and rubbed his burning, itching eyes. Six days. He was running out of time. And out of gas. Where had the two years gone? How had he let his cockiness lull him into letting his dream almost slip through his fingers? He was like that damned rabbit who'd napped by the side of the road and had to scramble to the finish line.

*Focus, McKay.* He sucked in a breath. *You can do this.*

He examined the options. Could he find a manufacturer with a quieter motor? Not in less than a week.

Could he move the sensors picking up the voice commands farther away from the motor? Dumb idea. Nobody was going to stand far away from the bed so they could *watch* it vibrate.

Maybe he could insulate the motor to muffle the sounds. But it would overheat without air circulating around it.

There had to be a simple solution. He laid his head on the desk, letting his mind scroll through scenarios, searching for one that would fix the error. Eventually they all ran together, dancing through his brain like puzzle pieces that almost but didn't quite fit.

A buzzing noise sounded close to his ear. He lifted his head from his desk. The late afternoon sun had all but disappeared from the high windows. *Shit.* It was six-thirty. He'd fallen asleep. And the answer hadn't materialized in his dreams.

His cell phone continued to vibrate. Warily he opened it.

"Congratulations, rich genius!" Paige's uber-cheery voice fought through the cobwebs in his head. "Where are you? We're waiting for you at the restaurant."

"Restaurant?" His mouth tasted like dry cotton.

"The club? Didn't Connor give you the message?"

"Connor didn't tell me sh--" He put on his glasses and read the yellow post-it note taped to his computer screen. *Paige called. Country club. Six-thirty.* "Sorry. I just now got it."

"No problem. We've only ordered drinks. How soon can you get here?"

His head ached like a two-day hangover. No way he could make it through an entire evening looking happy and lying through his teeth. "I can't, Paige. I'm really wiped."

"I know you must be exhausted. But you've got to eat." She blew a kiss into the phone. "I promise I'll get you home early." She giggled enticingly. "And tuck you into bed, if you like."

The offer sent a sharp ache to his groin and made him forget all about sleep. But nothing made him forget that his ass was on the line. He didn't want to lie to Paige, but he wasn't ready to admit that the

Suite was broken and he didn't have a clue in hell how to fix it. "Another time," he said. "You and Connor enjoy dinner."

"It won't be much of a celebration without you," she said petulantly. Brian heard the sound of clinking glasses and Connor proposing a toast. "But I'll give you a rain check, just you and me." She purred into the phone. "Get some rest, and I'll see you Thursday at camp, right?"

"Sure." Damn, the camp presentation. He was down to five and half days.

"Sweet dreams, Brian." The phone clicked off.

He stared at the numbers on the cell phone before setting it down. Well, what had he expected? That she'd pay for the drinks and walk out of the restaurant without ordering dinner, just because he wasn't coming? She did have to eat. And though he didn't trust Connor as far as he could kick his Mercedes, he did believe Paige would keep the implicit promise she'd made to him in the parking lot of Johnny Rockets.

So why did his throat burn and his stomach cramp at the thought of her laughing and smiling with somebody else?

\* \* \*

"Miss Paige, is today the surprise?" The little boy squirmed with excitement.

"Yes, Jesse. After quiet time." Paige bit her lip, feeling as anxious as the kids. She hadn't heard from Brian all morning and he hadn't answered his cell. Hopefully getting the rest he needed and so deserved but please, God, don't let him oversleep and miss the program. The children would be so disappointed.

The wind rushed playfully through the branches of the giant oaks as she settled the boys and girls down on their mats for afternoon rest time. She read a story, then played her favorite Rachmaninoff CD. Paige usually enjoyed this quiet time, letting her mind wander as the music mingled with the chirping of birds and soothed her spirit. But today her ears were attentive for a different sound.

Finally, she heard it. The sound that stirred her heart more than nature or music. The exhilarating roar of a motorcycle.

Within minutes Brian appeared at her campsite, wearing a black tee shirt, worn jeans, and a two-day growth of beard he'd managed to acquire in barely twenty-four hours. As Paige stood to greet him, her knees weakened.

"Car keys," he said, holding out his hand.

Were they back to two-word discourse? She'd expected him to be grinning with joy. Or at least not scowling.

She grabbed her keys from her satchel and pressed them into his palm. "Need help?" She could play the two-word game too.

He shook his head and shuffled silently back through the trees without another glance in her direction.

The air was heavy and humid when the campers woke from their naps and Paige led them across a grassy area to the covered pavilion where Brian had set up Victor. There were few clouds in the sky, but the scent of rain hung overhead.

"Children, we have a special friend visiting today." She brought them to within a few feet of where the robot stood on the concrete. Brian sat with his laptop at a metal picnic table. "He's going to talk to you for a few minutes, and then you will each get a turn to visit with him by yourselves."

In his denim overalls and flannel shirt, Victor looked adorable, a miniature version of his creator. Except that the robot had personality.

Paige nodded to Brian as he placed a CD into his laptop.

"Helloooo, boys and girls." The robot rolled forward on inline skate wheels and the familiar voice boomed in halting robotic tones. "I am a friend. I come from the planet Zepton."

An alien robot. Nice touch.

"My name is Victor."

The recording paused. Paige stepped among the children. "Say 'Hello, Victor,'" she prompted.

The children responded in singsong unison. "Hellooo, Victor."

The robot's welcome program continued with the script Paige and Brian had worked up. The children listened, spellbound. Paige smiled at Brian but he barely acknowledged her.

Why couldn't he ever be happy? He was about to realize his dream of financial independence, and he looked like he'd lost his best friend.

"Today is my birthday," Victor said. "Who wants to join me for cake and ice cream?"

"Me."

"Me!"

Victor's recorded speech continued. He described the camp as he "saw" it, as Paige had written it, combining visual details with the sounds and smells familiar to the children. A little boost for his credibility, she'd figured.

"And if you're wondering what your counselor looks like," Victor said, "I'm telling you, Miss Paige is *hot*."

The children giggled.

Paige's face flamed. She definitely hadn't written *that*. She glared at Brian, but he wouldn't meet her eyes.

Surely he wasn't angry that she and Connor had eaten without him? He'd *said* to go ahead and enjoy dinner. It wasn't like Brian to say something just to be polite. Polite probably wasn't even in his vocabulary.

The robot was back to the prepared speech she recognized, and was winding to a close. "I am soooo excited to be here on Earth and so happy to be making new friends," Victor said.

Paige had written that line, obviously. Confirmed loner Brian didn't seem to think he needed other people. She could hardly imagine a wish for new friends coming out of Brian's mouth.

But Victor's mouth was Brian's voice today. And if she talked to the robot, maybe she could provoke his master to respond...

Smiling to herself, she moved closer to the robot's platform. "I love making new friends too, Victor. Do you have lots of friends on Zepton?"

Brian raised a brow, apparently trying to figure out what she was up to. "Hundreds," the robot squawked as Brian typed. "Zippo and Yonora and Xavier and Waltifred and--"

"It's nice to have lots of friends," Paige interrupted before he named his way to the beginning of the alphabet. "And every one is special."

"They can't all be special," Victor said.

"Of course they can." She draped an arm around Elena's shoulder. "Elena is special because she draws such pretty pictures. And Jesse is special because he likes to build things. And Katie is special. And Mike. And Alan."

She read the frustration in Brian's eyes. He couldn't disagree-- or have the robot disagree--without jeopardizing the children's self-esteem.

Paige spoke to the children. "Does anyone have an extra-special friend? A best friend you can tell your secrets to?"

Several children raised their hands.

"Me too," Paige said. "Someone extra-special that I care about more than any of my other friends." She stole a quick glance at Brian, then faced the robot. "You didn't raise your hand, Victor. Do you have a special friend? Maybe a girlfriend?"

Two little boys tittered and made kissing noises.

It took all of Paige's composure to keep her eyes on the robot.

Not that the children could tell who or what she looked at. But Brian needed to see she was talking to his robot friend. Not him. Not exactly.

"I used to have a girlfriend," Victor finally answered. "But she turned into a butterfly and flew away."

The children laughed.

Butterfly? So he *was* jealous of her having dinner with Connor. Brian had to know, he *did* know, that there was nothing between her and Connor. And yet he resented the time she spent with anyone but him.

"Did you chase her with a butterfly net?" Jesse Ortega asked the robot. "You should catch her and put her in a jar."

"Butterflies need to be free, Jesse." Paige brushed a hand over his hair. "If you try to cage them in a jar they might shrivel up and die. They need to be free to fly all over the universe, and have all kinds of friends." She faced the robot. "Isn't that right, Victor?"

She waited an eternity for the robot's response. Finally he said, "Maybe. But I miss her."

Paige swallowed. She focused her wet gaze on Brian. "I bet she misses you too."

Thankfully, Jenna arrived then and gathered the children away from the pavilion area so Paige could pull them out from the group for their individual chats with Victor.

Brian stood and moved toward her. "You really had my hands tied out there."

She grinned. "I had your *tongue* tied." She curled an arm around his neck and kissed him, teasing the inside of his mouth in an attempt to do that literally. God, what was it about this man? Nobody else provoked her temper the way Brian did. No one else had ever made her feel *anything* as intensely as he did.

"Miss Paige, is my friend here?"

Paige gulped and broke the kiss. Katie Royce had lingered behind the others. The little girl was uncannily sensitive to Brian's presence, but she couldn't have Katie spoiling the magic for the other kids. "Mr. McKay brought Victor from his spaceship. You can talk to him after the program."

She escorted Katie back to the group and selected the first eager volunteer.

Jesse Ortega's interview went well. Brian had pre-programmed most of the responses needed. Jesse had a few questions of his own, about Victor's life on his planet and his girlfriend, but Brian rose to the occasion with quick, impromptu answers. With only an occasional mouthed prompt from Paige, they managed to convince and delight the six-year-old.

Things went even smoother with the second and third child. But then it was Katie's turn. *Let her believe*, Paige pleaded silently. The child was as distrusting as the cynical man at the keyboard. Hopefully Victor could lift her, if only for a few minutes, from her sightless reality into a happier world where all things are possible.

"Are you my friend?" Katie asked after the robot had run through his initial questions.

"Of course I am," Victor responded.

"Do you like me?"

Paige's heart lurched. Katie's first response to meeting Brian was to ask him to be her friend. How lonely it must be for a blind child who couldn't play easily with the 'normal' kids in the neighborhood.

"I like you very much." Brian's fingers flew over the keyboard. "You are special to me."

Yes! Paige shot Brian an approving smile. Even if he didn't quite believe himself that you can have more than one special friend, at least he'd absorbed the sentiment enough to convey it to the children.

Katie wrinkled her brow as if she were taking that in. Then she headed in Brian's direction.

So much for suspending disbelief.

Katie raised her hand, fingers spread, and touched Brian's lips. "You're making him talk."

Brian's fingers flew over the keyboard. At the same instant that the robot screeched, "I'm a big boy. I can talk for myself," Brian held Katie's hand on his mouth so she could feel his lips move and said in his own voice, "Then how could we both be talking now?"

Katie dropped her hand, confused. And went back to Victor.

Paige breathed a tentative sigh of relief.

When Victor asked her what she wanted to be when she grew up, Katie didn't choose a doctor, like her father. And she vehemently opposed the robot's suggestion of being a mommy. "I want to be a astronaut," she said after some thought. "So I can fly far away to another planet. Can I come with you, Victor?"

It took some dissuading, but Katie finally accepted that as impossible.

Elena's interview was last, of course, since the child never volunteered. Paige steered her in gently, scanning the dark sky. The clouds looked full and about to burst. Thunder rolled in the distance like faraway cannon fire. Would the rain hold off long enough to finish the presentation?

Victor greeted Elena as he had the others, but she didn't answer him. The robot rolled closer and repeated his "Hellooo." No response.

Paige frowned helplessly at Brian.

A clap of thunder roared overhead. Elena jumped.

"HELLOOO. MY NAME IS VICTOR," the robot boomed in a voice so loud it drowned out the thunder. "WHAT'S YOUR NAME?"

"Elena." Life flickered in the little girls eyes. Paige looked at Brian in wonderment. She hadn't known he could adjust Victor's volume. Was Elena's hearing the problem after all?

Victor asked another question, and another. Elena responded like the other children, with eager excitement. Then, following the script Paige had written especially for her, the robot asked casual questions about Elena's home life. How old were her brothers and sisters? Did they play together? Was she a good girl most of the time? Was she ever afraid to go home? Elena answered them all without hesitation, seemingly a happy child with a loving family.

As Elena hugged Victor goodbye, a drop of rain fell onto the concrete. *Perfect timing.* Brian packed up his laptop and rolled Victor under the protective awning.

Back at the campsite, Paige grabbed her satchel and directed traffic. "Bus children follow Miss Jenna. Car children come with me."

The rain was coming down in big splattering drops. Paige tied a plastic poncho around Jesse's neck and counted heads. "Where's Katie?" Mrs. Royce usually drove to the camp every afternoon to pick her up.

"She went with the bus kids," one of the boys answered. "Her mom not coming today."

Mrs. Royce must have had an afternoon appointment. "Okay, hold hands and let's go."

Paige led the line to the parking lot, deposited each of her charges with their parents, and ran to her car, where Brian was struggling to position Victor in the trunk.

"I'll hold his legs." Rain pelted her neck and back as they eased the robot inside trying not to jar loose any parts.

*       *       *

Brian's hair felt like a wet mop and his tee shirt stuck to his skin. It never rains in southern California? Like hell. He squinted to see around the droplets on his glasses. "Did Victor come through for

Elena? Do you still think she's abused?"

"Thank goodness, no. You were right about it being her hearing. But I swear, she was just tested recently."

"The problem may not be her hearing, per se." He turned Victor's head and aligned the robot's body inside the trunk. "If you noticed, I gradually lowered the audio back to normal volume and she still participated. My grandmother heard fine at home. But in a restaurant or a crowded area, especially outside, the distracting noises interfered with the reception of her hearing aid." Much like the motor in Suite Smart's mattress jumbled the voice commands.

"So trying to listen to one voice over the noise of the other kids may have caused her to give up and tune out. The thunder interfered with her focus on Victor until you turned up the volume." Paige shoved his laptop into the back seat and slammed the door shut. "You are one smart man, Brian McKay."

Smart about detecting problems, maybe. Damned incompetent at finding the solutions.

The rain was coming down steadily like pulsing shower needles, but Paige made no move to get in her car. Soft tendrils of blonde hair clung to her wet cheeks. Her thin blouse was plastered against her body, defining the shape of her breasts, outlining her taut nipples. Disregarding the rain splashing his glasses, Brian framed her face with his hands and held her for a deep, penetrating kiss.

Her fingers plunged into his matted hair. Brian ground his hips into her as his tongue thrust wildly inside her mouth. Every nerve in his body cried out with one voice, one need. It took all his control not to yank down her cotton shorts, push her against the car, and drive inside her until he exploded.

Paige broke the kiss, breathing unevenly. Her eyes met his. "Meet you back at the lab."

"You'd better." He couldn't stand much more of this torture. There was no way in hell she was going to keep him away tonight. As he watched her drive off in the late model Infiniti, his heart went with her.

Brian slung a sopping pant leg over the Harley, and was about to start the engine when he heard footsteps running up behind him. Small footsteps.

He got off the bike and turned. A wet child slammed into him, grabbing his thighs.

What the--? "Katie?"

She clutched him tighter, sobbing softly.

"Don't be scared." He squatted and folded his arms around her shoulder. "Did you miss your bus?"

She kept crying into his shirt.

"It's all right," he assured her. "Don't cry." Gently he pried her face from his shirt.

"Don't make me go home," she begged, her cold, purple lips trembling. "I'll be good, I promise. I want to live at your house."

# Chapter Twelve

K atie? Abused?

Paige sat in the backseat of her Infiniti, cradling the whimpering, shivering little girl next to her. She'd been five miles down the road when Brian called and told her to come back to camp. "Your instincts were right," he'd said in a shaky voice. "But you had the wrong kid."

What had Katie told him? Why hadn't Paige picked up on it?

Brian's fingers clutched the steering wheel as if he needed all his strength to keep the car on the road. His cheeks were drawn, his lips taut. Paige couldn't see his eyes, but she trembled to think what he might be feeling now.

Katie's sobs had quieted, but she was still awake. Paige settled back and rubbed a soothing hand over the child's shoulders. "It'll be all right," she said softly. But would it?

She racked her brain for clues she'd missed, hints she'd ignored. She couldn't think of one. If anything, Katie was more outgoing and assertive than the other children. Always seeking attention. With Dr. and Mrs. Royce as parents, she'd have labeled Katie spoiled, not abused.

Oh, God, Dr. Royce was Daddy's best friend!

And one of the nicest people she knew.

Surely this whole thing was a play for attention, a theatrical performance by Drama Princess Katie. Maybe she'd gotten spanked for misbehavior and blown the discipline out of proportion.

Brian accelerated onto a freeway ramp, not the highway that led to Katie's house. "Where are we going?" Paige asked.

"Don't take me home!" The little girl stirred in her arms and raised her head. Her eyes were wild. "You promised."

Paige's gut wrenched. Katie's defiant protest was more than a typical spoiled child determined to get her way. There was something else in her voice. Terror.

"I'm not taking you home, honey," Brian said.

Katie relaxed against Paige's side. "I'm going to live with Mr. McKay."

Paige swallowed. "Surely you didn't prom--"

"No," he said quickly. "We're going to Miss Paige's house."

Paige frowned. If Katie was really abused, they should take her to Child Protective Services. But if she was making it up...

She glanced at Katie, not wanting to upset her further. "The child is prone to e-x-a-g-g-e-r-a-t-i-o-n. Are you sure you're not o-v-e-r-r-e-a-c-t-i-n-g?"

"Trust me," Brian said.

*Trust me.* A clichéd phrase that could mean anything from I-am-in-complete-control to I-have-no-clue-what-I'm doing. "If you're this sure, shouldn't we go to CPS?"

"Maybe. We'll talk about that later."

She wanted to scream *Will you just tell me what happened in that parking lot?* But of course, he couldn't. Not now. Without specific information, Paige had limited choices. Take Katie to CPS and report her parents for--for what? She had no idea what the child had accused them of. Or she could insist on driving Katie home, possibly inviting more abuse.

Or she could trust Brian.

She pulled out her cell and shuffled through her bag for the camp phone listings.

There was no answer at the Royce home, but Katie's mother answered her cell phone on the second ring.

"Um, hi, this is Paige Anderson. I...well, as you know we had our special program today and the kids were so excited. I...well I kind of invited the girls to my house for a sleepover tonight." Oh Lord, she was going to hell for sure. Or jail. "I know this is short notice, but I hope you'll let Katie come." Lying got easier if she spoke faster. "I've got extra clothes and we'll all take the bus back to camp tomorrow..."

Amazingly, Mrs. Royce agreed. "That's so nice of you, Paige. And actually it works out well for me because I have jury duty today and they still haven't released us. I told Katie to take the bus home. Kyle said he'd watch her but this is so much better. Thank you."

"Sure. We'll have a great time." She didn't mention that no one had answered at home. Paige swallowed. At least she wasn't sending a seven-year-old girl to an empty house. It didn't eradicate the lying, but it made the liar feel a little better.

By the time they arrived at Paige's house, the car was humid with the smell of wet clothing. Brian's tee shirt defined every ripple and nipple on his chest. His bedraggled hair curled down his neck. Katie's teeth were still chattering.

"I'll give her a bath and put her in some dry clothes," Paige said as she unlocked the front door. "You should shower and change too."

She grabbed a Property of Stanford Med School tee shirt and a pair of sweatpants from Daddy's closet and directed Brian to the hall bathroom. Then she filled the tub in her own bathroom and helped Katie strip off her wet things.

*No cigarette burns.* Paige exhaled a sigh of relief. No cuts, bruises or welts of any kind. She examined the little girl as she shampooed her hair. If she'd been hit recently, it couldn't have been very hard.

179

"Did you enjoy the program today?" she asked casually as she dried Katie off.

"Yes. I like Victor."

"Why didn't you take the bus like you were supposed to?"

Silence.

"Were you afraid there wouldn't be anybody at home to meet you? Is that why you wanted to go home with Mr. McKay? So you wouldn't be alone?"

More silence. Then, "I'm hungry. Can I have something to eat?"

"Sure, honey." As Paige wrapped Katie in a towel, Shelly waltzed into the bedroom.

"There's a naked man in the shower," she announced.

Oh, great. Shelly had seen Brian naked and *she* hadn't? "Well, most men do shower without their clothes," she said dryly.

Katie giggled.

"Oops, didn't know we had company." Shelly entered the bathroom. "You're Katie, aren't you? I'm Shelly."

Katie nodded her head vigorously.

"Shelly, make yourself useful," Paige directed. "Go grab a pair of Phillip's pajamas from Helene's room."

"I don't want to wear boy's pajamas," Katie said disdainfully.

"They're for boys *or* girls," Paige amended. "I won't tell Phillip you wore his pajamas if you don't tell him I told you he sleeps with a doll."

Katie giggled again and slipped willingly into the pajamas Shelly brought, a normal kid enjoying the special attention.

*Brian is wrong*, Paige decided, relieved. Misguided. Well-meaning. But wrong. "Now about that food. Would you like a peanut butter and jelly sandwich?"

"I'll make it," Shelly offered, taking Katie's hand. And I'll put her in bed. "You need to change into dry clothes. And you have that n-a-k-e-d man to attend to."

"Thanks."

But, after his quick shower, Paige found Brian already dressed downstairs, pacing the floor like a dog on a short leash.

She led him to the sunroom, out of earshot of the kitchen. Perching on the sofa next to his chair, she said in a low voice, "I didn't see any evidence of physical abuse, thank goodness. My guess is she didn't get her way at home and she's made up some story to play on your sympathy."

He was quiet for a long minute. "I don't think so."

"Katie's parents are pillars of the community. They sponsor this day camp."

"So rich people couldn't possibly abuse their children, is that it?"

He was upset, rightfully so. But as usual, blaming people whose only fault was having money. "Dr. Royce is my father's best friend! You're accusing a wonderful man of...of terrible things." Paige's fingers trembled. Dr Royce was actually Katie's stepfather. And she'd never seen him alone with Katie, always with the mother in the same room.

No! She refused to believe...*that* about a man who'd visited often in her house, played poker with the family, delivered her sister's baby. "Brian, I know Katie. She embellishes and exaggerates just to get attention. Dr. Royce would never hurt a child, let alone his own disabled stepchild."

Brian drew in a deep breath. "It's not the father. It's the brother."

A chill passed across Paige's stomach. "Kyle?"

"And we're not talking about the kind of abuse that shows scars on the outside."

*Oh. My. God.* All the liquid in her mouth dried up. "What did Katie say?"

"The parents leave the stepbrother to baby-sit. Once when they were gone, Katie broke an expensive vase. Kyle cleaned up the mess and promised to cover for her, take the blame himself."

"And this makes you think he's abusive? If I'd broken a vase, my older sister would have been the first to tell on me."

Brian pressed his lips together as if reining in his impatience. And anger. "Later, he came to Katie's room and told her she owed him. Said he wouldn't tell on her if she did special things for him. Said it would be their 'little secret.'"

Paige shuddered. Classic. "Was she specific? How can you be sure--"

"She touched me."

Paige swallowed. "You mean, in an inappropriate place."

His eyes blinked in rapid succession but he didn't speak.

*Breathe in. Breathe out.* "It may have been unintentional," she said, her heart hammering with denial as her mind struggled against the awful truth. "Blind children have to touch everything. It's how they see. She didn't realize she was doing anything wrong." She let out a shaky breath. "She was probably reaching for your hand."

She leaned into his shoulder and placed her hand on his. "You were shocked. You over-reacted. It's perfectly understan--"

"Paige, she grabbed my nuts. And she knew exactly what to do with the equipment." He swallowed so hard he sounded like he was choking. "She promised to be *good* to me if I'd let her come live with me."

Paige was sure her mouth was moving but no words came out. They stuck to the back of her throat like dirty sandpaper.

182

"You don't believe me, do you?"

Her heart ached for Katie. And for Brian. "Of course I do. But..." Her eyes clouded. "Why you? Why would she trust a man?"

"I've been trying to figure that out the whole way here."

Paige buried her face in her hands. How could something this terrible happen under her nose without her having a clue? "Why didn't she come to me?"

"Maybe she tried."

Shame flushed Paige's cheeks. And rebuke. Katie had sought her attention since the first day of camp. But Paige had shunted her away, ignoring the poor little rich girl in her misguided attempts to focus on the economically disadvantaged children.

She raised her head. "Why wouldn't she have told her mother?"

"We don't know that she didn't."

She almost gagged. "Are you suggesting Mrs. Royce knows about this and lets it go on?"

"I'm not suggesting anything. I'm trying to make sense of this, just as you are." He heaved a low, heavy sigh. "How long have the Royces been married?"

"Three years. Maybe four. Why?"

"Mrs. Royce doesn't work outside the home?"

"No."

"And when she was married to Katie's father, she didn't work either? Does she have any professional skills or training?"

"I don't know. Brian, what are you getting at?"

"I'm not sure." He sighed again. "Just hear me out." He stood and paced toward the living room. "Here's a woman who is suddenly left with a disabled child, and no means except maybe minimal child

183

support."

He turned back to face her. "She meets Dr. Royce. He can support a more-than-comfortable lifestyle *and* provide the special education and benefits that a blind child needs."

"So?" This was a lot of words from Brian without having made his point. "What's wrong with that?"

"So she doesn't want to lose Prince Charming. If her daughter .tells her this horrible secret about her husband's son, is she going to jump to accuse him?"

"No mother would allow her stepson to molest her child!"

"I agree. If she heard and processed everything Katie told her." He stopped pacing and crouched on the floor beside her. "But you've said yourself Katie is prone to storytelling and exaggeration. Her mother knows that too. So what if she convinced herself that Katie was making this up, or overreacting to some innocent gesture?" He paused. "Just like you reacted."

"She didn't hear it because she didn't want to."

He shrugged. "You know the family better than I do. I'm just throwing out a theory."

Paige shuddered. If this was true, then she'd been blinder than her visually impaired campers. "Well, what if you're right about the mother? Why wouldn't Katie come to me? Why would she seek you out? I mean, you're a relative stranger. And a man."

"Thanks for noticing." He tried to chuckle but his mouth didn't seem to follow up. "I can't say for sure. But try to get inside that little girl's mind. 'Mommy didn't protect me. Mommy is powerless. Only men have power.'"

"But she has female teachers as role models." *And camp counselors.*

"Maybe she thinks they're ineffective."

Paige knew he wasn't referring to her specifically. But she'd obviously failed Katie. She'd been ready to believe abuse, just on a gut feeling, about a little girl from East L.A. But a child from a 'good' family, from her own social circle, those clues she'd missed entirely. The thought sickened her.

"She can't go to her stepfather for obvious reasons. Maybe she feels her real father deserted her." Brian hoisted himself to the couch beside her. "I have no idea why she formed this attachment to me."

*I do.* "She trusted you. Kids seem to know instinctively, better than adults, who the good guys are. She couldn't see you with her eyes, but her heart knew."

Paige's eyes swam as she considered the frightened little girl eating a peanut butter and jelly sandwich in the next room. Katie had been thrust cruelly into an adult world. A horrible, ugly world. No matter how hard Paige tried to focus on the positive, the dark side always found her. She couldn't escape her mother's legacy.

Before she realized she was crying, Brian's arms were around her, steadying her. Paige buried her face in his shirt, clutching him like the pillow she'd squeezed as a child, when her mother was on one of her rampages.

"It's okay," he whispered. "The truth can be frightening. But we'll get through this."

He thought she was crying for Katie, instead of mourning her own lost innocence. But his use of the word 'we' shored her up as much as his arms.

"We need to call CPS," she said, drawing strength from his support. Paige had always thought of Child Protective Services as the last hope for children who had no resources and no place to go, not for a well-off, well-loved little girl like Katie. But it was the only way to protect her and find out the truth. Whatever it was. "They'll probably want to question you."

"I'll talk to whoever I have to if it'll help that little girl. But why don't you discuss it with your father first?"

Her father. Oh, God, this nightmare was just beginning.

\* \* \*

Brian clamped his wrist against his thigh to keep from punching a hole in the Andersons' living room wall. Growing up was hard enough for a healthy kid with normal problems. Living in a world of total darkness made that tougher and scarier than he could imagine. But no child should be at the mercy of a sick teenage predator.

Bile rose in his throat. He'd acted calm for Paige but he wanted to throw something, smash something, break something.

For the first time, he considered himself to have had a privileged childhood. Being ignored by your father was cake with icing compared to being abused.

He walked quietly past the study, where Paige and her father still spoke in hushed voices. Probably deciding whether to kill the messenger. Paige had said she believed him, but he'd seen the suspicion in her eyes. Hell, the story sounded sketchy even to him. But it had happened. The fear etched on Katie's face was something he'd never forget.

What was going on in that little girl's head now? Was she peacefully asleep in the room upstairs, dreaming of rainbows and lollipops? Or fighting nightmares of monsters with grasping claws? Or was she lying awake feeling strange sheets on her body, in a room with strange smells, worrying what might happen to her next?

He wanted to check on her but he didn't dare go upstairs alone. He couldn't risk Katie sensing his presence and--

He closed his eyes, willing the image away. He almost gagged at the corrosion in his stomach.

He strode to the stairs and listened. No sounds came from above. But the voices in the study were raised and heated. He shouldn't eavesdrop. *Like hell.* It was his nuts the little girl had fondled. And his neck under the guillotine if Dr. Anderson didn't believe him.

He moved quietly to stand against the wall next to the door.

"These are good people," Dr. Anderson was saying. "Joe Royce is my close friend. This accusation could ruin their family."

Brian couldn't hear Paige's response.

"Katie's my patient, and in my home. I've seen no signs of abuse. You spend hours with her every day and you never got that impression. You're basing all this on Brian's word."

"On Katie's word," Paige said louder. "As told to Brian."

Brian closed his eyes and listened.

"Katie is a child," Dr Anderson replied. "She may have misinterpreted, exaggerated, or totally lied about her stepbrother's actions. I can't imagine a child initiating what you've described occurred today in that parking lot. It's more plausible it happened the other way around."

Brian's stomach cramped.

"What?" Paige's voice was pitched high. "Do you think that Brian--"

"If I thought that, he wouldn't be sitting in my living room right now, wearing my clothes. He'd be wearing an orange jumpsuit, locked up in a jail cell. I'm only trying to view the situation as an impartial party might. A jury, for example. A man alone with a blind little girl. He takes advantage of her and then makes up this family abuse story to cover himself."

Brian clenched his fist. Without even accusing him, Dr. Anderson had managed to convict him. And there was no response from Paige. She was throwing him under the bus.

Dr. Anderson spoke again. "How well do you know this man?"

Finally Paige answered, slowly and deliberately. "Well enough to trust his word. I don't care how 'plausible' your scenario is, it didn't happen that way. I can't vouch for the truth of what Katie told him, but I believe with all my heart that she said and did exactly what Brian told me."

There were no sounds from inside the study but outside the door. Brian's heart pounded like a jackhammer.

Dr. Anderson broke the silence. "Honey, I admire and respect your wanting to do the right thing and come forward about this. But the situation is more complicated than you may realize. Once this hits the fan, I'm going to lose a good friend. Maybe all of our friends, if the accusations turn out to be untrue and the community sides against us." His voice softened. "This could be eighth grade all over again."

*Eighth grade?*

Paige spoke in a strong voice. "I'm not thirteen anymore. And I'm sorry to put you in this position. But what if it *is* true? I can't sit back and keep quiet because it might make my life a little uncomfortable. What about Katie's life?"

Brian didn't know what Paige had experienced as a teenager, but he knew she was one hell of a woman.

"Mr. McKay!" Katie appeared at the top of the stairs. "Are you still here?"

"I'm here, Katie." Brian started to run up to her, to keep her from falling, but she was holding tightly to the banister, and didn't appear to be in danger. *Stay where you are, McKay. Don't invite trouble.*

"I'm scared. Will you come sit with me?"

His heart wrenched. But he couldn't follow its lead. He had to use better judgment. If Dr. Anderson saw him going into that little girl's bedroom... "I can't right now, Katie. Go back to bed and I'll get Miss Paige."

The child frowned, but shuffled slowly back to the bedroom.

Brian inched back to the study and knocked on the door. "Katie needs you," he said when Paige opened it.

"Come in, Brian," Dr. Anderson said as Paige left.

*Oh shit.*

He sat in a wooden chair opposite a large desk, trying not to drum his fingers on the arm rests. Dr. Anderson didn't say a word, apparently waiting for him to speak first. Well, screw that.

Seconds passed. A full minute. Brian kept his peace. If they were going to hang him, it wasn't going to be by his own words.

Paige appeared at the doorway with Katie in tow. "She wants her Raggedy Ann doll. And she'd like to say goodnight to Brian." She led the little girl to his chair.

He tried not to put his arms around her but when Katie hugged him, he couldn't hold back. She was a scared little girl and she had no idea her affection for him might have caused him trouble. "Good night, Katie," he said. "Miss Paige is going to help you. Be brave and try to sleep now."

Before walking her back upstairs, Paige retrieved a bright red backpack from the other room and unzipped it. Katie dug through the pack and extracted a worn, loved-on rag doll, dumping out in the process a pack of crayons, a candy bar, half a peanut butter sandwich, and a handkerchief.

Dr. Anderson picked up the handkerchief and unfolded it. Dark, dried blood stains encircled the monogram BGM.

*Double shit.*

Paige's father shot him a look he wouldn't want to see on a jury foreman before announcing a verdict. Placing the handkerchief in the little girl's hand, Dr. Anderson said gently, "Katie, do you know what this is?"

"Miss Paige's handkerchief."

Paige moved to stand next to Brian, draping an arm around his shoulder. "It was in my purse." She rested a stony glare on her father. "Brian gave it to me to wipe mayonnaise off my hand. I gave it to Katie when she had a nosebleed."

Dr. Anderson was silent.

Paige turned back to Katie and took her hand. "Let's take your

189

doll up to bed now." She led her out.

Alone in the room, the two men faced each other. Dr. Anderson gazed into Brian's eyes and said simply "I'm sorry."

He nodded as if the implied accusation was no big deal. "You and Paige don't have to get involved in this," he offered. "Katie confided in me. I'll talk to CPS alone."

Dr. Anderson raised a brow. Had he realized Brian had been listening at the door? "No," he said. "It's best if you don't get involved."

"But I am involved."

Paige's father sighed. "This is an ugly situation. Paige is the girl's counselor. If we do report this to the authorities, it would be better coming from her."

*If?*

"He's right, Brian." Paige came in and sat in the chair beside him, clasping his hand. "Katie has gone through enough anguish. Your testimony would only upset her more." She shot him a concerned look. "And it wouldn't be good for you."

"Don't worry about protecting me. What about you? You'd be committing perjury, telling the authorities something you heard second hand as if you'd experienced it yourself."

Her face paled. Apparently she hadn't considered it that way.

"There is another option," Dr. Anderson said quietly.

Paige's liquid blue eyes looked hopeful.

"I've always known Joe Royce to be an honest, reasonable man. Let me talk to him first. He may be willing to do the right thing and take care of this without involving the authorities."

Brian looked at Paige. Was she buying this?

He felt Dr. Anderson's eyes on him. "Please," he said. "Let me at least give it a shot."

# Chapter Thirteen

Brian's brain was a fried mushroom. His eyes were so blurry he could barely see the computer screen. Sounds of grinding motors and bobbing mattresses bombarded his skull. But even when he closed his eyes, he couldn't sleep.

He'd promised Katie she wouldn't have to go home, and he'd let her down.

When her parents arrived at Paige's house last night, the mother had gone upstairs to Katie while Dr. Royce grilled Brian for two hours, apparently trying to shake his story. Paige had sat quietly beside him on the inquisition sofa, her hand in his. Even without words, he'd felt the warmth of her support.

Finally abandoning his efforts to twist the truth away from his son's guilt, Dr. Royce had agreed to pay for counseling for both Katie and Kyle. His wife, carrying a half-asleep Katie in her arms, promised to keep an eye on Kyle and Katie at all times and not leave them alone together until this 'unfortunate situation' was resolved. As the Royces walked out with their precious bundle, everybody seemed pleased with the arrangements.

Brian wished he could feel as satisfied with the resolution as Paige and her father apparently were, but his gut wouldn't let him. He kept seeing the glassy look in Katie's mother's eyes as she followed her husband dutifully out the door. Damn, if something like that had happened to him when he was a kid, his mother would have scooped him away to safety before you could fire a shot.

But the image that wouldn't leave his mind was that frightened child's eyes as her mother carried her out. Katie's gaze had found

Brian's voice and stared at him in hurt accusation. *You betrayed me.*

Forcing Katie's problems to the back of his mind, he tried to concentrate on his own. Insulating Suite Smart's mattress motor solved one problem but, as he'd feared, created a worse one. Now the program could recognize the voice command to shut down. But if the massage ran too long, the motor overheated.

Different insulation materials offered varying results. But even using the best of them, after thirty-five minutes, max, the motor fried.

Damn, if somebody fell asleep without uttering the massage end command, they could set the bed on fire.

He didn't confide that to Connor when he waltzed in at noon, sober and in a good mood. Nor did he tell him what had happened after the presentation when his brother grudgingly drove him back to the campsite to retrieve the Harley. Instead, Brian dozed against the passenger door for most of the ride. It might be the only rest he got all day.

At three-thirty he called Paige's cell to see how she'd survived the day. It went immediately to voice mail. Maybe she'd turned it off at camp quiet time and forgotten to turn it back on. He tried several more times to reach her, always with the same result.

It was after eight that night before she finally called him.

"Oh, Brian, it's all a mess. I thought I could do it Daddy's way, but I couldn't."

"What happened?"

"When Katie came to camp this morning, she looked normal, like nothing had happened. But she wouldn't speak to me. Not once all day. When I talked to her she looked away. And when her mother came to pick her up this afternoon Katie started screaming. 'I'm not going home. I'm going to live on the planet Zepton.'"

Brian winced. Katie had figured him for her savior but he'd let her down, and now the child's only hope for deliverance was a box of knobs and wires.

"It tore my heart out." Paige muffled a sob. "I had an uneasy feeling last night, but for Daddy's sake, I hoped it would work out. But that child is scared to death."

Brian slipped on his sandals, determined to rescue Katie even if he got arrested for kidnapping. "Let's go get her."

"She's not home anymore. I went to CPS and reported what I know. What *you* know, mainly, so don't be surprised if you get a call from the authorities asking for your testimony. They picked up Katie and put her in a foster home." She sniffed again. "I had to, Brian. I couldn't risk leaving her in a dangerous situation."

"You did the right thing." He logged off his laptop and shut it down. "Where are you now?"

"I'm home. Daddy's not speaking to me. Katie's parents are furious. Dr. Royce is meeting with the camp directors Monday to recommend they remove me from my position."

"Well, that's no great loss. They're not paying you anyway."

He'd hoped that might lighten things up, but Paige didn't find it amusing. "I'm sorry about the way they all treated you last night. It wasn't personal."

The hell it wasn't. "Nobody wants to think something like that about one of their own. Me, I'm expendable."

"Not to me."

Closing his eyes, he imagined his arms wrapped around her body, her head against his chest. "Hang in there. I'll be over in twenty minutes."

She hesitated. "It's probably better if you don't."

"Your father doesn't intimidate me."

"I know. But I'm tired of fighting everybody. I'm tired, period. I just want to sleep."

"Me too." With her. He wouldn't even care--that much--if all they did was sleep. He wanted to hold her, comfort her, make her worries go away. Lie in her arms all night.

All right, so she wasn't the only one needing comfort.

The words rushed out before his brain switched on. "I'm going to Reno tomorrow for the weekend. Come with me. The change of scene might do you good." He gulped. *Are you out of your mind?* The Allied reps would be back in four days and he still had no clue how to fix the Suite.

"Oh, Brian, I'd love that."

He waited for the inevitable excuse of some social obligation she couldn't back out of.

"But--"

Called it.

"--are you sure it'll be okay with your mother? She's never met me."

"It'll be fine." Mom would probably turn cartwheels if he brought a woman home. A complication he didn't need. Brian closed his eyes. He must have lost a cog in his brain. But the weight pressing on his chest lifted. Maybe a couple days in the fresh air would free his mind too.

"We'll be back Sunday night? I have bus duty Monday morning."

"Why the hell would anybody care if you even show up? If they're going to fire you anyway."

"I care. I owe it to the kids. I want to at least say goodbye. I'm not slinking away with my tail between my legs."

"That's my girl." Damn, had he actually said that?

"But let's take my car. I don't think my butt can handle that long a trip on the back of a motorcycle."

"We're flying." Brian sucked in his breath. He was down to his

194

last Thomas Jefferson, but if he had a plane available, Charlie Haines would probably wait for his money until they sold the Suite.

He gave Paige directions to the airstrip and arranged to meet her at eight the next morning.

"I can't wait," she said. Then, more quietly, "I miss you so much."

"You just saw me yesterday."

"I've lived a lifetime since then."

He couldn't have put it better himself. His muscles tensed just thinking of having her to himself, well, almost to himself, for two whole days. "I lo--I look forward to it," he said, and hung up before he embarrassed himself.

Damn, he'd almost lost it. *My girl.*

Well, what would be so terrible, if, for once, he gave rein to his emotions?

*That she might not feel the same way?*

He ached for Paige to want him as much as he wanted her. Not just in bed at night. He wanted her in the morning, at Christmas and Easter, and all the days in between.

He *had* lost it.

After making arrangements with the airstrip, he called his mother.

"Brian? What's wrong?"

Damn, he'd forgotten how late it was. "Everything's fine, Mom, I just thought I'd fly up tomorrow if it's okay."

His mother agreed readily, cheerily brimming with plans to cook his favorite meals. "I'll have your room ready for you."

"I'm bringing a friend. If that's all right."

"Of course, dear, any friend of yours is welcome." She paused. "Not Connor?"

"Has hell frozen over?" He cleared his throat. "It's someone I've been working with on a project. She's had a bad week and I thought the desert air might do her some good."

"She?" The pitch of her voice rose.

"Don't start. Give her my room, I'll sleep on the couch."

A knowing chuckle filled his mother's voice. "Whatever you say, dear."

*     *     *

Paige parked the Infiniti on the gravel area next to the landing strip and hauled out her overnight bag. The sun danced on her face as if it were trying to lift her dark mood. Daddy had hardly spoken a word at breakfast this morning. His eyes were as cold as the ice cubes in his diluted orange juice. When she'd told him she was going away for the weekend with Brian, he'd clammed up entirely.

Until the other day, he'd liked Brian. But his benevolence had evaporated at the suggestion of scandal and social ostracism.

Apparently she hadn't inherited all her bad qualities from her mother.

Paige crunched her lower lip. She was a grown woman but inside she still felt like that scared eighth grader. Was the solid feeling of knowing you'd done the right thing worth the cost if all her friends deserted her?

*Yes.* The realization shocked her right down to her tennis shoes. What good was it to be liked by others if you didn't like yourself? There was only one person whose respect she cared deeply about, whose friendship she couldn't bear to lose.

When she saw him, her heart lightened. With his aviator sunglasses, his jean jacket slung over his shoulder and his motorcycle helmet propped against a cocked hip, Brian looked...sexy. He was talking to a tall slim man in his late thirties or early forties, and when

196

she walked up, he turned and actually smiled at her.

"Feel better today?"

"Starting to." Amazing, just his presence brought comfort. The smile pushed her all the way to almost happy.

He introduced her to Charlie Haines, a pilot and flight instructor who ran the airstrip.

"Now I see what the emergency was." Charlie grinned at Brian and patted the belly of the plane they stood beside. "She's ready to go."

Paige looked up at the one propeller plane with red stripes on its body and wings that made her think of Wilbur and Orville Wright at Kitty Hawk. Her stomach flip-flopped at the thought of how small and exposed it was. "Nice plane. Is it yours, Mr. Haines?"

"Yep." He smiled broadly like she'd complimented his baby.

So he would be their pilot. She examined Charlie Haines more closely, assessing his sobriety before risking her life in that little soapbox with wings. She was tempted to ask how much experience he had, but since Brian seemed to know him well, she supposed he'd covered all that.

Charlie took the motorcycle helmet from Brian and the men traded keys. "Just bring her back full of fuel and we'll call it even." Smiling at Paige, Charlie turned and walked toward Brian's motorcycle.

Where was he going? She grasped Brian's arm. "Isn't he our pilot?"

"Nope." He bent to move the blocks from the plane's wheels.

She faced him, arms at her hips. "Then who is?"

He stood. "You're looking at him."

A cold whoosh of air streamed into her lungs. "But I thought...you said you couldn't fly a plane because of your eyes."

He opened the door on the passenger side, and helped her up into the seat. "I can't fly for the military or for a commercial airline. But I can--and do--have a private pilot license." He took a plastic document pouch out of his jacket pocket and laid it on her lap.

"I believe you." She just hadn't imagined, when he'd said, 'We're flying,' that he'd meant he'd be doing the flying. And she'd be doing the nail biting.

She pressed her hands to her sides to keep them from fidgeting as Brian walked around to the pilot's seat. "So you leased this plane for the weekend?"

He strapped himself in. "Charlie and I sort of traded. He borrowed the bike, and he's letting me take the Skyhawk for a test run. I've been talking to him about buying it when I sell Suite Smart."

"Wow." She'd had no idea. She stared at the control panel, which looked like N.A.S.A. Mission Control. "You know how to use all these gauges and gadgets?"

"Every one." He started the engine, switched on the radio, and taxied down the runway while they waited for clearance.

Then they were up. And up. It wasn't scary at all. It was glorious. Compared to this view, looking out the window on a commercial jet felt like watching TV. On a small screen. Paige let out a cleansing breath. Cars and people got smaller and less significant. She and Brian became one with the sky, looking down at the world.

"Just one thing," he said. "Since it's my right eye that's bad, you can help by navigating your side of the plane. Let me know if we're about to hit any other planes, or plunge into a mount--"

"Oh my God." Panic grabbed her throat and her stomach lurched at three times the plane's rhythm. "I can't do that. I didn't know you expected me to--"

"Paige. I'm kidding." Seeing the alarm in her face, he squeezed her hand. "I can see fine. They wouldn't give me a license if I couldn't."

She fought to stabilize her rapid, pounding breaths.

He stroked her fingers. "I passed a Military Comp test and I just took a medical test and flight review test last year. I promise you I'm in complete control. And even if I couldn't see past my fingers, 'all these gauges and gadgets' would land us safely."

She grabbed the packet of documents he'd laid in the cockpit and slapped them against his shoulder. "How was I supposed to know you were kidding? I've barely seen you crack a smile before, let alone a joke."

"I'm sorry, honey, I didn't mean to frighten you."

*Honey?* The documents slid to the floor.

Brian didn't seem aware of what he'd said. He massaged her neck and shoulders until she relaxed and faced him. "You're safer up here than you are in a car. I swear to you, on my life, that I'd never take a chance with yours."

*Honey.* Paige let her breath out slowly and watched him. He had a confident air about him, not cocky, but relaxed and contented as he guided the plane. The demeanor seemed to fit him better than his usual tight-lipped behavior. "You're different up here."

"Better or worse?"

"I don't know. Different. Fun-loving. Dangerous." She lowered her eyes. "Sexy."

"I'll take that as better." His face was flushed, happy. Alive.

"Flying does something to you, doesn't it?"

"Oh yeah. Riding the bike gives me a sense of freedom, but nothing like this. A man can be up here alone with his thoughts. Or he can talk to God."

Brian seemed more at ease with either than in the company of her chatty, vacuous friends. She pictured him, once he sold Suite

Smart, retiring to a secluded cabin far from the social pressures of modern life. Not exactly Paige's cup of tea. But she wouldn't mind a week or two alone with him in that cabin.

About their present destination, she had mixed feelings. She was anxious to meet Brian's mother, curious to see the house he'd grown up in and learn about the childhood that had shaped the man. But she wished they were staying at a motel.

She'd never felt such intense cravings to be with a man. Brian McKay was not your usual heartthrob, muscle man stud hero. But she was itching with a primal desire to touch and be touched by him.

She laid her hand on his knee. "I'm glad you suggested this trip. Thanks for believing in me. You're the only one who thinks I did the right thing."

"It's the least I can do, since I'm the one who got you into the situation."

"No, Katie did that. You only reported it."

"And you only did as much as you could do. You're not responsible for the whole world."

To hide her brimming tears, Paige turned to the window. The splendor of Northern California lay below them, sturdy redwoods, shimmering lakes, lavish waterfalls. Why couldn't she see things this clearly from the ground? "How high up are we?"

"About ten thousand feet."

"It's beautiful."

"Yeah." Brian wiped a finger along a wet spot on her cheek. "Paige, what happened in eighth grade?"

She flinched. How did he-- "You were eavesdropping last night?"

He shrugged without apology. "You want to talk about it?"

She hadn't talked about it, to anybody, since it happened. "It

200

was really no big thing."

He didn't press her. Just waited silently. Why did that work on her? His infernal patience could draw her out easier than another person's badgering.

She sighed, disgorging the painful memories like stones lodged in her throat. "We had a new girl in homeroom that year, from Pakistan. She was shy and didn't know anybody. I always celebrate my birthday the first weekend of school, so I invited her to my party, hoping my friends would kind of welcome her and make her feel more comfortable."

"I gather they didn't."

"Oh, Brian they were horrible. They didn't say anything mean to Regina, they just ignored her as if she were a piece of furniture. But they were rude and snide to me. At my own birthday party! And after that, they didn't speak to me at all or include me in anything. I was ostracized the whole year." It shouldn't hurt, twelve years later, but it still did. "Even Regina found her own group and barely said hello to me."

He covered her hand with his. "I'm sorry."

He sounded like he meant it, but... "I guess you think I was immature to be so upset."

"I think you were brave. You stood up for what you believed in. Not as a protest, not in any dramatic way, just because you thought it was a nice thing--and the right thing--to do. You honestly didn't expect repercussions."

Would she have behaved differently if she'd known what would happen? Paige hung her head, not proud of the answer.

The plane's engine hummed as they soared over brown earth and gray mountains. Brian silently stroked her hand. Usually Paige felt uncomfortable when conversation lulled, but with him, she felt communication without words. Breathing in his aftershave, she leaned her head against his shoulder.

He was the first to break the silence. "Why is it so important for everyone to like you?"

She straightened. So much for wordless communication. "I knew you wouldn't understand. You think I'm a shallow Beverly Hills girl who only cares about what other people think." She dabbed at her eyes with her fist. "Well, I'm sorry I don't meet your high moral standards. But the truth is, if I'd known then what I know now, I would never have invited that girl." A lone tear escaped its barrier and trickled down her cheek.

"Paige, you were thirteen. At that age, being popular is the most important thing in the world."

"Not to you. I'll bet you wouldn't have cared a flip what the whole world thought, if you believed you were right."

He grasped her chin and tipped it upward. "I made myself not care. I was always an outsider. The geek, the nerd, the dork. Girls didn't know I existed. If guys paid any attention to me it was only to slam me against a locker."

*Oh, Brian.* Her heart hurt for him.

He let go of her chin and ran his fingers along her shoulder. "It's easy to be self-righteous when you have nothing to lose. But you were the princess, the beautiful popular girl everyone else wanted to be. And then, in one day, an outcast. That had to have hurt more than anything I ever lived through."

Paige furiously blinked back tears. *She* was the one who didn't get it. She'd had every advantage in life, but was still whining over her one miserable year as a non-person. Brian had been given nothing. His whole life had been broken promises and slammed lockers. He hadn't accepted it, but he'd made peace with it. And grown strong from it.

"It doesn't matter what you did then," he said. "Or how you'd act if you could do it over. What matters is what you did yesterday. You knew the social ramifications, but you followed your conscience."

Not that she deserved a ticker tape parade for that. A little girl's safety trumped her stupid social life any day.

Brian's face hardened. "You think I don't want to be liked? Of course I do. But I don't like the price. I won't kiss up to people I don't respect. Or pretend I'm somebody I'm not just to fit in." He focused his gaze on the lamb's wool cloud formations dancing above and below them. "I'd rather be special to just one person than barely tolerated by the whole world."

Was that what she was doing? Pretending to be someone else just to fit in? She smoothed her hands along her jeans. "I'm not special to anybody, not even myself. I'm not as smart as Helene, or as pretty and funny as Shelly."

"You're the peacemaker. The glue that holds your family together."

She drummed her fingers against her knees. What would happen if she were to quit being the resident nurturer? Did she really believe her family couldn't get along without her? "I work at it. But if I ever stopped..." She stared at her hands.

"You're afraid they wouldn't love you just for yourself."

Hearing the words said out loud brought them too close to the truth. "I'm not sure they'd love who I really am. I don't even know the real Paige myself. I'm not sure anybody does."

"I'd like to."

She turned to him, trembling inside. She wished she had the courage to let him. Part of her wanted to strip off her clothes and reveal herself to him, physically and emotionally, holding back nothing.

Part of her feared she'd showed him too much already.

She'd made it her mission to seduce Brian out of his loner shell, to encourage him to open up and share his feelings. But she hadn't expected him to make the same inroads with her. She hadn't foreseen that this quiet, unassuming man would breach her defensive walls and see inside her heart.

Suddenly she felt trapped in this small plane with the one person who could expose her dark places, her hidden fears. There was nowhere to run. Not from him. Or from herself.

# Chapter Fourteen

"She's lovely," his mother said after the lunch dishes were done and Paige had retired to the bathroom to freshen up.

Brian swilled his beer and grunted.

"Does she know you're in love with her?"

His shocked stare was only partly feigned. "Why would you think that?" He'd hardly spoken a word since they arrived. Paige and his mother had hit it off immediately, chatting away over lunch like old friends at a high school reunion.

"You never take your eyes off her." His mother winked. "You might fool her, and you may even try to delude yourself, but you can't hide anything from your mother."

He grinned sheepishly.

She sat next to him on the sofa. "You haven't told her how you feel?"

"Nope."

"Planning to?"

"Not today."

She let the remark pass. Mom knew better than anyone not to pressure him to talk. Instead, she took up her embroidery from a box beside the sofa and threaded her needle. "It's nice to have you home."

"Nice to be home." He propped his feet on the old oak coffee table that still bore the scratch marks of his toy jeep and tank convoy. He'd told himself he was making this trip for Paige. But as he sank into the worn sofa cushion that had molded itself to his butt after years of sitting in this exact spot, he realized how much he'd needed to come home. To unwind in the place where he felt most like himself.

"I'm glad you brought Paige with you. She's not what I expected, given your distaste for the Beverly Hills set. But I like her."

"She's down-to-earth, warm and caring. Always looks for the best in everyone." He frowned. "But she has the commitment span of a Hollywood celebrity."

Mom's brown eyes studied his. "So why are you with her?"

*Because I can't not be with her?* He searched for words that wouldn't make him sound like a lovesick fool. Couldn't find any. Opted for the truth.

"She makes me feel...like I'm somebody. Like I matter. She cares what I think and wants to know how I feel. She laughs at my stupid attempts at humor." He stared at the geraniums in the middle of the coffee table. "Because she lights up a room when she walks into it. She can tease me out of my worst funk. She makes me smile."

"For that alone, she deserves a medal." His mother patted his hand. "You *are* somebody, Brian. You've always gone after what you wanted and made your own success." She pecked his cheek. "By this time next week, you'll be rich."

Rich or flat broke. His chest tightened. Even here, he couldn't escape his worries. But he couldn't tell Mom he might not sell the Suite as promised, any more than he could tell Paige.

*Shit.* One more nagging fear. Paige might think he was a genius now, but how long would her admiration last if instead of a successful entrepreneur, she saw him as a failure who'd wasted his last chance?

\* \* \*

After refreshing her lipstick and combing her hair, Paige studied the bedroom where Brian had grown up. Glow-in-the-dark planets and asteroids of the universe dotted the sloped ceiling. The juvenile wallpaper, red and yellow trains on a blue background, was almost completely covered by a giant bulletin board and dozens of posters, photos, and newspaper clippings.

A faded clip of Brian at about ten years old holding a second place trophy. A photograph of him in a high school track uniform. He'd gone out for sports? Well, track made sense, given those long, lean, muscled legs. And it required minimal interaction with team members.

There were half a dozen Star Trek posters, an aerial map of Nevada, and a dozen notes and quotes on the bulletin board, some typed, some in handwritten chicken scratch.

She pulled the push pin off one. *The strong defeat the weak,* it read. *But the smart triumph over the strong.*

"Paige."

She jumped.

Brian stood at the doorway, his eyes on the paper in her hand. "Want to ride down to the park?"

"Sure." She pinned the quote back on the board and followed him to the kitchen, where he loaded beer and chips into an insulated pouch.

"You can use the truck." Mrs. McKay bustled into the kitchen. "I won't need it this afternoon."

"Thanks, but I figured we'd just take the bikes." He turned to Paige. "Okay?"

He had another motorcycle in Reno? Or two? "I'll just ride on the back of yours," she said. "I don't think I could drive one of those things."

207

"You can't ride a ten-speed?"

Oh. *Bike.* The non-motorized kind. "Okay, I'm an idiot."

He grinned at her red face. "You look more like a ripe tomato."

"Don't mind him, Paige. Brian has a warped sense of humor."

She smiled at Brian's mom. It wasn't hard to see where the real Brian came from, the one Paige had glimpsed when he let down his cynical guard. "Actually, I'm glad for any humor. Usually he's a crabby old sourpuss." She winked at him.

"One at a time, ladies." Brian took her elbow and led her out the back door. "I can't defend attacks from two fronts."

He removed the padlock from the door of an aluminum shed and retrieved two bicycles.

"I like your mom," Paige said. "She's sweet."

"She said the same about you."

As he loaded one of the bikes with the food and a picnic blanket, Paige looked around the shed. In one corner stood a little red tricycle and next to it, something that looked like a steel canoe with wheels. A racing car? "Did you build that?"

He looked up to see where she pointed. "Yep. I won second place in the Vallejo soap box derby stock division when I was ten. Only sixty-two thousandths of a second behind the first place winner."

The newspaper clipping she'd seen on his bulletin board. Of course he would remember, twenty years later, the exact statistic. "You are such a geek."

"Smile when you call me that." He growled playfully but his eyes were bright and his expression light, almost joyful.

She couldn't help obeying his order. "You're different here too. Better," she added, before he could make his next remark.

She expected him to grumble or say something flippant.

208

Instead, he pulled her inside the shed, placed his hand behind her head and leaned down to give her a short, penetrating kiss.

He tasted like Irish stew and root beer. Paige wrapped her arms around his back and leaned into his chest. He felt like a redwood, steady and strong. "It's nice here. I see why you like it."

"I like it better with you here."

He kissed the top of her forehead, and then helped her onto her bike, a blue and green striped ten speed that was rusty but still serviceable.

They cycled through a pleasant neighborhood of tall, shady trees and modest frame houses fronting small yards. Bicycles and skateboards cluttered narrow porches. Paige glimpsed swing sets and jungle gyms in the backyards. No swimming pools, no houses more than one story, but the hedges were neatly trimmed and the grass mowed.

As they pedaled past an elementary school, Brian slowed.

"Is that your old school?"

"Yeah." He rode up on the grass and stopped. Weeds overgrew a concrete slab supporting a basketball backboard and a hoop that had lost its net. Nearby a half-deflated soccer ball lay almost hidden in the weeds.

Paige dismounted from her bike and took a run at the soccer ball, kicking it toward Brian's chest. He caught it and tossed it up into the basketball hoop.

"Two points."

"It's a soccer ball," she said.

"Use your imagination." He grabbed the ball off the pavement as it hissed out another ounce of air and held it against his chest. "Try and take it from me."

She ran at him, but he swerved aside as she made her grab, making her feel like Charlie Brown when Lucy pulled the football

209

away. After Brian made another shot, Paige caught the ball under the hoop and threw it up again with all her might. It didn't make it even halfway up before landing with a soft splat.

Brian laughed. "You throw like a girl."

"Oh, yeah?" It was the best retort she could come up with.

He tossed the ball back onto the grass and pressed her into his arms, locking his lips against hers. She took his tongue inside her mouth, teasing and tasting him.

"Mmmmm." He pulled away slowly. "You kiss like a girl, too."

Back on the bikes, they cycled along the Truckee River, through the downtown area. Paige noted a couple of flashy hotels and a lot of cheap-looking casinos with neon lights blinking in the early afternoon sun. Reno seemed like a run-down Vegas wanna-be.

Brian pointed. "That's the hotel where my Mom works." He seemed proud of his mother, and she was so button-bursting proud of him an adoring grin lit her face whenever she looked at him. And he earned that measureless devotion, apparently, just for breathing. He hadn't even helped with the dishes.

Leaving downtown, they biked past aging warehouses, apartments, and a large trailer park complex. At the road's end, they came to a parking lot, and beyond it, a pretty park.

"Oxbow Nature Study area," he informed her, as they rode through brush and greenery past a fishing stream.

Something furry flashed, then disappeared at the far end of the stream. "Omigod, is that a beaver?"

"Could have been. You might see rabbits, muskrats, quail, sometimes even a deer if you're quiet enough." He braked the bike at a secluded area off the track. Thick trees and heavy brush hid them from the path and made it seem as if they were alone in the deepest part of a wood. "Let's camp here."

Sweaty from the ride, Paige slipped off her windbreaker. A

light breeze cooled her bare arms. Behind them, the river rippled softly like the artificial waterfalls in the foyers of so many Beverly Hills home. But this was natural. Beautiful. And she wasn't responsible for any campers here.

Brian spread out the blanket and unpacked the beer and snacks. "I would have brought wine, but aluminum cans transport better on a bicycle."

She took the Budweiser he offered and popped the tab. "Beer works fine." She touched her can to the one Brian held and raised it to her lips. "To a brilliant inventor and his wonderful Suite Smart program." She took a sip. "When is Allied coming back with the money? Tuesday?"

"Yeah." He took a swig of beer and turned away to stare at the fluffy clouds in the blue Nevada sky. A thin line of perspiration streaked down the middle of his back.

She touched the cold beer can to his neck. "You should take off your shirt."

He turned to face her. "Why?"

"Because it's the middle of summer and you look like White Christmas. Get a little color."

He shrugged. Lifting his face to the shaft of sunlight beaming into their sanctuary through an opening between the trees, he stripped off his blue polo shirt and tossed it onto the blanket.

Paige tried not to lick her lips at the T-shaped pattern of light brown chest hair dusting his nipples and straggling down his breastbone. But she couldn't help staring at the place where it arrowed and disappeared inside his jeans. As he kicked out his legs and rolled onto his back, his rib cage muscles rippled in graceful sequence.

Suddenly hungry, Paige ripped open the bag of chips and stuffed one in her mouth.

Brian stretched out his left arm and patted the place beside him. "Come here."

Her heart skipped a beat. "Why?"

"To look at the clouds."

It was as flimsy an excuse as her tanning reason for his removing his shirt, but she lay beside him and snuggled her head into the crook of his arm.

"That one looks like a single engine Cessna." He pointed. "See the wings and the propellers. And that one over there looks like a lighthouse."

Paige thought it looked like an erect penis, but that was probably attributable more to her state of mind than the cloud's features. "I didn't know you were into cloud watching."

He rolled her closer. "I'm into beautiful sunny days, smog-free air, and a pretty girl in my arms."

He smelled like Right Guard and summer sweat. Paige lay on her side facing him and draped her arm over his chest, swirling her fingers through his chest hair. She flicked a thumb over his nipple, felt it stiffen, and followed it with her mouth. He groaned softly as she kissed the taut pebble, then took it between her teeth and sucked.

He tasted like a fruity sucking candy. When she touched his other nipple she found it already hard, waiting for her kiss. She raised herself to her knees, then slung her left leg over him and straddled his hips.

Brian closed his eyes. Gently Paige removed his glasses and set them next to the beer carrier. He didn't protest.

She massaged his chest with the heels of her hands, then leaned down and caressed his skin with her lips.

"How am I supposed to get a tan if you're blocking the sun?"

She raised up. "Like me to move?"

He pulled her down again, and slipped his hands under her tank top. "Absolutely."

His brows wiggled, gleefully, when his fingers didn't meet a bra hook. Paige rested her arms on either side of his head and pressed her lips to his. His tongue met hers and mated with it as his fingers kneaded circles on her back.

She wanted her breasts on his skin. Without breaking the kiss, she shoved her shirt up to her neck and pressed against him, nipple to nipple. From head to waist, they fit perfectly.

Digging her knees into the blanket, she tightened her grip on his thighs. He grabbed her bottom with both hands and pulled her against his groin. Hot waves of desire pulsed between her legs.

Too fast. Too soon. *Slow down.*

She moved down his body, kissing his stomach as her fingers fumbled with his snap and zipper and spread the denim flaps of his jeans. Clorox white briefs barely restrained his erection. She leaned forward and gently kissed it through his underwear, leaving wet traces. Then, sliding her fingers inside the waistband, she unleashed him.

Her mouth went dry, her panties, wet. She cupped her hand around the base and licked the thick shaft up to the tip, then captured him with her lips and took him inside her mouth.

Brian jerked and groaned as she indulged herself in giving him pleasure. Taking pleasure in the act herself as she never remembered feeling before. She wanted to nurture him, consume him. Swallow him whole.

Leaves crunched nearby. Voices, a man's and a woman's, drifted through the trees. Paige lifted her head. "Someone's coming," she whispered, yanking down her tank top.

"Not quite yet. But give me a minute."

"Brian!"

Grumbling, he pulled up the waistband of his briefs and tugged on his zipper. "Damn." It wouldn't close. He rolled, flipping Paige beneath him, and tossed the edge of the blanket over her. "Quit giggling."

213

She couldn't help it. The image of Brian fumbling to hide his boner reminded her of Donny Wilkins kissing her against the fence in seventh grade and his acute embarrassment when Mrs. Long, the history teacher, discovered them. Of course it hadn't been funny then.

A few feet away, she heard lip-sucking sounds. "Baby, baby, my sweet baby," the boy moaned as the couple passed close by their blanket. Smothered under the scratchy wool, Paige stifled a snicker by pressing her lips to Brian's skin. Would they be discovered?

More aroused than afraid, she slid her hand inside the back of his jeans and cupped his butt. He let out a muffled groan.

More leaves crunching. The couple passed on. She waited a minute, snuggling under Brian's warmth. Finally, he rolled to his side, then his back. "All clear."

He hadn't lost his erection. As Paige slipped out from under the blanket, he raised his hips and shoved his jeans and underwear to his knees.

All the moisture in her body pooled in one place.

He grabbed her hand and placed her fingers on him.

He was so hard, so firm. So ready. Paige got to her knees, overcome by the need to touch him.

A crazy, totally irresponsible need. "What if they come back?" she whispered, even as her hand moved over him, stroking his length.

"They won't. They've got better things to do." He pushed himself into her hand.

She squeezed, caressing his tip with her thumb. The smell of wood smoke drifted through the air. Someone was building a fire not too far away. A yellow kite floated high overhead, its tail dancing in rhythm with the rustling leaves. They wouldn't be alone for long. Maybe they should wait until--

Her unfinished thought rushed away on a breeze as she glimpsed Brian's eyes. He sat up and hooked his thumbs into her jeans belt loops. "C'mere," he said hoarsely.

She couldn't make him wait. Not this time. And she couldn't wait any longer, either.

He pulled her down until she lay on top of him. Her lips caught his mouth. He sucked her tongue inside, then grabbed her bottom and crushed her against his body. Opening her legs, she rubbed herself against his hard length.

*Ecstatic torture.* She cursed the thick denim separating her body from his. She wanted to feel him closer. Rolling to her back, she unzipped her jeans and wriggled out of them, leaving just her satin panties between them.

But before she could move to straddle him once again, he reached for her, grabbed her panties and slid them off.

He stared longingly.

Paige swallowed short breaths. They hadn't planned ahead. The nearest drugstore was probably miles away. And somebody could walk up on them at any time. But her need wouldn't be denied. She had to feel him, just the tip of him, just for a minute.

"I want you." She pushed him to his back and climbed on, positioning herself for the pleasure she craved. She moaned as he touched her where she needed him most. But it wasn't enough. Despite her limited access plan, her body opened for him. He slipped inside. A cry of pleasure escaped as he filled her, satisfying one craving and inciting a stronger one.

Was she out of her mind? Having unprotected sex in the middle of a public park? They had to stop. But before she could get the warning words out, he lifted her and moved her off him.

Paige let out a breath of disappointment and relief. "I'm glad one of us has the good sense to be practical."

He grinned. "I'm always practical." Reaching into his jeans pocket, he produced a slim packet.

She cupped his cheeks and kissed him.

They could barely get the condom on fast enough. He held his sheathed organ as she settled over him and sank down with a pleasured moan, so helpless to her desire she forgot where they were, who might be watching, losing all consciousness except the exquisite thrill of being one with him.

She tore off her tank top. Brian tugged the edge of the blanket over her in a too-little, too-late attempt at modesty. She flattened her hands against his chest, bracing herself.

He let her take the lead. She rode him slowly at first, savoring the sensation of him full and firm inside her. But each gasp of pleasure from him elicited stronger need. She rocked harder, faster. He pumped steadily at whatever pace she required, meeting her thrusts and teasing her higher.

The blanket slipped from her shoulders. Paige grabbed for it once, then batted it away, blowing the sweaty bangs off her forehead. She didn't care about modesty, didn't care about anything except the need to satisfy this singular, intense craving.

She rode him in a frenzy of passion, sinking onto him faster and harder until her head was so light the world seemed to float away. She couldn't have stopped if she'd wanted to. All the sensation in her body centered in a throbbing, exhilarating, joy of pleasure.

And then everything, inside and out, gave way, and she cried out his name. With a final pump of his hips, he convulsed inside her. Love and lust filled her body, comforted her soul, and expanded her heart. Shuddering with blissful aftershocks, she lowered her head and collapsed against Brian's chest.

For the first time since she'd taken leave of her good sense she heard the chirping of birds, felt the cool breeze on her sweaty, naked body. Her lungs strained for air. She felt like she'd been through a time warp, lost minutes, hours, maybe days.

In all her life, she'd never acted with such abandon, such disregard for decorum. She'd completely lost control of her body and mind.

And she couldn't wait to do it again.

# Chapter Fifteen

Brian lay on his back on a sliver of blanket, using the rest to cover Paige. Her eyes were closed, her breaths slow and shallow. He slipped his hand between her legs and felt the lingering tremors of their lovemaking.

She didn't push his hand away. Instead, she pressed against his palm and gazed into his eyes. "In all the time I've known you, I've never seen you smile as much as you have today."

He grinned. "Today I have something to smile about."

She outlined his lips with her finger. "If I'd known the effect it would have on you, I'd have had sex with you sooner."

"If I knew that's what it took, I'd have smiled sooner."

She laughed that bell-like tinkle that lightened his soul. "It was lucky no one walked up on us."

Had she not heard or seen the older couple strolling by in their Bermuda shorts and tennis shoes? "Yeah, we lucked out."

Paige ran her hand down his stomach and stroked him until he responded, then rolled to her back and urged him on top of her.

He took a deep breath and allowed himself one last caress of her full, ripe breasts. "But let's not push it." He grabbed his glasses, and then reached for his jeans and underwear. "Get dressed, hon."

With a petulant frown, she pulled on her panties and jeans and searched for her tank top. "Do we have to leave?"

"Negative. Just clean up our act a little. In the late afternoon, there are lots of family picnics out here." It took three tries to get his jeans zipped, but eventually he succeeded. He found his shirt wet and reeking of beer. Apparently they'd kicked over an open can in their heated frenzy.

He stuffed it in the bag and picked up the trash while Paige shook out the blanket. The strap of her tank top fell lazily over her shoulder and her nipples puckered against the thin cotton.

They spread out the blanket again and lay down. Paige snuggled eagerly into his arms. He cradled her head against his bare chest, caressing her hair. When he was with Paige, he couldn't help but share her joyous, life-loving passion.

"Thanks for inviting me here. I'm so glad I came."

"I'm glad you came too. As soon as we get some damn privacy, I'd like to help you do it again."

She giggled, tracing sensuous circles around his nipple. Making him wish for privacy right now. But there'd be other times. He could be patient. Their bodies had claimed each other, and he knew with certainty that his heart belonged to her. What he could only hope was that her heart belonged to him.

"Am I sleeping in your bed tonight?"

Damned if that simple question didn't get him hard. "Yeah. But not with me." He smoothed his hand over hers. "It's my mother's house."

"I understand." She kissed his hand. "It's a homey house. A place where everyone seems happy, even you."

He shrugged. "It was my grandmother's. We moved in with her after my father bailed. She babysat me at night when Mom was at work, but she died when I was eight, and then we were pretty much on our own, just the two of us."

Paige rolled to her side. "She she took you to work with her?"

"Every damned day. I had to report in by four o'clock or she'd

218

call the school. She made me sit in her office and do my homework. When I was old enough to stay home by myself, she still made me come to the hotel and work. She said it would keep me out of trouble."

"And you're complaining?" Paige sat up and hugged her knees to her chest. "I would have given anything to have a mother who worried so much over me. With my mom, it was always about her." She clasped her hands together and rocked.

He gave her a minute, then pulled himself up to sit beside her. "Tell me about your mother."

She shook her head. "I shouldn't have said that. My mother was a good person. She tried her best and she--"

"Paige." He touched his hand to the back of her neck. "I don't know anyone in your mother's social circle." And he'd probably despise them if he did. "Whatever it is, your secret is safe with me."

She sighed and took a big breath. "I was close to my mother too, but not exactly like you. I was Mom's little helper. She was sick most of her life. Nerves."

Nerves? A rich woman's disease, if he'd ever heard one. His mother hadn't had time for such luxury.

"Actually," Paige modified, "Mom was bipolar. In her manic moods she planned parties, was really into the social scene. But then she'd crash in the middle of a party and I had to take over."

Good girl Paige. Always picking up the pieces. Always fulfilling others' responsibilities. A bitter taste formed in his mouth.

Paige kept her chin on her knees, not looking at him, but her hand reached out for his. He stroked her fingers. "How did she die?"

"I killed her."

*Whoa.* And she'd called Katie a Drama Queen? "Paige, you couldn't kill a living being to save your own life." He resumed caressing her hand. "Anyway, you were in D.C. when your mother died. What really happened?"

Finally she turned to face him. Tears dotted the corners of her eyes, but she blinked them back. "Official cause of death was overdose of prescription meds. We told everyone it was an accident, of course."

"Why do you feel responsible?"

"Because I wasn't there!"

He reached for her, wanting to soothe her guilt, but she pushed him away. "I'd never lived on my own before. I was so excited about teaching on the east coast. Mom didn't want me to go. Said she needed me here." She paused. "This isn't very nice, but..." She eyed him warily.

What was she looking for? Disapproval? Condemnation? "Go on," he said.

She scanned his face, testing, as if deciding whether to trust him. Apparently, he passed. "I was fed up with responsibility. Being her nursemaid, keeping the rest of the family whole. I thought I'd earned the right to do what I wanted. I told Mom she was perfectly capable of taking care of herself, and if she wasn't, she could pay somebody else to be her personal slave.

"Three months later...she was dead." Her voice broke. "I never even got to make peace."

He grabbed her shoulders and pressed her close, holding her tight against him as she wept into his chest. "She was sick, Paige. Anything could have set her off, even a broken fingernail. Most likely, it had nothing to do with your declaration of independence." He brushed the top of her head with his lips. "And even if it did, she's forgiven you. Forgive yourself."

"It's not that easy."

"Yes, it is. So you're not Mother Theresa. You're still deserving of love." He pulled back, lifted her chin, and kissed her. ""Accept the fact that you're human."

She kissed him back, this time not with the raw desperation of their frantic mating, but with a promise of sweet fulfillment. Her arms encircled his waist, her soft skin embracing him in a warm cocoon.

"Brian, I'm scared." Her body trembled and withdrew from his arms.

"Of what?" Suddenly he was scared too, of his own emotional deficit. Paige was vulnerable now and needed big time support. All he knew to offer was a shoulder and some trite platitudes. What if that wasn't enough?

She crossed her legs and sat primly on the blanket. "I'm afraid of being like her. She had such dark moods, such angry outbursts, my sisters and I were terrified she'd hurt us."

His fingers clenched. "Did she?"

"Just once. Daddy was at work and Shelly was being a typical preteen brat. Mom had had enough. She tried to wash her mouth out with soap, and when Shelly fought back, Mom started hitting her with her fists, kicking at her. I tried to block her blows until Shelly could run away, but Mom came at me with a kitchen knife."

The sordid tales behind the walls of Beverly Hills' finest families. He wanted to put his fist through those fancy facades. "How old were you?"

"Fourteen, fifteen, I guess."

And he'd thought he'd had it bad having to make beds and wash laundry and wheel those room service carts to the rich and beautiful people. He wondered how many of those fat cats went home and beat their wives, how many of those Botoxed ladies attacked their teenaged daughters with a knife. "Paige, you're nothing like her. You're the most upbeat, cheerful person I know." He placed his hand on her shoulder. "You could never--"

"Don't you get it?" She swatted his hand away. "It's all an act." She scrambled to her feet. "I make myself act happy so the dark thoughts and depression can't surface. I'm afraid of what will come out." She stalked to a gray-barked cottonwood tree and laid her forehead against its deep furrows.

Brian walked up and stood behind her, not touching her. "Were you acting before when we were on that blanket?"

She turned to face him. "No."

He wanted to take her in his arms and kiss her, to tell her everything would be all right. But instinct held him back. "Paige, what's inside you that's so terrible?"

"Anger." She pressed her hands to her sides. "I keep it locked inside. I'm afraid if I ever lose my temper, I won't be able to control myself."

Had she forgotten that day in the lab, before they made up at Johnny Rockets? "You've gotten angry at me."

Her lower lip quivered. "You're the only one."

She'd never lost her temper with any of the other men she'd been with? No wonder they were all still her friends. "Why me?"

"I don't know. You get to me somehow. You make me...feel things I don't want to feel." She was trembling like little Katie had when he'd carried her to the car. But this was Paige. The confident, competent woman who always saw the glass as half full had been replaced by a terrified little girl.

"Paige." He clasped her hands. "You can't keep your anger bottled up inside. You have to acknowledge it."

She looked at him with hard, un-Paige-like eyes. "And what would that get me?"

He floundered for an answer. "It might get you past it and on with your life."

"Really?" She gave him a cool, Dr. Phil smile. "And how is that working for you?"

God, he was out of his league. He was struggling to try to understand her needs and fears, and she'd zeroed in on his in a heartbeat. "I guess we could both stand to work on that," he said sheepishly. "Maybe we can help each other."

"I'd like that." She moved back into his arms.

He'd never in all his life received a kiss so tender. Her tongue teased his lips sweetly. Her hands splayed against his bare back, warmly, lovingly. She smelled like soap and Chanel and tasted like his own spent desire. He folded her in his arms, wishing this moment would go on forever.

*I love you, Paige.* The words danced in his brain but something kept them from traveling to his mouth.

Her lips trailed down his neck. She rested her head against his chest. "Brian, let's not go back to L.A. Let's stay here forever, making love and enjoying each other."

His heart jerked. "You mean that?"

Slowly she raised her head. "No." She sighed resignedly. "It was just wishful thinking. You have Suite Smart to sell. And I have...well, obligations. Monday night is Junior Art League meeting. Tuesday I promised to help with decorations for the church bazaar. Wednesday is Helene's baby shower."

When she separated her body from his, a cool breeze fell across Brian's chest like a drawn curtain. The special moment faded. In an instant, the vulnerable woman he'd held in his arms disappeared, leaving in her place the normal, repressed, self-assured Paige, mentally checking her appointment book for her week's activities and responsibilities. Her father, her sisters, her church, her social commitments. Brian swallowed disappointment like a bitter pill. Was there any room in her schedule--in her life--for him?

* * *

Paige swiveled on her bar stool, clutching the Teddy bear Brian had won for her at the arcade. She'd lost forty dollars on the roulette wheel, but he'd made it back, and more, at Blackjack. The man was a genius at card counting. Growing up in Reno had its advantages.

Bells rang, sirens whizzed, and coins rattled out of a winning slot machine. Brian didn't even look up. He was deep in concentration, studying his cards, probably calculating standard deviations in his head.

In the piano bar glasses clinked and a singer warbled a ballad from Cabaret. *Maybe This Time...*

Paige studied the contours of Brian's back as he leaned forward to sweep his chips, longing to run her fingers over every rib and muscle. This afternoon, with her heart beating next to his, she'd almost told him she loved him. And she would have meant every word. Today. But those words had made a liar of her too many times. She'd said them because she'd felt they were expected, to men with whom she'd shared her time but never her heart. She wouldn't say them again unless she was sure she could keep their promise.

Brian turned to her and smiled, then left the table to cash in his chips. Paige jumped off the stool, leaving her half-full bourbon and coke, and pushed past brassy cocktails waitresses and raucous revelers. She met Brian walking away from the cash window.

Her eyes bugged at the sight of him stuffing a huge wad of bills into his wallet. "This ought to take care of the Skyhawk's fuel." He kissed her, his breath faint with beer and heavy with mint.

She hadn't realized how much it cost to fuel a small plane. Despite the free rental, this was an expensive weekend. And he'd financed it all with a few hours' play. "If Suite Smart doesn't work out, you could be a professional gambler."

He glared at her, his eyes suddenly hard. Then, as if she'd only imagined their anger, they relaxed into quiet pools. "I only take risks if I'm convinced I can win."

His intense look sent a chill slithering up her spine.

He took her arm, steering her through the crowds, past the dinging slots and flashing lights. Outside the casino, the clanging din silenced. Though people milled about, Paige felt like they were alone in the night. She breathed in the dry cool air and melted into Brian's arms.

She was glad she'd come here, to his world. Away from the southern California distractions he hated. Here the music was just as loud, the lights just as annoying, but she could tune it all out and focus on the only thing in this desert town she cared about. Brian.

Such a romantic evening. When they broke the kiss and moved on, Brian tucked the stuffed bear under his arm like a toddler in a football hold. They cruised through the next casino hand in hand like the dozens of honeymoon couples they passed. Paige dared to dream, to pretend they were a couple too.

But it was foolish to harbor hopes of Happily Ever After. Her track record bore out the reality: Paige wasn't a Forever girl. Within six months he'd be gone. Or she would.

But Maybe This Time...

Paige twined her fingers through Brian's and wished for a magic potion that would make this last.

# Chapter Sixteen

A noise in the kitchen woke Brian from a sound sleep. He kicked off the blanket, knocking two sofa cushions to the floor, and sat up. A female voice hummed softly. Suddenly hungry for some of that lasagna left over from dinner--and other things, Brian pulled on his jeans and trod barefoot into the kitchen.

Paige stood facing the open refrigerator, staring inside as if she were viewing museum art. She wore a thin little pajama top, pink with lace straps, and striped cotton bottoms that rode down in the back almost to her crack. Without turning around, she said quietly, "Sneaking up on me again?"

She'd heard him get off the couch? He really must be losing his edge. "It's a son's duty to protect his mother's home from marauders." He stepped closer so he wouldn't have to whisper. "Raiding the refrigerator is a serious offense. Punishable by kissing."

As she turned, he splayed a hand on the nape of her neck and lowered his face to hers. She smelled like strawberries.

Paige placed both hands on his cheeks, returning his kiss, then raised her lips to kiss his eyelids. "You go after possible intruders without your glasses?"

"I see some things better without them."

She closed the refrigerator door with a thrust of one sexy hip. "I was only looking. It would be rude to raid the refrigerator in someone else's house."

"Your defense doesn't wash. I taste the strawberries on your breath."

She smiled. "If I shared them with you, would you go easy on me? First offense."

"A likely story."

She retrieved a bowl of washed strawberries from the countertop and dangled one over his mouth. He opened his lips and tilted his head back like a trained seal as she dropped it in and he snapped it up.

He'd never tasted anything so sweet. It tasted even better when she popped one into her own mouth, licked it, and then fed it to him. He took a bite and returned the favor, passing it into her mouth with his tongue.

"Mmmm."

The way she sucked that thing almost made him lose it.

He backed her against the refrigerator, his tongue probing her mouth, his hand cupping her breast over her thin camisole. She was soft and warm in his palm, a perfect fit. When he pinched her nipple she flinched, then kissed him deeper. Her fingers raked through his hair. Her body ground against him.

*Control, McKay. Keep it under control.* "I think you're enjoying this punishment too much."

"Oh?" She widened those baby blues, fluttering her lashes, and whispered breathlessly. "You're not going to be too *hard* on me, are you?"

*Getting harder by the minute.* He lowered his head to her left breast and suckled where his fingers had been, drawing the cotton fabric into his mouth. Slipping a hand under her silky shirt, he massaged the other breast. Both nipples responded. He teased the one between his teeth with a gentle bite. She threw back her head and whimpered.

"Quiet." He returned his lips to her mouth. "Or I'll have to take drastic action."

227

He dropped one hand to her waist and loosened the drawstring on her pajamas. The tie unraveled as if she were a package waiting for him to open. He dipped his hand inside. He felt her body tense, then relax, as he pressed her tender spot.

"Brian," she moaned.

*Hope Mom took her sleeping pill.*

He slipped a finger inside. Her moist flesh closed tight around it. Brian felt both awed and aroused by his own power.

He teased her until she let out a little whimper and spread her legs to allow him deeper. He burrowed in with two fingers, making his own path.

When she moaned again, he thrust his tongue in her mouth. She sucked him in above and below. Grinding her hips, she danced at first in rhythm with his finger thrusts, then faster, in wild gyrations.

"Brian?" His mother's voice came from the bedroom.

His fingers froze. Paige clasped his shoulders and breathed into his ear.

"You're not getting into my apple pie, are you, dear? That's for the church social tomorrow afternoon."

If he hadn't been so tense, he would have laughed. "No, Mom. I'm not getting into the pie."

"Well, don't eat too much of the lasagna, either. You know you don't sleep well when you overeat."

"'Night, Mom."

"'Night, Son."

He let out a breath. Paige relaxed her grip on his shoulders. Shooting her an apologetic look, he started to retract his fingers, but she grabbed his hand.

"Don't stop," she whispered.

He glanced pointedly toward his mother's bedroom.

Her eyes pleaded.

Kissing her softly, he resumed, skipping over the slow tease and going right for the chase.

It only took a minute before she exploded against his hand.

"Oh my G--"

He stifled her scream with his mouth and held her tight against him until the orgasmic ripples subsided.

"Brian." Her voice was breathy and faint. She wound her arms around his neck and rested her cheek on his chest. "I'll never eat another strawberry without thinking of you."

\* \* \*

Paige stacked the lunch dishes next to the sink and grabbed a checkered apron from a magnet hook on the refrigerator. A baseball game blared from the television in the den. She plunged her hands into the soapy water.

"You don't have to do that." Belinda McKay strode into the kitchen, still wearing her spruce green church dress and sensible, low-heeled pumps.

"I don't mind." Since the kitchen didn't have a dishwasher, the least she could do was help with the cleanup.

"Paige." The TV noises stopped and Brian appeared in the doorway. "You packed? We should leave soon."

"What's your hurry?" His mother folded her arms. "I thought you and Paige might come with me to the church social this afternoon."

"Sorry, we can't." Brian looked anything but sorry. "Paige has to get back to prepare her camp activities for tomorrow."

A smoothly told lie. By this time tomorrow she'd be unemployed. But Paige was pretty sure he was anxious to get back for the same reason she was. She couldn't wait to be alone with him, to make love all night and sleep in his arms.

She cupped her hands over her flaming cheeks and faced the sink, hoping Brian's mother hadn't seen her blush. When she turned, Mrs. McKay was focused on her son. "You're not going anywhere until you fix the garage door like you've been promising."

"What's wrong with it?" Brian opened the refrigerator and swallowed a swig of milk directly from the carton. "Came off the track again?"

"No." Paige recognized Mrs. McKay's I'm-trying-to-be-patient-but-I'm truly-exasperated tone. "I told you. It's the security code program."

He frowned. "That could take a couple of hours."

"For a regular person, maybe. For you, forty-five minutes."

Paige smiled as Brian went grumbling to the garage, clanging an aluminum ladder. She loved listening to the good-natured banter between mother and son. She felt at home here, accepted. Her smile faded. Probably more accepted than she would be at her home right now. She wondered how Katie was faring in the foster home. Elena, and Jessie? Would they adapt well to their new counselor?

*You're not indispensable, Paige.*

Mrs. McKay set a jar of plum jelly and an index card on the kitchen table. "Thought you might like some of that jam you raved about at breakfast. And I wrote down the recipe for my Irish stew like you asked."

"Thank you." Paige wiped her hands on her apron and glanced at the card. "Where's the one for your ultra-fantastic special herbed and spiced lasagna?"

Mrs. McKay shot her a mock menacing look. "Don't push your luck."

Like son, like mother. Paige felt so comfortable with both. "Thank you so much for having me," she said after rinsing the dishes and setting them in the drainer.

"My pleasure."

"Maybe I'll see you again when you visit Brian in L.A."

Mrs. McKay's face darkened. "Don't get to that city very often. I used to live there, you know. Never liked it."

"Brian told me." Paige picked up another dish towel and a spoon. "My family used to live next door to--to Mr. McKay."

Mrs. McKay frowned.

*Stupid, Paige.* "I'm sorry. I didn't mean to--"

"It's all right. That was a long time ago. My biggest regret about the divorce is how much it hurt Brian."

Paige tread the thin tightrope between curiosity and tact. "He seems bitter about... his father deserting him."

His mother sighed. "It's made him very cautious. He doesn't trust easily."

Paige swallowed. The first week she'd met him, he'd said he'd rather never marry than risk divorce. The man wanted more than a promise. He wanted an iron-clad guarantee.

"Gil could have been a better father." Belinda McKay twirled the jelly jar in her hands. "I guess he tried to make up for it with Connor by throwing money and presents at him. But he didn't do right by that child, either. Both those boys needed love more than anything."

"I don't think Brian's lacked for that."

His mother shrugged. "I did my best. He's a good boy." Her tone sharpened. "A good man."

Paige folded the dish towel over a shiny gold rod, apprehensive about the edge in the woman's voice. "Yes he is."

Mrs. McKay set down the jelly jar as if it were fragile glass.

"He cares about things, deeply. But you can't tell it to look at him. He holds his emotions close."

*I've noticed that.*

Earthy brown eyes swept over Paige. Like Brian's eyes, they were warm but wary. "Please, don't hurt him."

\* \* \*

Brian stared out into the darkening skies as he navigated the plane over the Sierra Nevada peaks, one hand on the contols, the other on Paige's shoulder as she slumped against his side. She hadn't spoken a word since they'd left Mom's house and had fallen asleep almost as soon as they took off, apparently physically and emotionally exhausted.

He caressed her arm through her thin cotton blouse. He would have appreciated her light chatter to keep him alert and focused. Instead he was left alone with his worried thoughts. He had only one day and two nights to fix whatever was wrong with the damned Suite.

Make that one day and one night. Tonight was spoken for.

Paige stirred against him.

He brushed a loose hair from her cheek. "Good trip?"

"Wonderful."

"Me too." He kissed the top of her head. Incredibly, the innocent gesture got him hard.

He'd never been so anxious to return to the city before. He was going to sleep with her tonight. All night. No interruptions from park-goers or nosy mothers. Just the two of them with nothing but time to satisfy every yearning. She could damn well call her father and tell him she'd see him in the morning.

The faint scent of Chanel teased him as Paige dozed against his shoulder. She didn't wake up again until he landed the plane in Los Angeles, and taxied to a stop at the end of the runway.

She sat up and rubbed her eyes. "Did I fall asleep?"

"You were out for two hours." He set the brakes and shut down all the controls. Grabbing the keys and his duffel bag, he swung himself down and then went around and helped her out of the plane.

The night air was cool for this time of year. Paige rubbed her arms. He blocked the wind with his body, enclosing her in a protective hug.

"Thanks, Brian." She kissed him. On the cheek. "This was a wonderful weekend."

"Not over yet." He nuzzled her neck. "Come home with me."

She stiffened. "I can't. Not tonight."

"Don't tell me you have some party tonight or some charity event you have to hostess."

"No, just need to go home. Tired."

"I'll let you sleep." He grinned. "Later."

She shook her head. "It's better this way."

Ice rivulets chilled his blood. "What's better?"

She winced. "Look, this weekend was wonderful. Better than wonderful. But it all happened so fast. Maybe we got carried away, got ahead of ourselves. I think we should step back a little."

His breath froze in his throat.

"I'm sorry." She averted her eyes. "I didn't mean for this to be... I...I'm sorry."

He barely felt her extricating herself from his embrace.

"I'll see you," she said, in Beverly Hills-speak for *I'll never see you.*

She walked to her car. She didn't look back.

Brian stood rooted to the spot, unable to move or speak. His soul had left his body. His lifeless carcass watched as she started her Infiniti, switched on the lights, and drove off into the darkness.

He could not believe this. He was not fucking believing it.

Did he have LOSER stamped on his forehead? A sign on his butt that said Kick Me? How could he have been so gullible?

Connor had been right. She'd gotten what she wanted from him, then thrown him away like a used rubber. He'd spent hours working on Victor's program for her camp presentation, hours he should have spent on the Suite. And what had he gotten for it? Practically accused of being a child molester.

He'd squandered his whole goddamned weekend trying to put a smile on Paige's face instead of working to assure financial independence for Numero Uno. Now he could lose everything. Unless a bolt of genius hit him between now and nine o'clock Tuesday morning and told him how to fix the goddamned mattress program, he was completely, totally screwed.

All because he'd been thinking with his dick.

He'd believed their lovemaking was special. When she shuddered in his arms and called his name, he thought he'd finally found the soul mate who loved him for himself, who wanted to be with him forever and always.

But she'd just been horny as hell, and his happened to be the only cock available. Now that they were back in Tinseltown, she'd dive right back into her normal, geek-less life of parties, art exhibits, and beautiful, shallow people. 'Thanks for the fuck and the hand job, Brian, but I've really gotta run. See you around.'

The worst of it was, he still wanted her.

*Jesus, please kill me now.*

## Chapter Seventeen

"That is so not fair." Shelly swiveled on the kitchen barstool leafing through a *People* magazine. "How can they fire you for reporting suspicion of abuse? Isn't that what a counselor is supposed to do?"

Paige ripped lettuce leaves into shreds, struggling for composure. "When the people you reported are in a position to fire you, fairness sort of goes out the window." She blinked back the tears that had dogged her since last night. "Looking on the bright side, now I'll have the rest of the summer free to...free to..."

Free to be alone. Without Brian. She lost her battle with composure. Tossing the lettuce ball into the sink, she propped her elbows on the counter and buried her face in her hands.

"Paige!" Shelly jumped down from her perch. "It's just a volunteer job. You look like you lost your best friend."

"I did."

Her sister quirked a brow, then nodded with an Oh-I-get-it expression. "I wondered why you hadn't talked about your trip to Reno."

"I broke my own record, Shel." Paige dabbed at her eye with a tissue. "My previous shortest relationship was three months. I killed this one in three weeks."

Shelly giggled. "Well, you'll get over it in three days."

She sighed. "Not this time."

Shelly's blue eyes widened. "Is this a Paige Anderson first? Did *he* break up with *you*?"

Paige sniffed and shook her head.

Shelly steered her to a kitchen chair. "Talk to me, Sis. If you like this guy so much, why end it?"

"I don't want to hurt him."

Shelly furrowed her brows. "Well, you know him better, but the man doesn't look that fragile to me."

The thought of his hard body almost broke Paige. And his strong, comforting presence. He hadn't run away when she'd showed him her dark side, shared her secret fears. He'd accepted her, supported her, been the solid rock she'd always needed. Brian was so good for her. But she was poison for him.

His mother had recognized what Paige hadn't wanted to admit to herself. She couldn't handle a serious relationship. She wanted him now, missed him so badly her skin actually ached for his touch. But she knew herself too well. When the blissful sheen wore off, and reality settled in, she'd leave him, just like all the others.

But Brian wasn't like all the others. He did care deeply, intensely, and though he hid it well, more passionately than any man she'd ever known. She wouldn't just hurt him. She'd devastate him.

She repeated the mantra that had kept the pieces of her heart together through a long, sleepless night. "I'm doing the right thing."

"For who?" Shelly fisted a hand on her hip. "Paige, I love you, but after twenty-one years, your martyr routine is starting to wear a little thin."

"Excuse me?"

"Oh, don't get all pissy. I offered three times to help with the salad but you waved me off. You 'had it.' It's a freaking salad, Paige. Do you have to control even that?"

"So, I'm a control freak?"

"Does Superman wear a red cape?" Shelly paced the length of the kitchen. "You can't relax for a minute. You have to manage everyone and everything."

"If I didn't, nothing would ever get done around here." She rose, wrapped up the lettuce in cellophane and took out a knife for slicing cucumbers.

"There you go, assuming the world would fall apart if you didn't personally hold it together. You think you know what's best for everybody." Shelly stalked back. "Including Brian."

She couldn't say what was best for him, but she knew he deserved more than she could give. "I'm doing him a favor." She blinked under Shelly's hostile stare. "You know my relationships with men don't last."

"Oh, the great and noble Paige." Shelly smirked. "Your relationships with men lasted exactly as long as you wanted them to. Those guys fell at your feet and when you broke it off you did it so nicely, they probably didn't even know what hit them. They still show up for Fourth of July barbecue, for heaven's sake." Shelly narrowed her eyes. "I don't think it will be like that with Brian." A triumphant smile played on her lips. "You can't control him."

"I didn't try to contro--" She whacked a cucumber so hard the slice sailed across the room. Did she?

She'd flirted with him from the start, trying to coax a smile to his austere face. And when he'd responded, she'd reeled him in gently, drawing close, later edging away. Pretty much Paige modus operandi. As long as she was pulling the strings, seducing him to like her, she was in her comfort zone.

Except he hadn't reacted as predicted. How had he turned the tables, on her, making her want him as much as he did her? When had she started to care what he thought of her values and decisions, to need his approval and validation?

She'd shared her body with others. But he was the first man she'd ever let inside her heart. What if...

"He scares me, Shelly."

Her sister raised an apprehensive brow. "I see that."

"He's so deep. So intense. I'm afraid he'll demand something I can't give."

"Kinky sex?" Shelly's eyes lit up.

"Love." Paige whispered the word.

Shelly looked askance. "Love is your talent. Every guy you've dated has proposed to you. Everybody loves Paige."

Paige winced. The last person to say that hadn't meant it as a compliment. "Not everybody," she whispered. "Paige doesn't love Paige. In my past relationships, when I got close enough for someone to really know me, I just walked away."

"But Brian's the one man you care for too much to walk away from. So you blew him off before it got too intense."

"Too late for that." Disobedient tears streamed down Paige's cheeks "I'm a terrible person, Shelly. I wasn't ready to commit to Hale or any of those guys." Cold reality slapped her in the face. "I just used them and dumped them."

Shelly led her to a kitchen chair and wrapped her arms around her. "Yeah, you can be a real bitch sometimes. But I still love you. I never was too crazy about Perfect Paige." She winked. "And I'll bet Brian isn't either. If you give him a chance, I think he'll love you warts and all."

*You're still deserving of love.* He'd already accepted her imperfections. All she had to do was accept his love.

But could she give him the love he deserved? Could she commit to him, share herself with him, body and soul?

"Call him, Paige."

"He won't answer. And even if he did, what would I say?"

Shelly looked at her as if she were dumber than dirt. "You're asking me? My big sister Paige who knows all the answers is asking ditzy Shelly for advice?"

"Right, what was I thinking?" A slow smile edged its way to her face as she hugged her sister. "I love you, Shel."

"Back at ya."

*I'm out of my mind,* Paige thought when she finally worked up the courage to ring Brian's cell phone that night. *Out of my comfort zone. And out of control.* The neat pieces of her well-ordered life were hurtling apart at warp speed, and the only one who could put them back together was a lanky geek whose kisses set her on fire.

As expected, the call went to voice mail.

She tried again. And again. Finally, after ten o'clock, he answered.

"Wrong number."

"Please don't hang up."

He growled. "What do you want?"

She caught her breath. "To talk."

"I don't want to listen."

"Brian please, I feel as bad as you do."

"Want to make book on that?"

"No. Not with a man who can clean up a blackjack table." She'd hoped that might make him chuckle, but the only response from his end was stony silence. "Please." A dull ache weighted her chest. "Can't I just talk to you?"

His moment's pause gave her hope. "You've got two minutes. And you've already used one."

"Not on the phone. I want to see you."

"You had your chance."

"I'm sorry about last night. I know you won't believe this, but I thought I was helping you."

"If you ever want to hurt me, I'm in real trouble."

*Stubborn man.* She wanted to stalk over there and punch him in the chest. And then kiss the bruise. But she didn't have a clue where 'there' was. "Tell me where you live. I'll come over."

"No."

She dug her fingernails into her palms. "We. Have. To. Talk."

"No. We. Don't. And your two minutes are up. Have a nice life."

"Brian, I lo--"

The phone went dead.

Paige buried her face in her pillow and cried. This must be love, because she'd never felt so miserable in her life.

Even after a glass of wine and a hot bath, she couldn't sleep. Slipping into a pair of low-cut jeans, a white camisole, and a pink linen blouse, she grabbed her car keys. Maybe a drive to the beach would help.

The stairwell passed in front of Daddy's office, and the light was still on. Darn. They hadn't spoken since she'd gotten home from Reno. The last thing she needed right now was a confrontation. Hoping to avoid one, Paige, slipped off her shoes and tiptoed down the steps toward the back door.

"Princess."

She sighed. "Yes, Daddy." Resignedly, she put on her shoes and went into his office.

Her father looked up from his computer. "Kyle Royce was arrested today and placed in juvenile detention. Apparently he pushed a little neighbor girl off her bike, and kicked her in the stomach. She's in the hospital with internal bleeding."

*Oh, my God. If Katie had been home...*

"The Royces are getting a divorce. Mrs. Royce is petitioning Child Protective Services to allow Katie to come home. The child will stay in the foster home until the matter is settled."

She closed her eyes. "I'm sorry, Daddy."

"Don't be." He patted her shoulder. "You're the only one who saw this thing clearly, and responded appropriately."

*Not the only one.* She jingled her keys. "I'm going out for a while."

He nodded. "Apologize to him for me."

Him? She wasn't going to see any 'him.' She was just driving to the beach, trying to clear her mind. But when the Infiniti reached Santa Monica, it cruised only briefly down Ocean Avenue, then turned almost by itself onto a street of run-down glass-fronts and warehouses.

A dim light glowed from the back of one of the warehouses. Paige pulled into the gravel lot and parked next to Brian's Harley. What was he still doing here, at midnight? He might as well live in his precious Suite Smart laboratory.

The street was quiet, almost too quiet. Cold shivers ran down Paige's arms. She locked the car and walked quickly up the half-flight of wood steps to the front door.

She knocked.

No answer.

She pressed the buzzer, then leaned on it, then pounded on the door. "Brian! I know you're in there."

No answer.

Three or four cars squealed to a halt in the alley outside. Voices rang out, cursing in English and Spanish. What was going on here, a drug dealer's convention?

241

*Oh my god.*

"Yo, mama." A man in his early twenties, with arms as thick as tree trunks, sauntered up to her. "You're a long way from Beverly Hills. Want me to give you a ride home?"

"Brian!!" She slammed her hand against the door and it gave way to her touch.

"The lady isn't interested." Brian pulled her inside, slammed the door behind her, and dead bolted the locks. He must have been standing just inside.

"Welcome to my world," he said dryly.

She let out a slow, shaky breath. "I'm sorry to disturb you so late." She fluffed her hair with a sweaty palm. "I was out for a drive and I saw your bike outside...."

She couldn't read his expression behind his thick glasses. Paige lowered her gaze to his naked chest. He was barefoot and his jeans were zipped to only half-staff, as if he'd been suddenly aroused from sleep. Or... She swallowed.

Brian followed her gaze and zipped his pants. "Why are you here?"

He had to start off with a hard question? She didn't even remember how she got here. "I still have Victor in the trunk of my car." She tried a smile. "I brought him back."

His brows furrowed. "That couldn't wait until morning?"

"Victor could wait. I couldn't." Placing her palms on his shoulders, she caressed his arms from his eagle tattoo to his elbows, then slipped her hands around his waist and pressed her cheek to his bare chest. "I'm miserable without you." The words tore out of her soul. "I want to be with you. I want..."

He grabbed her hair and brought his mouth down to hers in a crushing kiss. Pulling her hard against his full erection, he slipped his hands inside her back waistband and kneaded her buttocks. He hissed in her ear. "Is this what you want?"

Her breath hitched. "Yes. I want to make love with you. All night."

"You're twenty-seven hours too late."

"I apologized for last night. I made a mistake."

"No, I made the mistake, thinking Miss White Bread Beverly Hills could care anything about a guy like me."

She fought a tear. "I do care."

"Tell it to the next sucker." He snarled and released her, then walked away silently into the bowels of the lab.

"Brian!"

He disappeared into the darkness without even a two-word dismissal. His cold tone and rough touch offered no hope of forgiveness. But he hadn't asked her to leave. And she wouldn't back off just because the going was tough. Not this time.

Groping her way in the shadows, stepping over coils that felt like live snakes, Paige picked her way into the laboratory. In a far corner of the electronic jungle, a light shone like a small beacon. There was a room back there. A plywood board room, like the one housing the Suite Smart demo, closed off by a curtain made from an old sheet and hung from a shower rod. Her mouth dropped open as she examined the cot-sized bed, the small round table, brick-and-board shelves. One lamp, a sink, and a combination refrigerator and microwave crammed the small quarters. *My God, he did live here.*

*Where did you think he lived, Paige, some beachfront condo?* Brian didn't have a trust fund income like Connor, only whatever modest savings he'd accumulated before starting the Suite Smart project.

He sat on the bed, pressing his palms to his thighs. Since there was no chair, she stood in front of him. "Please." She touched a hand to his cheek. "I want to be with you."

He swatted her hand away. "Prove it."

243

Paige jumped at his commanding, dangerous tone. "How?"

"I want you naked."

She let out an uneasy breath. She'd never undressed in full light with a man's eyes watching every move. But she wouldn't let him intimidate her. Seductively, she opened the top button of her blouse to expose her throat, then slowly continued her way down.

Too slowly, apparently. Brian jumped up, grabbed her shirtfront, and made short order of the last buttons, then tossed the garment to the floor. Greedily he yanked her camisole up and over her head. Barely pausing to ogle her breasts, he unsnapped her jeans, inserted his thumbs inside, and tugged them down to her knees. "Take them off."

She sat on the edge of his bed, kicked off her flip-flops, and slid the pants off, leaving only her panties.

"I said I wanted you naked."

A shiver ran down her spine. His tone was so cold, almost frightening. *This is where you walk away, Paige. Where it gets ugly and uncomfortable and you've lost control of the relationship. But if you walk, don't expect him to come after you.*

Never taking her eyes off Brian, she stood and slowly removed her black lace panties.

His gaze roved over her as if he were evaluating merchandise at a slave auction. Not the romantic interlude she'd envisioned. He stepped around her. "A dove," he said, bending to rub her tattooed butt cheek. "Peacemaker Paige. Figures."

Swallowing her embarrassment at being scrutinized and prodded like a lab specimen, she caressed the tattoo on his shoulder. "The dove flies with the eagle," she said suggestively.

If he recognized the paraphrase from the Crosby Stills and Nash song, he didn't comment. He walked around her, his eyes chilling every inch of her nude body. The rigid, unyielding planes in his face scared the hope out of her.

"Brian?"

He ignored her as if she weren't there, as if *he* wasn't in the room with her, but off somewhere inside himself, his sharp mind feeding his anger.

But his body was totally present. When he took off his glasses and dropped his pants, he was hard, full and ready. Muscles rippled across his chest and down his legs, primed for combat.

Rough hands shoved her backward onto the bed.

No kisses, no endearments. No foreplay. Paige caught her escaping breath as he climbed on top of her, sparing her little of his weight. His elbows pressed against her sides as his knees nudged her legs apart.

She whimpered from fear, not arousal. She wasn't ready. It was going to hurt. Determined not to plead or protest, Page squeezed her eyes shut and fisted her hands into the mattress.

# Chapter Eighteen

The assault never came.

Heaving a sound somewhere between a groan and pained howl, Brian rolled off her. His tortured breathing fanned the air across her breasts. His chest nudged her side. "I'm sorry, Paige. God, I'm so sorry."

She opened her eyes and stared into his. He looked anguished, beaten.

"I could have hurt you." He brushed a damp blond hair away from her cheek, and blinked. "You would have let me."

She touched his chest, holding her hand over his beating heart. "I didn't know how else to prove that I love you."

His arms enfolded her, enclosing her in an embrace so tight it set her heart on fire. "I swear to you, on my mother's life, that I will never treat you like that again." He kissed the corner of her mouth, her chin, her neck. "I didn't want to let you in tonight. I was afraid of myself."

"Into the lab? You were afraid you would hurt me?"

He covered her hand that still touched his chest. "Into here. I was afraid of losing my heart, and you walking away again." He heaved a deep sigh. "Why didn't you come home with me last night?"

"I was afraid too. I've never felt so...intensely about anyone else before. I was scared of things not working out between us. Of not being able to give you what you need. Especially after talking to your mother--"

"My mother?" He moved away from her. "What did she say to you?"

Paige took a breath. "She asked me not to hurt you."

He scowled. "My mother should mind her own business."

"Don't be angry at her, Brian. She was just trying to protect you. She loves you and wants you to be happy."

The cot creaked as he stood and switched off the lamp. "I am happy. Now."

But for how long? "So you believe that I love you? I gave you the proof you needed?"

"No. There is no such thing, and I won't ask you for any again. I accept your love without proof, without guarantees. Because I love you too much not to take that risk."

Moisture trickled down her cheek. "I love you, too." She reached in the dark toward his voice. "Come here." When he moved back into her arms she felt...complete.

What a crazy thing love was. Two hours ago, she'd felt so low, she'd finally understood her mother's deep despair. Now her heart was so full it could barely contain the happiness. Being in love was like being bipolar. Ecstatic highs, but there was always the risk of a crash.

She had to take that risk. He had. "I love you, Brian." She huddled against his chest. "I want to be with you for--"

*Forever.* Nestled in Brian's arms, as if she were swaddled in a warm blanket, the word didn't sound so scary. She felt safe with him. They fit together like connecting puzzle pieces, their tongues entwined, her breasts against his chest. The bed was as narrow as an army cot but it was more room than they needed. Paige pressed herself against him, wanting his skin touching hers everywhere.

She worked her fingers into the back of Brian's neck. He caressed her breasts, teasing her nipples to stiff peaks. She arched, wanting his mouth there. He made her wait, blowing his breath over the crests until the anticipation drove her wild.

She grabbed his hair and pulled his head down. His lips surrounded her breast. She pushed herself into him, loving the feel of his teeth lightly scraping her skin.

He transferred his attention to her other breast, then southward. Paige opened her legs and he crawled between and kissed her stomach, swirling his tongue inside her navel. Slipping his hands under her buttocks, he pressed his mouth to her most tender spot. Delight followed delight as he teased and tortured.

His breath was feathery soft, fanning the heat created by his lips and tongue like a tropical breeze. She closed her eyes, letting him take her away to a paradise where waves lapped gently against the shore. She was the land. He was the sea. She resisted his power, and then, as mounting tidal waves buffeted her senses, gave into its force and let the waves rush over her.

She raked her fingers through his hair, scraping his scalp. "I want you inside me."

After slipping on protection, he entered her slowly and gently, but the extra care wasn't necessary. Wet and eager now, she grabbed his buttocks and lifted her hips to draw him in deeper. Within seconds she came again, quivering under his body.

"More?" he asked when her breathing slowed.

Only one more thing could make her joy complete. "You," she said, moving against him in renewed rhythm. She wanted the sensation of him exploding inside her.

He thrust harder, faster, breathing raggedly. Then, calling out her name, he collapsed against her.

"I love you, Brian."

He trembled in her arms. She held him close, wanting to keep him inside as long as she could. But finally he slid out, and rolled off.

There wasn't much room to roll in the narrow bed. Instead of facing the wall, he took her in his arms, his body sticky with sweat. "Stay with me," he said, drawing her into his warm cocoon.

Paige tasted her own scent on his breath. He rested one leg between hers and slung the other over her hip. She slipped one arm around his neck and the other between his thighs, cupping him.

She could lie with him like this forever, their arms and legs entwined, barely recognizing where her body ended and his began. But after a few minutes, Brian changed positions, rolling her with him. He'd hardly settled in before he moved again.

"Can't get comfortable?"

"Can't sleep."

She kissed the part of his shoulder where her lips had landed. "What's bothering you?"

He hesitated.

She gave him a minute. Sharing his feelings wasn't easy for him. *Trust me, Brian. I've got my hand between your legs. If I wanted to hurt you....*

"It's the Suite," he said finally. "It's got a glitch. I don't know how to fix it. The sale is screwed."

The sale! "Oh my gosh, it's tomorrow!" She'd totally forgotten what day it was. "What's wrong with it? Is it something you can disable and sell later as an add-on feature? Or sell as it is?"

"It's the massage bed. It won't shut off by voice command. I can't sell it without that feature and I won't sell it as is. The motor could overheat and catch fire."

"Well, of course, you can't do that." She extricated herself from his arms and sat up. "What can you do now?"

"Nothing. It's over."

It was almost pitch dark, but she didn't need to see his face.

The anguish in his voice said it all. Why hadn't he said something? When had he--Oh my god. "Did you know about this problem before...before this weekend?"

"Yes."

Guilt squeezed like a vise. "And you took time to fly me to Reno?"

"Don't pin any medals on me, Paige. My brain was blocked anyway. I figured if I couldn't resolve my problem, maybe I could help with yours."

God, she loved this man. "Surely Allied will wait a few more weeks for the product. You'll just explain to them--"

"You don't get it. That's not the only deadline I'm working under."

The partnership agreement he'd signed with Connor. "It's been two years?"

He nodded. "Next week. Even if I could fix the mattress in time, it would take longer than a week for their corporate bureaucracy to schedule another appointment. If I don't have a signed contract by month end..."

"Connor owns the Suite and gets all the money." Paige clenched her fists. She could go to Connor and beg him to be reasonable, but Brian would never agree to that. And if she went behind his back and he found out... he'd hate her for interfering even more than losing the sale.

Brian's deep sigh filled the room. "So my father had the last dig after all. I worked two years for *nada*. I wanted to rub the arrogant bastard's face in his fucking dollar and laugh my ass off as I waved goodbye to his rich Beverly Hills crowd. Now I have nothing."

"You have me."

He sat up and draped his arm around her shoulders. "We can't live on love. I have two hundred dollars in my wallet. That's all

250

that's left of the money I'd saved, all spent on living expenses these last two years in sunny California. I'm broke, Paige. I can't even afford to take you out for a hamburger, let alone a steak dinner."

"And you think I care?"

"You will," he muttered under his breath.

She wrapped her arms around him. "Brian, you are the genius behind the Suite. But you're not the Suite itself. Even if you lose it, you'll make and sell something else. You're smart and capable. I believe in you." A thought occurred to her. "Will your mother be upset if you can't buy her a new house?"

"Nah, she never cared about that. It was what *I* wanted for her."

She'd figured as much. Brian wanted to show gratitude to his mother for her love and support. As well as prove he could take care of her as Gil McKay hadn't. Always, always, it came back to his father.

"You told me the other day that I should forgive myself. Why can't you forgive your father?"

"You didn't produce a child and then walk away from it." He edged his back to the wall. "The bastard doesn't deserve my forgiveness. And where he undoubtedly is, he doesn't need it."

"But you do." She took his hand between hers. "All your anger isn't hurting him. It's imprisoning you. Holding you back because your energy is tied up in some kind of emotional revenge. Let him go, Brian. He screwed up your childhood, but you don't have to let him keep ruining your life."

Predawn light teased the skylight above their heads. "It's almost morning." She kissed his finger. "Try to get some sleep." She sucked his finger into her mouth and then pressed it between her breasts. "Shall I sing you a lullaby?"

He lay down and pulled her beside him. "Sing me the song you were humming at the refrigerator the other night."

*Maybe This Time.* She crooned it softly in his ear, this time daring to believe the words.

"More," he said when she'd finished.

She sang another chorus. And another. "You should program me," she teased. "Like those sleep buttons on the clock radio that lull you to sleep. If you touch my right breast I'll sing for five minutes. Touch my left breast if you want ten minutes."

He kissed both breasts and massaged her stomach. "And what do I touch if I want forever?"

Slowly she opened her legs and pressed against his hardening erection. "Start here."

*     *     *

It was so amazingly simple he could kick his own butt for not seeing it. Brian keyed in the program changes as fast as his fingers could fly over the keys, barely able to keep his weary eyelids open, but pumped by an adrenaline rush that could keep him going for days.

Unfortunately he only had a few more hours. Allied's representatives were due at two o'clock.

"Brian?"

Paige appeared in his peripheral vision, eyes squinting, hair tousled. She looked so delectable wearing the blue work shirt he'd worn yesterday and, he'd guess, nothing else.

"It's almost ten." She rubbed her eyes. "Did you sleep at all?"

He could barely keep from cheering. "I got it, Paige. I fixed the problem."

"You did?" She clapped her hands like a child over a Christmas toy. "How did you figure it out?"

"You gave me the answer. With your singing snooze alarm." He explained the programming he'd just completed, requiring the customer to order the massage for a certain number of minutes, after which it shut itself off. The program would accept commands up to a maximum of thirty minutes, then go into a mandatory cool down period. The motor could never get to the thirty-five minute danger zone. "You're my muse, honey."

"Every brilliant man needs one." She kissed him on both cheeks. "It makes more sense this way. You want a massage to lull you to sleep and shut off by itself. If you have to wake up enough to order it to stop, it kind of ruins the effect."

Of course she was right. He was such a damned geek he'd ignored common sense. "Muse, I'm putting you on the payroll."

She saluted. "What's my first assignment, boss?"

"Quality control manager." He led her to the Suite Smart module and gestured for her to lie on the bed. "We're testing the program. You can order a massage for five, ten, or fifteen minutes."

She sat at the edge. "This is a Honeymoon Suite, right?"

"Sure. It can be."

She shot him a cute little frown. "Well, if I were a new bride, I wouldn't likely be on this bed by myself." She held out her hand. "Join me."

"That wouldn't be scientific," he protested. "I have to track the shutoff time."

"Use your super geek watch." She grabbed his arm and dragged him down beside her. "Massage, five minutes."

He set his digital watch alarm as the mattress buffeted his body, sending ripples of pleasure down his back. "Not bad." He closed his eyes. Why hadn't he tried this when he was stressed?

Paige leaned into him, sandwiching his ribs between the massaging coils and her equally gratifying body. He slung his leg over her hip. Together they rode the waves like a raft on a rolling sea, kissing and cuddling as their bodies swayed.

His watch alarm beeped. Within seconds the massage shut down.

"It works." Paige kissed him slowly and deeply. "You're going to make the sale today."

He grinned. "Looks that way." He started to get up but she held his arm. "Paige, I've got to--"

"You've got to finish what you started." She fluttered her lashes. "We're on our honeymoon, remember?"

"Not until we've said our vows." Propping himself on one elbow, he cupped her cheek and stared into her eyes. "I Brian, take you, Paige to be my wife, my lover, and my friend."

"And I, Paige, take you, Brian, to have and to hold from this day forward."

"For better, for worse."

"For richer, for poorer," she said significantly.

"In sickness or in health."

She took his hand as they recited together. "To love and to cherish 'til death do us part,"

Paige tilted her head back. "You may kiss the bride."

She accepted his kiss, then urged him onto his back and unzipped his jeans.

"Paige, we don't have time for this now."

"Fifteen minutes. She slipped out of his blue denim work shirt. As he'd hoped, she had nothing else on. "We need to finish testing the program. She pressed her irresistible body against his bare chest. "Massage," she ordered, "fifteen minutes."

He was out of his jeans and underwear in seconds. "I'm only doing this for science," he said as her lips tweaked his nipples and her hands caressed him...everywhere.

He could never have imagined the erotic sensations generated by Paige's alluring body, the rocking of the mechanical bed, and his own escalating desire. First she rode on top, undulating in rhythm with the movements of the mattress, teasing him with exquisite tenderness. Then, as the bed rippled beneath him, he rolled her over and mounted her.

It was the ride of his life. His breath left his throat. His blood drained from his veins and puddled in his groin. He was one with Paige. His arms and legs tangled with hers. She cried out his name, bucking and weaving and rolling under him.

He couldn't say when the mechanical massage shut down. At some point, the hum of the motor quieted and the bed slowed to a stop, but Brian kept going, oblivious to everything but Paige. He strove with her like a rapacious animal, need and desire driving him to a peak of frenzy so high he feared coming down.

They exploded together with a mutual cry, incinerated in a violent blast of lust.

Gasping for breath, Brian rolled to his side, sweaty, sapped, his knees and elbows weak as a newborn's. Gradually his eyes focused on a large, hulking figure at the foot of the bed.

"Just a test run, right, Bro?" Connor sneered.

## Chapter Nineteen

Brian tossed the rumpled bed sheets over Paige. "Get out, Connor."

A lascivious gleam lit his half-brother's eyes. "Slumming, Paige?" Connor advanced toward her side of the bed and reached a hand toward her cheek. "If you were this desperate, you could have come to me."

Brian shot off the bed, shoved Connor's face flat against the wall and twisted his arm behind his back.

"Brian!" Paige sat up and tucked the covers under her armpits. "He's not worth it. Connor, go away so I can get dressed."

"I won't look."

*That's for damn sure.* Brian held Connor's face against the wall while Paige scuttled out of the Suite, trailing bedclothes. Once she was gone, he released Connor and grabbed his jeans.

Connor flexed his bruised arm. "So you finally got some Beverly Hills pussy," he said with a menacing smirk. "Hope Miss Goody Two Shoes has improved since high school. When I had her, she was about as much fun as a log with a hole in it."

"You're a lying sonofabitch." Brian's fist clenched, but he held it in check as he zipped his jeans.

Connor grinned. "Yeah? I can get any woman I want."

"Not Paige."

"Oh, you think this is 'true love?'" Connor snickered. "You really are a naïve sap. Did you think about why she paraded her tight little pussy for you today, of all days? When you'll just happen to be a millionaire in a few hours?"

*Don't go there. Don't let him bait you.*

An evil gleam danced in Connor's eyes. "Enjoy it while it lasts, 'Bro. You don't have the class to keep a girl like Paige. After you've dropped a bundle on her, she'll get bored with geek cock and move on. And now that you've warmed her up for me--"

Brian landed a solid punch to Connor's gut. Caught off guard and out of shape, his brother hit the floor with a satisfying thud. Brian's fist throbbed. All his life he'd held back his anger. Determined to use his brains, not force, to take what he was owed. But that punch felt so damn good.

Conner slowly got to his feet, swiping at the trickle of blood from his lip. "You're gonna be sorry for that, 'Bro. We've still got to work together. And I can make your life miserable."

"Not after today. Once Allied signs on the dotted line, I'm out of here. I'll go to Chicago to install the system and give the hotel programmers six month's training as promised, but I won't be looking at your ugly mug any more."

"Guess again." Connor kept his eyes trained on Brian's face. "The contract calls for two years of maintenance by our technical team." He grinned. "And you're the team."

Brian's eyes narrowed. "That was *not* the deal."

"It's the deal I made."

Brian's temples throbbed. "But you were supposed to tell them--" His veins threatened to burst through his skin. "You bastard. You never went back to Allied and told them it's a one-time sale."

"Why should I?" Connor stiffened and actually showed a hint of backbone. "I put half a million dollars into this business. It's mine and I'm not giving it up with one shot. I'm putting Suite Smart in every five-star hotel chain in America."

Connor reached into his back pocket and took out his wallet. "You want out of the deal?" He pulled out a single bill, wadded it in his fist, and threw it at Brian's chest. "I'll buy your share of the business."

The dollar bill floated to the floor.

Brian's eyes blurred with fury. He shoved Connor against the wall. Connor shoved back. Brian jerked back his fist to wipe the smug smile off his half-brother's face, but somebody grabbed his arm from behind.

"Stop it!" Paige let go of his wrist and moved in front of him, shielding Connor's designer suit with her body as she glared from one to the other. "You're brothers!"

"He's not my brother," he and Connor said in unison.

Connor taunted like a bratty five year old. "He was a mistake."

Brian sucked in his gut. "So were you."

Connor's haughty expression downshifted into wary. "What the hell does that mean?"

He didn't know? He'd never counted backward from his birth date to his parent's marriage? Brian considered sparing Connor the same indignity he'd suffered, but he wasn't feeling charitable. "Your grandfather was the creator-director of Medical City, USA. Gil McKay wanted the part of Mike Devlin but he couldn't snare an audition. So he made a play for the director's daughter. Careless and selfish bastard that he was, he got her pregnant. The result: a part in a tasteless soap, and you."

"Dad loved my mother," Connor said hotly.

"Face it, 'Bro.' You're no better than me. We were both mistakes." He moved closer, sandwiching Paige between them, meeting Connor's eyes over the top of her head. "I feel sorry for you, Connor. Your genes come from a worthless user and a shallow woman who doesn't have two brain cells to rub together."

Brian saw the blow coming but when he turned to push Paige

out of the way, Connor's fist slammed into his side.

Paige squealed and ran to the door of the Suite.

Brian took a second too long to make sure she was okay. When he turned back, Connor caught him with another hard punch to his stomach.

Rage boiled inside him. Fighting for breath, he maintained his balance, but the room spun around him. He blinked until it stopped. Refocusing, he stared into the cold blue eyes inherited from Gil McKay.

Brian's gut seethed with pure hatred. "Go ahead," he dared, "hit me again. That's what you've always wanted to do, isn't it? Beat me into oblivion and erase me from your life."

He got what he asked for. The punch knocked his glasses to the floor and bashed the corner of his eye.

"Oh my god!" Paige moved into the fray, stooping to rescue his glasses as she waved her other arm for a Time Out. "This is stupid. Stop it, both of you."

He nudged her aside without taking his eyes from his adversary. "This is between him and me."

They faced off. Brian landed a punch to his father's nose and watched the blood trickle down to his perfectly shaped lips. "The smart triumph over...self-absorbed assholes."

Gil McKay's fist caught Brian's jaw. "You're not as smart as you thought, are you? And you're as weak as a pussy."

"And you're a man?" Brian elbowed a hard jab into his father's ribs. "You let your wife support you until you got your break. Then you threw us away as if we never existed. You never acknowledged me as your son. But that wasn't enough for you." Gil McKay's face morphed into Connor's, then back again to his father's. Brian rubbed his eyes. "You had to insult me after you died with that godforsaken dollar. And left millions to your nitwit son who'll waste it in your memory on booze and coke."

A hit to his midsection left Brian fighting for breath, but he put his hand to his stomach and straightened. "That your best shot?"

Like a pitched fast ball, the fist zeroed in on his left eye. His good one. In the last nanosecond Brian deflected the blow, ramming the fist's arm and wrist against the wall. Following with a body slam. His ears rang with the sound of drywall tearing and the crack of particle board.

"Son of a--" Two hundred pounds lunged toward him with intent to kill.

Brian kicked high and fast, then spun out of the way. The big oaf went down like a felled tree. A bedside lamp crashed to the floor with him.

Ignoring the broken glass, Brian jumped on his antagonist, lashing out with both fists. Raw anger, unleashed after decades of vigilant control, took over. The little boy inside him punished and pummeled the powerful man who had rejected him and ruined his and his mother's lives.

The buttons of the fancy white dress shirt snapped as Brian straddled his enemy and landed another brutal punch. Blood spewed from the patrician nose. Gasping noises croaked from a reddened face as his fingers tightened around his father's throat.

"Brian!" Small hands grabbed at him. "Stop! That's enough." A horrified feminine face loomed in front of his.

He blinked Paige into focus. She kept yelling at him as she tried to pull him off Connor.

Connor?

Brian released his hold from his brother's neck and staggered to his feet. Holy shit. He'd gone completely over the edge. He'd seen his father's eyes, the same face, the same haughty attitude.

Brian's head pounded as loud as his heart. He stared in horror at the misdirected revenge he'd taken on Connor's face. Instead of throttling his hated father, he'd just punished another victim.

He leaned against the punched-out wall. As if he'd stumbled into someone else's dream, he watched Paige help Connor to his feet and onto the Suite Smart bed.

"He's psycho," Connor gasped, clutching his throat.

Considering his recent separation from reality, Brian couldn't really argue. He surveyed the Suite's damages. The glass splinters embedded in his hand came from what used to be the bedside lamp, now shattered on the floor. The wall had a hole in it eight inches around. He and Connor both looked more like street fighters than urbane businessmen.

"I'm done," he said simply. "Tell Allied the deal is off." He held out his arm to Paige. "Come on, I'll see you out."

"Oh, sure walk away." Connor's eyes looked defeated but held a strange live spark. "You're no better than him, you know. He got what he wanted and moved on. Never gave a crap about the people he stepped on when he did."

"Don't compare me to that monster." Brian nudged Paige to the door of the model suite.

Connor sat up and planted his feet on the floor next to the bed. "He didn't love me either!" His blue eyes looked almost vulnerable. "At least he respected you. He left you that damned dollar because he knew you didn't need his money to survive. 'Brian can take care of himself,' he'd tell me. 'He joined the Air Force and made something of himself.'" Connor fought for breath. "He said I was a millstone around his neck and that I'd never be anything on my own."

"Well, now's your chance." Pausing at the door, Brian stopped to pick the blood-stained dollar bill off the floor. He stuffed it in his jeans pocket. "The Suite's all yours now. Find another programmer."

"Brian, wait! Allied won't buy outright," Connor yelled after him. "I can't do this without you!"

Brian tried to shut out Connor's pleading cries as he walked Paige to the front office.

Paige gently led him to Connor's desk chair. "You okay?" She ran her hands over his shoulders, scanning his face with worried eyes.

"I'm fine." But he sank into the chair.

"You're bleeding."

He looked down at his fingers. "It's nothing."

Paige pulled up a chair next to him and took his bloody hands in hers. "Oh, Brian." A lone tear trickled down her cheek. "Your hatred for your father is destroying you. You almost killed Connor." She brushed her lips against his shoulder. "Did you mean what you said about letting him have Suite Smart?"

He felt in his pocket for the dollar bill he'd picked up in anger. "I...well, I...."

"You should. Walk away from it, now, before you lose your sanity."

Was his sanity worth a couple million dollars? "It's two years of my life, Paige."

"I'm more worried about the rest of your life." Her eyes braised his. "We don't need that money. We don't have to be rich to be happy."

Sweet, naïve Paige. "You say that now, but you've never lived without money. You don't know what it's like."

"We won't starve. You're a talented programmer. You'll work. I'll work. We'll be okay." She laid her head against his chest. "I love you. I can't stand to see you hurting like this. Please, let your father go. Walk away."

Her eyes were so blue he could almost see the ocean in their depths. Brian closed his and saw another blue pair, the deceitful eyes of Gil McKay who'd never given a crap about anybody but himself. Did he have his father's genes after all?

"Get your things," Paige urged, nuzzling his cheek. "Come home with me."

Brian blinked and saw yet another pair of blue eyes. Connor's eyes. Begging to hold on to his one chance at self-respect.

"I can't." He wiped a trace of blood off his lips. "For me, it's just about the money. For Connor, it's his whole identity." He kissed Paige lightly on the mouth. "You were right about him. He needs this business more than I do. And he can't run it without me." And if he walked away and stole his brother's dream, Brian would be no better than his father.

He stood. "Go home, Paige. I'll call you--I'll come by-- afterwards." Over her worried protests and offers to clean up the Suite he bundled her out the door and returned to the Suite.

Connor was still on the bed, head in hands.

"Get up, Asshole. Go buy a new lamp, then clean yourself up." Brian strode to the Renoir print hanging over the bed, yanked it off the wall, and re-hung it over the damaged plaster. "We've got a lease agreement to finalize."

# Chapter Twenty

Paige paced back and forth in front of the bay windows, listening for the sounds of a motorcycle, watching the sun lower over the tree-lined street. How long could a business meeting last?

She should have stayed. The place had needed cleaning up. The boys needed cleaning up. She should never have left those two alone. If they couldn't even be civil to each other, how were they going to broker a multi-million dollar business deal together? And if they did cinch the deal, how long before another argument tore the partnership apart?

She'd never seen Brian out of control. He'd actually believed, for a moment, that Connor was his father. Now that all that venom had sprung from his soul, did he feel free, cured of his hatred? Or had he unleashed a tiger whose rampage was only beginning?

When he finally pulled up in front of the house, he looked tired, but he was smiling. He was wearing an expensive gray suit, but his computer and a bulging blue duffel bag were strapped to the Harley. When Paige rushed out to meet him, he took her in his arms as if he'd waited all day to hold her.

He smelled like Connor's cologne. His face was puffy where he'd been hit, but the bruises had been covered by makeup.

"Are you okay?" she asked between kisses. "How did it go?"

He reached into his suit jacket pocket and pulled out a cashier's check for one million five hundred dollars.

"Congratulations." That answered only her second question. "I thought the lease was for two million." With Brian's share only a million. "Did you renegotiate?"

"Not with Allied," he said. "With Connor." He leaned against the Harley. "If he wants me to stick around and service an unlimited number of lease licenses, I want a bigger take for the startup. He got his initial investment back. However much he makes in the future is up to him."

Most of his explanation swam by her ears but Paige heard one thing he didn't say in words. "You don't hate him any more, do you?"

"Connor?" Brian lifted a brow. "He'll never be one of my favorite people, that's for damn sure. But...he can't help the way he is, given who raised him."

She smiled. "He might turn out okay, thanks to you. When you conned him into going into business with you, that might have been the best thing to ever happen to him."

Brian shrugged but she glimpsed a proud smile in his eyes.

Paige studied his 'stuff' crammed on the back of his motorcycle. "So if you're 'sticking around,' why are you carrying what I assume is all your worldly possessions?"

He grinned. "I don't have to stick around here. I'll have to fly up to Chicago next month for the first installation. Then San Francisco, Dallas, and Atlanta. I can live anywhere I want. So I'm going home."

Home? Paige's stomach muscles tightened. "Reno?"

"Yep."

"Now?" She'd envisioned them spending the day together. And the night. And the next day and night. And the next.

"As soon as I deposit this check." He kissed her on the eyes, drinking in the wetness that had somehow formed there. "Come with me. We'll get married."

"Married?" Her heart stopped a full beat. She drew back to examine his face.

He was smiling. "We've already said our vows and enjoyed the honeymoon suite. Might as well make it legal."

Not quite the romantic proposal she'd imagined, but she knew it was sincere. Paige traced her finger around the outline of his lips. "I do want to marry you. But I can't just take off. I have commitments. Helene's baby shower is tomorrow night." Not to mention the absurdity of riding four hundred miles on the back of a motorcycle, sharing the space with a laptop and duffel bag, and no luggage of her own.

"Guess you're right." His smile faded. "I'll have to live without you for a few days. Take all the time you need to get your things in order. You'll drive up this weekend?"

Pack up her entire life in three days? Her heart twisted and strained between *want-tos* and *can'ts*. "Brian, I love you. I want to be with you. But there's no way. It takes time to arrange a wedding. And--"

"There's no waiting period in Nevada. We can get our license and get married the same day."

Without her family present. Paige felt an invisible knife poised at her breastbone, threatening to slice her in two. "You don't understand." She took a deep breath. "I don't want to live in Reno."

Hard brown eyes raked her face. Brian sucked in his breath. "O-kay," he said slowly. "How about Hawaii? Or Santa Fe? You name it, we'll go there."

"But I don't want to go anywhere. I want to live here."

His eyes neither wavered nor blinked. "I hate L.A., Paige. Don't you know me well enough by now to understand that?"

"But this is where I belong. Where my heart is. I want to be near my family. And my friends."

He stared out at the Beverly Hills landscape. "And every old boyfriend you ever went out with."

"And what would you have me do? Live alone with you like a hermit in some secluded place in the desert? Seeing my family only a few times a year? Having no friends unless they met your rigorous standards?"

"If you really loved me, living alone with me would be enough."

The knife pricked her chest, dividing her heart. "I love you more than I ever thought I could love anyone. And I've given you more of myself than anyone else in my life." She paused to let the choked-up air out of her lungs. "But I love my family too. And I need them. And they need me."

The hardness in his eyes softened, but only to change to hurt. "To play nursemaid anytime any one of them is sick, or needs a babysitter?"

She sighed. "Brian, family isn't perfect. But it is family." She touched his arm. "They could be your family too. My dad apologized for treating you so badly. He likes you. Shelly adores you. I want us to be a part of a loving circle."

"So I should just quit my family and join yours?"

He was impossible. "Of course not. Your mother could come down here and stay with us as often as she likes."

"Why did I not see that coming? The family circle just gets bigger and bigger. And when do I get to see you? Every other Tuesday night if there's no family emergency?"

"Brian, please."

He stretched his arm out toward a street lamp and pressed his hand so hard against it the metal moved. "Connor was right. You're a damned butterfly. Spreading sweetness and light and what you think is love everywhere you go. For a smile and a little attention, anybody can have fifteen minutes of Paige."

She staggered back as if he'd slapped her. "That's a horrible thing to say!"

"I'm just stating the truth." He fisted his hands at his sides. "You can't really love anybody. You can't commit to a real relationship."

"I'm trying to. If you'd be reasonable." Fury rose up like acid and tears stung her eyes. "Secluding yourself away from the rest of the world isn't love, Brian." Her voice shook with desolation. "Love isn't selfish and insecure. Love doesn't require a person to give up their entire life."

The muscle at his jaw ticked. "Sometimes when you love someone you have to make a choice."

"You're not giving me a choice." Holding his hot gaze, she swiped at her wet cheeks. "You don't trust me to give my love to you freely. You want to lock me up in some tower so I can't walk away and leave you like your father did!"

Brian's eyes blazed with a fire that scared her as much as his violent actions this morning. Tears flowed down her face unchecked. But she wouldn't take back her words if she could. He wanted the truth? Let him hear the truth about himself.

He turned and strode back to the motorcycle and slung his leg over, then pierced her with a furious glare. "My father walked away from a wife who loved him and a son who could have adored him. But love wasn't enough reason for him to stick around. And it's not enough for you either." He started the Harley's engine. "It's been a nice fifteen minutes," he said coldly. "Tell the next sucker I said Happy Fourth of July."

He revved the bike into gear and took off without a backward glance.

The invisible knife slashed through Paige's chest, leaving her heart on the pavement.

*    *    *

Paige refilled the appetizer tray and mixed up another batch of punch. Thank goodness she had this baby shower to worry over. It had kept her mind busy, pre-empted it from thinking about Brian. Except for the sleepless hours she'd lain awake all night.

She was waiting to serve the cake until after Helene opened the presents, but two of her sister's law colleagues hadn't shown up yet, and the six women in the living room were still making small talk and munching on chocolate covered strawberries.

The doorbell rang. Finally. Paige turned the blender on Pulse until the ginger ale and lime sherbet danced in frothy waves.

"Paige!" Helene called out from the living room. "Could we get some more punch, please?"

As she lifted the pitcher from the blender, Paige tried not to feel resentful. She was needed.

*To play nursemaid anytime any one of them is sick, or needs a babysitter?*

His words stung with more truth than she wanted to admit. She preferred another 'truth.' She loved her family. She was happy to help them, and they appreciated it. Shelly's engagement party. Helene's baby shower. Paige tried to ignore the nagging voice in the back of her head. *Always a bridesmaid.* Would she ever know the feeling of being the center of someone's world?

"Thanks," Helene said after she'd refilled the punch bowl, then leaned close to Paige's ear. "There's someone here to see you. He's in the study."

*He*? Paige's heart jumped. When it started beating again, she looked to Helene, but her sister was suddenly immersed in an animated conversation with her friends.

Paige walked quietly to the study, stopping just beyond the door when she heard Brian's voice. She closed her eyes and tried to still her pounding heart. Had he changed his mind? Was he here to apologize?

She tiptoed closer, casting a quick peek inside. Brian had his back to her and he was reading from a paper in his hand. He wore the suit pants he'd had on yesterday, looking rumpled and worse for wear, and his white shirt looked as if greasy dirt had been rubbed into it.

She edged just inside the doorway and strained to hear his words. He seemed to be rehearsing something.

"Paige, I was wrong." Oblivious to her presence, he cleared his throat and rubbed the paper between his fingers. "I shouldn't have asked you to choose between me and your family. I know how much they mean to you and I guess I was a little jealous. I wanted you all to myself. I wanted to be number one in your life. But I was selfish and child--immature."

He scratched the paper with a pen and read it again. "I was selfish and immature. I promise not to keep you away from the people you love. I just want to be part of your life."

Paige blinked back tears. "You're the most important part of my life."

He whirled around, stuffing the paper into his pants pocket. "How long have you been standing there?"

"Long enough." She grinned. *Finally gotcha.*

His shirt was only half tucked into his pants, with the top and bottom buttons open. The bruise along his jaw was a puffy, iridescent blue. His normally shaggy hair was uncombed and wilder than usual, and day-old beard stubble shadowed his cheeks. He could have been mistaken for a homeless person. An incredibly sexy homeless person.

"You look like you slept in your clothes." A clump of sand shimmered in his hair. "On the beach."

"I did."

Somehow that pleased her enormously. "Not a lot of beaches in Reno."

He gave her a tired smile. "Obviously, I didn't make it that far. I couldn't."

"Oh, Brian." She tried to throw herself into his arms, but he held her off.

"Wait. I'm not finished." He reached into his pocket. When he retracted the crumpled piece of paper, sand fell out onto the floor. Brian scooped it up in his palm, then smoothed out the page and began to read. "Paige, I used to--"

She grabbed the paper from his hand. "No. Not from a paper. Not through a robot. From your heart."

He grinned sheepishly. "I used to ride out on the beach to escape the city. Every time I saw those movie studios and that Hollywood sign, it reminded me of my father. This time, when I looked back, all I could see was you. And then I realized that none of this--not the money, not the glitter, not the fraud and deception-- means a damn thing to me anymore. It's just a town. I could live here or anywhere--as long as it's with you."

He wrapped her in his arms and kissed her. He tasted like salt and his lips were gritty from sand. He smelled like the sea--and like Brian. "I love you, Paige. I don't need anything else. If you want me to tear up that check and throw it in the ocean, I'll do it."

She nuzzled his neck. "You don't really think I'd ask you to do that."

"I hope not. Because I've already spent some of it." He reached into his other pocket and pulled out a small square Van Cleef & Arpels box.

She caught her breath. Tremors circled around her heart but she tried to be cool. "I'll bet you got some serious attention from Security when you strolled down Rodeo drive looking like that."

He grinned. "Even stranger looks when I paid cash."

She opened the box and caught her breath when she saw the ring. An exquisite marquis cut. Platinum setting, at least two carats and set off by baguettes. The diamond's sparkle seemed to fill the whole room. Or maybe it was the reflection from the light in Brian's eyes. "It's beautiful."

"I don't know anything about jewels, but they tell me a

271

diamond is forever. And so is my love. Will you marry me and share my life?"

"Yes!" She flung herself back into his arms. "Oh Yes."

Brian's kiss was as thrilling and demanding as the first time, in the Suite Smart lab. Only this time it was filled with promise. He ravished her with his lips, pulling her hard against him. Paige took his tongue deep in her mouth, forking her fingers through his matted hair, melting and joining with him.

"I love you, Brian McKay. Forever. I will live with you anywhere." She pressed her body into the hard evidence of his love, secure in his arms, never wanting this bliss to end.

"Paige." Shelly's annoying voice shattered the perfect moment. "They're ready for you to cut the cake."

*   *   *

Paige's warmth slowly slipped away from his body. Brian fought to hold back his disappointment. He'd promised to share her, agreed to accept her social needs and obligations. But the frustration of being reminded, so soon, that he wasn't number one in her life, almost broke him in half.

And then, in the blink of an eye, she was back in his arms, her cheek touching his, her fingers clutching his neck. Her eyes fixed on him as she yelled to her sister.

"You cut it, Shelly." Paige's clear blue eyes met his, radiant with the light of eternal love. Her body melted against his, promising forever. "I'm busy kissing the most important person in my life."


THE END

Also by Linda Steinberg


*The French Deception*

Romantic Suspense

Tourist or Terrorist?

When her backpack is stolen in a Paris museum, American tourist Megan Chandler is stranded in Europe with no passport, no money, and no cell phone. Unable to contact family or friends, with no place to stay, she can't imagine things could get any worse. Until she discovers she's the main suspect in a terrorist bombing.

Computer geek Paul Bernard isn't having a good day. On his way to his job at the British Embassy, the building explodes before his eyes. The security photo of the perpetrator looks exactly like his hot French girlfriend. Who seems to have disappeared, along with his security badge. And when he finally catches up with her, she claims she's someone else.

Did his girlfriend bomb the embassy? Or is Megan the terrorist? Paul isn't sure if he's the biggest dupe in Europe or the hero Megan seems to think he is. All he knows for certain is that he can't let this deceptively innocent look-alike out of his sight. Or into his heart.


*Coming Soon*

*Suspicious Heart*

Contemporary Romance


*She's determined to uncover the truth.*

Maddie Walker has never trusted her enigmatic brother-in-law, Chase Harrison. When her sister, Laura, calls with a chilling plea for help, Maddie flies to Cleveland, determined to protect her.

But she's too late. Minutes after that phone call, Laura was killed in a car accident. Maddie is devastated. And suspicious of Chase, believing he intimidated her once-vivacious sister into a withdrawn shadow. Guilty for not protecting Laura, and fearful for her niece and nephew, Maddie vows to do whatever it takes to keep them safe. But the more time she spends with the grieving husband and devoted father, the more he melts her suspicions--and her heart. Can she discover Chase's secrets without falling prey to the fire in his dark intense eyes?

*He's sworn to keep the truth from her.*

Before his wife died, Chase Harrison promised Laura that he would never reveal her secret to her sister Maddie. Exhausted from parenting two traumatized, now motherless children, he's tempted to accept Maddie's help with the kids. But he can't risk letting her stay in his house and discover the truth about her sister. And he can't trust himself to keep the passion Maddie begins to stir in him from exploding into emotions he's afraid he can't control.

Sign up for Linda Steinberg's Announce Only newsletter to be notified when *Suspicious Heart* is available.
http://www.lindasteinberg.com/contact.html#newsletter